SPEAKERS

OF THE EARTH

Book One: The Fireweed Entrance

SPEAKERS

OF THE EARTH

Book One: The Fireweed Entrance

RICHARD JONES

SEATTLE

2020

CONTENTS

Author's Note

The Fireweed Entrance is Book One of a two part work titled *Speakers of the Earth*. The second book is titled *A Mountain Spruce*. These two volumes are the first in a collection of closely related—though not at all chronologically ordered—tales that I think of as "The House of Windy Gap Stories." While it is possible that I may, some time in the foreseeable future, write a story unrelated to these places, people, and this way of looking at the workings of the world, I believe it is highly unlikely.

—Richard Jones, Seattle, 2019

Part One

The Fireweed Entrance

I can't live this way any more. I am heartsick from uselessness, from pointless roaming. The trees, the plants, birds and animals, the ground itself all talk to me constantly, expecting me to know their meaning, and I understand none of it. I am exhausted from wandering, driven from one place to the next by humans who are afraid of me, and all the other peoples who want something from me. I come to the point of refusing to move any more, while to stay where I am will bring disaster.

Now a complete stranger sends me away, like a rock flung out over a chasm with all of the thrower's strength behind it. As much as I hate and fear the sensation of falling, it is a familiar feeling, a well known waking nightmare I can cling to, for I know exactly how to fear it. Where and how will I fall this time?

(Seattle, Aug. 2000)

Chapter 1

I walked aimlessly through Occidental Park, in the heart of Seattle's Pioneer Square, on a break between the breakfast and lunch shifts at the restaurant where I was working. Washing dishes isn't a glamorous job, but it's easier to find—and refind after they fire me—than farm or loading dock work. In any case, I was never strong or mean enough for the other jobs where the bosses aren't particular about the origins or status of their employees. Being a dishwasher is about as high as I had ever climbed in the twenty years of scuffling between 1980 (aged 15) and that day in the Park. This working life is much like my father's was; I don't want it or like it, but what tears me apart is the thought of ending up like him, locked away in a mental institution until his dying day.

The park was sun-dappled, and filled with Normals, sitting singly or in small groups. Normals are those happy people who fit in, who live *in bounds* and stay within our society's requirements and expectations safely and easily. Outliers are people like myself and my father, who died after years of confinement, for refusing to acknowledge that he lived forever *out of bounds*. For true Outliers like us, people who are uncontrollably different, sometimes other Outliers, but *always* Normals—even those who mean well—are dangerous. Nothing is ever easy, and everything and everyone is perilous. And that includes a simple walk in the park.

Occidental Park, more or less in the middle of Pioneer Square, takes up half a city block. It's cobbled with bricks that date back to 1890, as do the brick and faux stone buildings that surround it. They were all put there after the Great Fire of 1889 that ate everything in the area, since everything had been made of wood. Sometimes I thought the park just looked old and beat up, but it always held itself with a dignity that I admired. I had been through Seattle many times, and this place always seemed to draw me in.

The trees that crowd the park provide welcome shade in the short summers, and drip rain on passersby the rest of the time; they too are old and dignified. They are called London Plane trees, a natural hybrid of the Oriental Plane and the American Plane. They were first discovered in Spain in the eighteenth century, in a neighborhood where the two parent species had been planted near each other. The Londons, therefore, have a slightly mongrel history, the kind that has always appealed to me.

They are strong and tall, with broad, maple-like leaves that are tougher than maple. The variety planted in the park was the kind whose bark does not peel off in great long strips. They made less cleanup work for the parks department than other varieties, which is likely why they were there.

One of the Plane trees near the center of the park caught my eye. I walked over to see what had attracted my attention. As I neared the tree, a sensation I knew well began to steal over me. Try as I would, I could not resist the tree's call; it pulled me over to it as if I had no will of my own.

I stood near it, already a captive, and regarded its rough brown bark, the straight trunk about two feet in diameter, the long branches forking out above, starting about twenty feet overhead. The tree meant me no harm—none of them ever had. It was initiating a conversation, and I had never been able to say no. I had never really wanted to say no, even when—as in the middle of Occidental Park—the time and the place were absolutely wrong. What do trees know about things like that?

My vision began to constrict, narrowing down until I could see nothing but the trunk. I stood as rooted to my spot as the tree was rooted to its own, and I could feel my breathing grow shallow and slow.

Some trees put thoughts in my mind that become words, describing things and ideas I can understand. Others seem to be unable or unwilling to do that, and instead fill my head with images and feelings for which I have no reference. This tree was one of the latter; my eyes remained fixed but unfocused on the tree's scaly bark while a stream of images flowed through my mind. There were flashing, momentary glances at mountains, hills and valleys, and sometimes other trees that flew by so fast I couldn't identify them. There were also views of places I could not begin to identify; whether they were deep within the earth, inside some living creature, or somewhere I couldn't even think of, I had no idea. All of these images were somehow connected to a parallel stream of ideas that were more like feeling or emotion, with no words to reveal their meaning. I knew that this tree wanted something from me, wanted me to do something. It seemed clear that it had to do with more than a single London Plane tree in Occidental Park; but it had all happened this way many times before in many different places. It was like being stopped in the road by someone who needed help, but someone who moved and spoke in a way so foreign that I could never begin to understand what they needed, or why they were in the road at all, or why I might be the one who could help them. I wanted to help, wanted to understand. More than anything, I wanted to do something that felt useful and worthwhile, something that had meaning in the world beyond ensuring the next day's food, and with luck a place to spend the night. The images and the alien thoughts of the tree continued pouring through my mind, rushing in for an instant and then speeding out of me again, and still I did not understand.

Something was happening apart from what came to me from the tree, and it began to break through the tree's strange and rambling discourse. The stream stopped abruptly; its absence created a void in which for a moment it seemed I had no senses at all. Slowly, my body began to reassert its ownership. The first thing I realized was that someone had a firm grip on my upper arms, and was shaking me with an authoritative persistence. The next thing to return was my hearing, which registered a raspy baritone in front of me, speaking loudly and slowly, as if to a mentally disabled person or a very small child.

In another moment my vision was restored, and I turned towards whoever was holding me. My fears were confirmed, for it was a policeman. When he saw my eyes focus on him he stopped shaking me, but kept his grip on my arms. A quick glance around showed a knot of five or six people—Normals, certainly—standing nearby, close enough to hear and see, but not so close as to be at any risk of exposure to whatever would happen.

It was an older cop, and it took a moment to see that while he probably wasn't especially worried or angry, neither was he in the mood for a complicated talk.

"What's going on here? You all right?"

"I—I was thinking." My mind was still reeling from what the tree had tried to place in it, still trying to scrabble its way back to the world of humans.

His expression went from wary cop to one I was more accustomed to: a mild, sceptical contempt.

"You've been standing here for three hours with your mouth hanging open, making what I have to say are some pretty weird noises. Is that you thinking, or the drugs?"

A quick look beyond the cop showed that the shadows had changed from mid morning to mid afternoon. It had probably been more like four hours. The knot of people—office workers, by the look of them—whispered together excitedly, but they stopped when they saw I was watching, and looked nervously away. I turned back to the cop. Speaking still required me to remember how it was done.

"These trees are—fascinating, officer. They're, um, they're called London Plane trees, and they're a, a hybrid that was discovered in Spain—"

"Never mind that. You have identification?"

I fished a tattered card from a hip pocket, and handed it over. His eyes rolled.

"Oregon I.D. card, expired last year. That's the best you can come up with?"

"That's all I have, officer."

He sighed. "All right, look. I've called for the paramedics to come check you over. They'll be here in a couple of minutes."

A hot jet of panic ripped through me, and I prayed he hadn't felt it. My father's fate began to close in on me again. I had evaded or escaped for so long—were they going to get me this time? I took a deep breath, and shrugged my shoulders slowly. The cop remembered he was still holding me, and let go of my arm. I almost lost my balance but recovered just before falling; after a conversation like the one with this tree, I am usually left weak and unsteady.

"Um, no, really, officer, I'll be fine. I have to get back to work now, my meds are there and as you can see, I'm a little overdue. Thanks so much for your concern, but I'll be going now."

The cop looked unconvinced. "I can't keep you here because you haven't done anything, but you really should get checked out. Your job can wait a few minutes more if it can wait three hours."

I could feel beads of sweat on my forehead. "Thanks again, but I'd better be going. I appreciate the help."

I turned and started walking away, as smoothly as I could manage, trying desperately not to run. He let me go, and I did not look back, either at him or the gawkers. I felt unconsciously with a hand for the pack on my back. It was there, and along with not falling into the hands of the authorities again, that was one of the few good things of the moment.

I had missed the lunch rush at the restaurant where I'd been working. This was the second time in a week that had happened, for much the same reason, and I knew from long experience that I would be fired the moment I returned. Since I had been paid the day before, there was little point in going back at all.

Nor was there any point in staying anywhere near here. Attracting attention twice in a short period was too much to ignore; in the past, when I had been stubborn and stayed in a place, the consequences had been unpleasant and unhealthy, to say the least. It would be at least six months before I could even consider passing through this part of Seattle again on my never-ending cycle of movement, confrontation, and flight.

My mind was still struggling to be fully human again. I needed someone to talk to, a person who knew nothing whatever of what had just happened, somebody who would simply talk about and listen to ordinary things. I had learned through long, hard repetition of scenes like this that if I could find that kind of person soon after a difficult encounter with the trees, I could quickly re-establish my own thoughts and feelings. When it came to getting out of town—whatever town that might be—it went much better when I knew who I was, at least within the human community. And if it took hours, or days, to get my bearings again, as sometimes happened when I could not find anyone at all to be human with, the risk of falling into trouble I couldn't talk my way out of was dire.

Once around the corner I kept walking, as quickly as I could without running. I needed to get away from the park and its police, medical and mental health responders, before they could find me. I moved without worrying about exactly where I was going. I had not even decided if I would head north, south, or east, or even west, perhaps into the damp, silent hinterlands of the Olympic Peninsula. I had to do whatever it would take to get away from humans who either feared and despised me, or thought they should or could "help" me. Before getting all the way away, though, I needed some bit of interaction—almost anything, so long as it wasn't hostile or dangerous—with someone (anyone!) hopefully closer to Outlier than Normal.

While it's sometimes possible to stay out of trouble when you talk to people, if you *listen* to them there's no telling what will happen. It is, in fact, a gamble—and for me, the stakes are high—to talk to anyone and everyone, in the cities or the countryside, who is willing to talk to me. Talking is necessary but almost trivial; listening—listening can change you.

The old guy in the battered bomber jacket caught my eye in a way that people do once in a great while. He was leaning against the worn, dusty brick front of the Commerce Café, one of the oldest and most egalitarian eating establishments in the city. Everyone tells you to never make eye contact with anyone when you walk the streets. I do it all the time; usually, as now, out of need. He looked back with a glint of amusement.

"What's up, bub?"

His posture was casual and relaxed. He probably didn't need anything in particular, which was fine with me. I took one shoulder out of its backpack strap and let the pack hang from the other; there wasn't much I could do to be less recognizable, but just maybe, standing here talking to someone who looked reasonably legitimate, I would seem less like the crazy person from the park.

I responded to him with what was expected: the most common lie in all of human interaction, and the obvious next question.

"I'm doing all right, how's it with you?"

"I'm hungry. And I mean *hungry.*"

So I was mistaken, but this particular problem was a clear and—for the moment, anyway—easily remedied one. Only talk and very careful listening would tell if there was a murkier, more dangerous hunger at work here.

"Okay, I can probably help out a bit with that. What do you need?"

He hadn't stopped looking right at me. This kind of person is unusual. They make me pay strict attention—for safety's sake—and remind me how alive and lucky I still am at this stage of my life.

He said, "I just need a full belly. Compared to what you need, I'm in fat city."

People say surprising things often enough that I chose not to walk away until I had heard a little more. Maybe this encounter could still eventually help me settle back into my skin. There were no clear danger signs yet, and there was a chance he was some kind of Outlier. It was worth a bit more probing.

"Tell me more."

He spat on the pavement. Right up against the wall, where nobody would step in it. There was no doubt it was his intention to spit that way.

"To put it bluntly, you need a life. No, let me rephrase that. You need *your* life."

My feeling towards the situation shifted abruptly; this probably wasn't going to be the kind of human exchange I needed. I started to pull out my battered wallet to give him a couple of bucks, and then move away.

He put up a rough, brown hand. "Nope. Not yet. Come in, buy me some food, and listen to what you need to hear."

I had looked him over with some care before, but it was clear I needed to do it again, even more closely. Sandy colored hair, short enough to be easy to comb straight, just long enough to not declare an ideology either way. Forehead and eye corners with long, neat lines of deep wrinkles. They made me wonder if he had spent a great deal of time thinking hard while facing the sun. The bomber jacket looked like the genuine World War Two article; it was faded almost to gray, but the leather was soft and clean. Dark gray pants with a few old stains on them, but no fresh ones, and a pair of battered hiking boots. I'd seen much scarier.

I mentally ticked off the points: to my experienced eye he didn't look violent or psychotic, he sounded intelligent, I could almost certainly run faster than he could, and I would soon become desperate to find someone who wanted, or was at least willing, to talk. Not only that, if we went inside, the paramedics would be much less likely to find me if they were still looking. We turned and walked into the café.

On the street food comes first, unless you have a different sort of medical emergency. He ate in perfect silence. I went through three cups of tea, since anything else is too much for situations that demand clarity. When his plate was empty, he put down his fork and looked me over as carefully as I had done to him.

"Good. You know how to shut up for a few minutes."

I needed human conversation, but that didn't include insults. I neglected to reply, returning his gaze instead. He waited for about three relaxed breaths, and smiled.

"We could play, but I won't. Your need is greater than mine, and we both know it. I can tell you something about that, if you're interested."

"Am I to take it you saw what happened in the park just now?"

His eyebrows lifted slightly. "No, but I did see you down at the waterfront day before yesterday. Happened again, did it?"

It was a lot easier to get a half hour of human contact if the other party knew nothing about me. I started to get up to leave, but something in his eye caught my attention. Was there the remotest possibility that this man knew something useful to me? An Outlier might not panic when he saw the types of things that happen to me, but he could still be someone to avoid.

Feeling wary and uncertain, I eased back down into my seat. Without acknowledging my temporary change of heart, he continued.

"Okay, here it is. You already know that when you start reciting to yourself all the reasons to live, you're in serious trouble."

"I've been in serious trouble for most of my life, and I recite those reasons on a regular basis. So what?"

"All right," he said imperturbably, "You're a tough case that's been knocked around a bit. It's clear you're a survivor, and you've seen and done things, and had things done to you, that you won't be telling me or anyone else about any time soon."

My pack was on the floor, resting against the table leg. I moved my foot to touch it in an unconscious prelude to getting up and actually leaving this time. "I'd like to say this is all very interesting, but it isn't. What is it you want? What's wrong with just getting fed?"

He looked at me thoughtfully. "I'm a curious bastard, and there's nothing I can do about it. Right now I'm curious to know why a smart fellow like you hasn't asked the important question, at least not lately."

I said coldly, "I don't take tests, and I'm not interested in guessing games. Nor, for that matter, am I all that concerned with satisfying your curiosity."

He held up a hand, palm facing me, as if it were a universal signal of apology. "Bear with me just for a minute, bub. Whatever it looks like, I'm not trying to mess with you. The question is this: 'How and why did I end up here, and why should I have to put up with it?'"

He paused long enough to drain his coffee cup, and politely signaled the waitress for more. "Perhaps you've asked it, perhaps not; if you'd answered it correctly, you wouldn't be buying an old bum a late lunch—you'd be off somewhere else, doing what you were meant to do. Maybe you just haven't looked at it right. If you want, I can offer you another way to see that might work better than what you've tried so far."

Ah. I got it then—an evangelist. I wondered what psychic rut he wanted to push me into. This exchange was not what I had been looking for, and I could feel any control over it I might have had slipping away. But something about this lean, tough looking old man kept me sitting across from him, and that compulsion to stay began to make me afraid. I remained ready to leap to my feet and leave—but I remained, working hard to stay calm.

I cleared my throat, trying to sound impatient without provoking an outburst of rapture. "I'm still listening. But not for much longer."

He should have leaned across the table towards me, and whispered his message in a dramatic undertone. Instead, his voice and stance were as casually conversational as they had been all along.

"It's not hard. Your life was stolen from you shortly after your birth. It isn't uncommon or anything. What *is* uncommon is when someone realizes it, at the level of thought or just a bit below. To be honest, that seems to be the main thing that makes you unusual, and it's why you keep up this vagabond kind of business," as he glanced at my pack on the floor, "never quite figuring out who and what you are, and how to live with it."

How strange he should use it; the word *vagabond* describes me perfectly. Like many words, it carries small secrets, long buried by the humdrum of common usage and association. It stretches back to the fifteenth century, poking its way up into Middle French as *vagabonde* from the Latin *vagus*, which meant 'wandering, undecided.' It has exactly the same origin as the word *vague*. And it describes me. My life had held many of the troubles, much of the loneliness and the empty, aimless wandering of the 'undecided' vagabond, and none of the carefree romance so often tied to the word.

The clatter of a pot being dropped in the kitchen brought me back from the dark, silent place I had fallen into. I heard the clink of silverware on heavy duty restaurant china, the murmur of quiet talk elsewhere in the café, and remembered to breathe. "So you're telling me my life is a complete mess, but it's not my fault."

"It may not be your fault it started out that way", he said, "but it's your own doing that keeps it that way."

"Okay, who stole it?"

He waited while the waitress poured his coffee, and gave her a smile that left her humming on the way back to her station. "That's not important—yet. You're at least a little patient, and that serves well."

"How do you know I'm patient?"

"Anyone who will be quiet for even one minute just to piss somebody off has more patience than most of this civilization does."

I had to agree with him there.

Every time I looked at this man there was something more to see. The nails on his hands were clean but chipped and dented, as if he did a lot of brick or stonework. His knuckles were rougher than the rest of his hands, and the elbows and shoulders of his jacket were permanently scuffed.

"Were you ever a stonemason, or something like that?"

That got another smile. "Nice try, but nothing like it."

No point trying to squeeze a story out of someone. But it seemed like my initial impression was wrong: whatever this guy was, he wasn't likely to be pushing religion on me. I began to wonder a bit more seriously if this strange old man could mean more to me than a few minutes of hiding out—and maybe even have something I really did want to hear. I felt myself relax very slightly, just enough to think about being mannerly.

"My name's Ray Holdman."

"I'm Henry."

"Just Henry?"

He laughed. "That's it, bub."

Now it was my turn to laugh. A little. "I'm in no position to be suggesting things, I can tell. So look—you have my undivided attention. What are *you* suggesting?"

A long, slow sip of coffee first. "I'm suggesting that you possess qualities you don't understand very well, if at all. And that you aren't entirely powerless to retrieve that life that was stolen from you."

"You're not going to try to sell me something, are you?"

"No. You want to hear more, or just keep asking stupid questions?"

"All right—you talk, I listen," I said.

"It's clear that you're willing to hear what people have to say, in ways most folks won't. What do you think of when I say, 'The Mountain'?"

That was easy enough. "I think of what's commonly referred to as Mount Rainier, though there must be a better name for it."

"Good. Now you might think about taking your considerable talent for hearing people and going up there to ask some questions, and listen to some answers."

The waitress had begun to look earnestly in our direction, which was the politest way I've seen to say our time was up, and we should make room for someone else. It was likely a consequence of Henry's rough charm, but it felt nice anyway.

"What kind of questions?"

"I can't do all your thinking for you. Just take some time, go there, and try it."

It didn't take a lot of thought; not only was there nothing holding me here, it was imperative that I go somewhere else.

Whether or not I was going to tell this Henry person anything, I had already decided: I would head up to The Mountain. I loved it there. Not only had I hiked through its exquisite landscapes, I'd seriously thought about finding a way to live there, in secret, free to talk to any tree or human I cared to, and free to avoid the rest. It was a lovely fantasy, and it had always remained exactly that.

"All right," I said, "I'll give that some serious thought. Anything else?"

He looked at me steadily for a long moment. "Nope, that's about it. Thanks for the food, bub. I'll see you around."

He rose from his seat and made for the door in a single motion. I briefly wondered if I actually would see him around. But he had given me something to think about, and for a time Henry himself slipped out of my mind as smoothly as he slipped through the door of the café.

Chapter 2

I asked the last driver I'd caught a ride with to let me out about ten miles from the Carbon River entrance to Mount Rainier National Park. It wasn't so much that I needed to be alone, or that I wanted to sneak into the Park without paying. It seemed more natural, I guess, to walk in rather than sit in a car. I was there to listen, not to make noise; it would feel right to be doing what I came to do as I entered.

Ten miles from the park entrance is about a mile beyond the turnoff to Carbonado, the last town before the northwest side of the Park boundary. The two-lane road is narrow and battered, its shoulders cramped and uneven. The few people who live in this part of the landscape conceal themselves well, and when the traffic dies away and the wind is calm, the quiet is profound.

I had been through Wilkeson many times, and Carbonado, another town a few miles to the north, several times. They were hacked out of the "endless" forests of virgin Douglas fir that surrounded The Mountain until the late nineteenth century. The towns sprang into being in order to rip coal from beneath the ground for fuel, and the trees from above it for factories, houses, furnishings, tools and toys, and more fuel. The coal—which had certainly never asked to be torn from the earth in chunks, or taken on a train ride—was dumped into rolling hoppers and trundled off to Tacoma and Seattle. There, it was sacrificed to the smelters, the brick works, and the stoves of this land's new tenants. The trees received the same respect and gratitude as the coal, which is to say, none whatever. When I say it this way it sounds callous, thoughtless, and criminal, and perhaps it was. But how, after all, were those people supposed to live? Shall I pronounce angry judgment on the historic arrogant ignorance of a nation, or shall I instead acknowledge its profound wrongness, try to understand, and move on? Lots of responses are appropriate, but history tends to fill me with grief rather than righteous indignation.

The only family I had ever known was my father. When my grandparents—whoever they may have been—were children, these two towns were lonely islands in a sea of forest; visitors and newcomers were few and far between. The people who lived there did their work and sent away first the coal, and then the ever-increasing trainloads of timber that replaced it when the mines were played out. Today the towns are lonely islands in a ragged, patchy sea of second- or third-growth forest interspersed with ravaged, hundred acre rectangles of clearcut devastation, and there is little work to speak of. The visitors roll by in an unending stream, but their destination is the National Park, and the newcomers are as rare as ever.

Almost all of this land has been clear-cut at least once since the 1860's. The area I walked through had been worked over again, much of it some time in the last thirty years, and some of it within a few months. When you're driving through at fifty, you mentally cluck your tongue in sympathy, and soon you're inside the Park, where the trees are huge and ancient, dignified and imposing. When you walk through it at two or three miles an hour, you have a lot of time to look at these blasted landscapes, and think too much about them.

I ponder the resilience of life: the lizards, snakes, insects, birds and small mammals that either hang on stubbornly or actually move in after a catastrophe like a clearcut. Or I consider the possibility that totally destroying a forest opens strange opportunities for other plant forms to come in and start it over, maybe in a different way. Or the fact that much of what those trees were sacrificed for was used once, or wasted. Or, more distressing still, the incredible truth that for thousands of years human civilizations have willfully destroyed the enormous systems their livelihoods depend on, and we're still doing it.

For some time now no cars or trucks had come roaring past to make me jump farther away from the road, out of the way. For the moment I could afford to look around me attentively, and think about whatever I wished. On this warm, clear August day there was no wind, and the lovely quiet was broken only by the crunch of my footsteps in the coarse, gravelly dirt of the road's shoulder, and an occasional creak from my pack.

The only time I ever thought about having a pack on my back was when it made noise. I had lived out of it for nearly twenty years, and carrying everything I owned inside it was the only way of life I had known since I was fifteen. The pack's grommets, its buckles and straps had all been replaced several times with random parts cadged from wherever I could find them. It was speckled with gracelessly-sewn patches, as if it were an ancient, beloved pair of blue jeans.

Most of the times I heard a sound from my pack, it was because something in it was not right, as if the pack was calling my attention to something I should have noticed long before. This time was no exception; the rounded corner of the plywood box deep within the pack was jabbing my side. No matter how I packed that box, it always worked its way into some position that poked, or prodded, or pushed in some way that gave me no peace until I had pulled it out and tried again to place it.

I had made the box from quarter-inch plywood, ten inches wide by twelve inches long, and about four inches deep. The top was hinged, and a hasp that was much too heavy for the box held it closed with a cheap combination padlock. I had tried to shave down the sharp points at the corners, but it was a clumsy job. All in all it was not something a conscientious backpacker would lug around. The box held both my torment, and my salvation. I found a place to take a few steps off the road and slipped out of the pack. I rooted around for the box until I had extricated it, and sat with it in my lap.

The box held a fat, battered, canvas-covered three ring binder so filled with notepaper it pushed against the lid. There was no more room in the binder for new pages, and no room in my pack for another binder. The box was lined with a plastic sheet, now turning brittle, and the lid was made to overlap the box. This was my attempt to protect the most important thing I owned.

I unlocked the box, took out the binder and opened it. All but the last few pages were filled on both sides, written as small as I could manage. The first pages had been written twenty years before; the last one had been written the day before. To hold this binder open in my lap meant to read from it, the only way I had to remember from day to day that I am a real person in a real world. I opened the it at random and found myself eight years in the past.

July 17, 1992 (Crater Lake National Park, Oregon)

Fired again today. Dishwashing jobs, especially at resorts, are so easy—I wish I could keep them longer. I clung to this one for a month before the welter of voices from the land pulled me away. I went for a walk in the woods near the resort. The trees drew me in, pulling me farther and farther away, until I was deep inside the forest, disoriented and forced open to them. They passed me from one to the other, filling me with images and ideas I did not understand, and to which I had no reply. The next thing I knew, I was crawling back to the human world, weak and famished. At the restaurant they told me I had blown off three days of work, and it took all my powers of persuasion to get paid for the hours I was owed. I had to pay for a meal, and then was summarily tossed out.

> *All the trees, and in fact, all of the not-humans are*
> *so powerful here. The very rocks on the ground seem*
> *to murmur at me, adding their incomprehensible*
> *talk to that of the wildflowers, vines, bushes and*
> *grasses, as well as the trees, whom I sometimes*
> *understand. I love to hear them in my mind—*
> *whether I understand their speech or no—and at*
> *the same time I hate and fear them, for they make*
> *living among humans impossible for me.*
>
> *If I knew what they wanted of me, if I could find*
> *sense and meaning in what they say when I am*
> *their captive audience, perhaps I could accept the*
> *lot of the outcast, the role of crazy, unpredictable,*
> *and therefore dangerous man, when among men.*
> *As it is, an impossible life is simply impossible, and*
> *it continually tears me to pieces. How long will I*
> *bother to reassemble myself, and to what end?*

A moment to put the box and the past away, and I was back to walking. About three miles past the Carbonado turnoff I began to pass a clearcut that had stripped the land almost down to the road. A thin veil of trees and brush at the roadside obscured the view without really hiding it, a tattered and disreputable-looking curtain vainly trying to hide the crime beyond. On an impulse I turned from the shoulder where pitted asphalt met dirt, and clambered up a small embankment and through the screen of trees. I made my way a hundred yards up the slope to a flat spot ringed with stumps about three feet tall. Half my mind protested, citing all the reasons for going back to the road: moving on, getting to where I was headed, no time for this. The other half said simply, sit down, shut up, and *look*. I sat down.

Everywhere I glanced the ground was churned, chopped and laid back down in utter disarray. Everywhere. The dense forest understory was torn to bits by the methodical chaos of heavy machinery, and scattered like a grisly salad across the landscape.

Stems and fronds, now limp and brown, were lying flattened or sticking up grotesquely from the soil. Short stalks with ragged ends protruded at weird angles from mounds of upturned earth. The stumps had jagged tags sticking up on one side, from where the trees had been torn away from themselves as they fell; if I were to fall on one of those tags it would run through me like a bayonet. The slash piles—heaps of disordered limbs and branches so completely unlike the true chaos of a mature forest floor—were twice my height, and long and wide as a small house.

How can we do this to our home? We are the greatest natural disaster of our time; in previous ages it might have been an asteroid, a titanic eruption, or some other unimaginable, impersonal force. But in this human era it is us, and we will it so. It's personal and painful, something my eyes, mind and heart are incapable of closing themselves to. I turned to the stump nearest me. I tried not to do this, but in my mind I spoke to it:

It must be horrible to be cut down like that, in the prime of life, for no reason that has anything to do with you.

Somewhere in my mind, the stump answered.

It must be horrible to be so terrified of change.

The only real surprise in this was that, to all intents and purposes, this was no longer a tree. I had talked to trees for as long as I could remember, they had talked back for that long, and once in a great while I understood what they were saying. What did it matter? When it came to living in a society of humans, it mattered very much. Keeping these conversations a deep secret had been ingrained in me long ago, and the many times that people had seen me experiencing them were generally followed by very bad times indeed. Nevertheless: here and now, there was no one around to be afraid of the crazy man, no one to think, 'what's wrong with this guy?', no authorities to call. Besides, the conversation could be interesting; I had spoken to trees since I was a toddler, but never had I talked with a stump, and neither had they talked to me. And to actually understand what it said was a rare thing indeed.

So, then: *Meaning,* I thought to it, *that you have no fear of death? If that's so, how does the will to live, to procreate, the will to survive when the elements are trying to knock you down—how does all that happen?*

Your notions of 'living' and 'dying', said the stump, *are mysterious. How you manage to split it all up like that is beyond me. New moon or full moon, tree, seed, or rot, I am. You are. What else do you need?*

I need to understand. I need to be a lot less confused, and a lot less afraid.

It is well that you see these needs, the stump replied. *I have my path of regeneration. So do you. It's time to get busy and do some regenerating.*

What kind of regeneration can someone like me hope for?

But the stump had apparently decided the conversation was over.

Most people would be frightened, or at least seriously worried about going crazy if they were talking with a tree stump. But the world—the human world, that is—told me every day that I was already irretrievably crazy.

If you asked me during a moment when I was willing to tell the truth, I would answer: Yes, I talk to trees. Yes, they often talk back to me; in fact, they are usually the ones that start the conversation. No, I am not making it up, and I am not deluded, no matter how alien it seems. When I was a child, a long procession of foster parents and orphanage staff almost convinced me I *was* making it up. Almost. How it is they failed I don't know, but they did fail—at least in some measure—and I had found through the passage of years that trees are often safer to talk to than people. Human talk lost me my home and my childhood, and since then it had periodically landed me in small town and city jails,, and a handful of other institutions I will not describe.

When the trees speak to me, I can't refuse. They are always strong and quiet; when they talk they fill my mind to the exclusion of all else, and I can't respond to anyone but them. Sometimes I can speak my responses to them in English, but sometimes I say other, less decipherable things, and they are all said out loud without my knowledge. All this is frightening to most people, as is the behavior of most "crazy" people. I have learned time and again that to be helpless myself, and to be frightening someone, is a deeply dangerous position to be in.

None of this has led to a safe and happy life. I'd been able to stay away from the most horrid times and places for a good while, but recently I had felt my will and my resourcefulness weakening. My life was wearing me down, and I did not know how to live any other way. A clear-cut was as good a place as any to look for answers, and it was a good day when a tree stump was kind enough to remind me that there's more to life than danger, destruction, and death.

It was time to be moving along. I got up, dusted off my pants, slung my pack over my shoulders without thinking about doing it, and headed down the slope back to the road.

The most common way to reach the northwest entrance of Mount Rainier National Park is to take Highway 165 heading south from the town of Buckley. After only a few miles the highway bends further south at a T-intersection. The northwest branch of this road is called Pioneer Way. The southeast branch that heads towards the tiny town of Wilkeson and then to The Mountain looks like it's been around long enough to have earned the name "Pioneer." It does actually possess asphalt, but the road is narrow and faded, and in many places the patches themselves have been patched repeatedly. It looks like the land and weather hammer it mercilessly each year, and of course, they do.

Land, air and water are restless, and roads here are no match for them.

But the land can't teach us anything we don't already know about restlessness, and I had never been an exception to that. When I was younger I didn't mind the constant motion, never staying in one place through even a single season of the year. By the time I was walking towards The Mountain, though, I was sick of it; nothing sounded better than stopping for a good, long while.

I had never felt attached to any place or time, but The Mountain was the one place that always drew me. Most places, I sauntered or trudged or ran full tilt along roads, sidewalks, or trails, mentally cataloging and then forgetting potholes and plants, people and place names. The Mountain was different, but even there I had always wondered just what I was looking for. What could fill my own potholes?

This road, like the one that ran through my heart, had more than its share of holes, cracks, humps and divots. Like mine, it had a narrow shoulder that made it hard to stay out of the way of the traffic barreling through, and the landscape on either side tended to be chaotic and disturbed.

But the vine maple's electric green leaves glowed brilliant under the sun. The bunchgrasses sent up sheaves of rough, brown, hearty seed. And the fireweed—the ultimate pioneer—was indomitably, unpretentiously beautiful where it covered the ravaged ground I passed.

The word "pioneer" comes from the Old French *peonier*. Its literal meaning is 'foot soldier', but for many generations it has usually referred to those people—generally of low social status—who venture out well beyond the easier, settled life; those who go to open up new (to them) territories of existence. Despite the myth of the 'pioneer spirit', I believe it's a good bet that most of them would have stayed home and passed on the danger and hardship, if only they'd had a safe and comfortable way of life where they were. Hence the *peon* part of the equation, taken from the Latin for 'foot', pronounced "pawn": the lowly ones booted out into the frontier.

Fireweed is a true pioneer. In our culture, anything called 'weed' qualifies as having low social status. Fireweed comes into any area where the land is disturbed, rendered inhospitable to its previous tenants. It reproduces with astonishing speed using a combination of rhizomes (traveling, underground stems) and as many as 80,000 seeds per plant. And no matter what it's called, fireweed's blossoms have a beauty that is at once delicate, brilliant, and strong.

Its name comes from often being the first plant to establish itself after an area has burned over. It grows where nothing else is able to, and fixes nitrogen in the soil so its less hardy relatives can follow. Older cultures gave it due respect, recognizing its properties as an astringent and tonic, and its ability to ease the pains of rheumatism and age.

So my entrance into this place is in the company of a humble medicinal pioneer. Perhaps if I listen carefully, it might have some words of advice for me.

About four miles from the Park entrance the road dips sharply down towards the Carbon River. This is when I know I'm really there, really coming close to The Mountain. The road itself, which up to this point has been abused by the winters and the logging trucks alike, becomes even more battered and uneven. The ground is grittier, the plants more sparse. The river bed is about a hundred yards wide, though the river itself here digs a chaotic series of fair weather channels, none of which are more than twenty feet across. There are boulders the size of piano boxes scattered casually along its course, and the gravelly bed is littered with smaller stones, like unabridged dictionaries embedded in the coarse sand, their own secret vocabularies carefully locked away.

This place where the road comes down to the river is no more than eight miles from the lower end of the Carbon Glacier, one of several located on the north slopes of the mountain, where the Carbon river is born. As I stood at the road's edge looking out, the water was milky with rock flour ground in the glacial maw, and when I approached the river's edge I could hear the muffled clack of stones being shoved along the bottom, at the rate of perhaps a mile a century. The riverbank was as unsettled as its bed. It is never quite the same from one year to the next, and the population of low-growing salal and the tangles of willow, alder and vine maple are always vulnerable to being swept away or mown down by flood-driven stone. If I kept from stomping on the downed branches, my footsteps in the sandy spots were silent.

I had never walked the riverbank on this part of the route before. Sometimes I had stopped somewhere along it to watch and hear the river. This time I abandoned all pretense of making steady progress towards the park entrance and stayed by the river, picking my way up the gentle slope that led to the mouth of the glacier's canyon.

Three miles from the entrance a National Forest Road intersects this one, which by now is called the Carbon River Road. The National Forest Road crosses the river heading north on a bridge that had to be rebuilt just a few years ago. It used to be a rickety timber affair, made as short as possible by building up dirt embankments as close to the river's edge as could be managed, with the bridge's road raised up to the level of the Carbon River Road. This arrangement was swept away one winter when the river felt either frisky or angry—it's hard to tell which. The new bridge sports concrete and steel with its timber, though the embankments were built up again to keep the span short and the cost down. At any rate, it will work until the next hefty flood. Things are built here with the foreknowledge of their destruction, the only question being when the river will roar over its banks again.

This river crossing road goes into the Fairfax Forest Preserve, a stretch of National Forest, much of which has been "preserved" by clear-cutting. The road bears the same name, and the Fairfax Bridge is the only place for several miles where you can easily and safely cross the river's numerous channels to poke around on the other bank. So, as a matter of curiosity, I crossed it.

The other bank is sufficiently similar that a person who operates mostly on logic wouldn't feel compelled to explore it. I walked slowly on that bank, passing the time with games of observation and whimsy. Most of the plants within a hundred feet of the river are less than two years old, everything else getting washed away each fall or winter. But once in a while you come across a willow so tenacious it has outlasted more of the floods, and survived five or more years of winter battering. I crouched down near one of these, absently noting first that the light was changing: late afternoon, and no way of entering the Park before dark. It didn't matter, because there is open space in abundance here.

I spent a while considering this six foot tall willow tree. How does this tree persevere, when most are swept away by the floods? I wondered how much of its root structure's placement was the result of a lucky accident, and how much was intentional. I really wanted to know—what kind of intention does a willow manifest? I've tried to ask, but have never been able to hear a reply. Always one to try again when presented with an interesting person, I settled cross-legged in front of the willow, and tried to quiet down enough inside to form a question. I worked on slowing my breathing down, getting my attention focused on the tree; with a little luck there would be no one to come by this isolated spot and wonder what was wrong with me. After a time that could have been a few minutes or a few hours, nothing existed in the world but the tree, and my desire to ask it things.

I didn't hear anyone approaching, but from behind, a low, rough voice made it through the wall of my concentration. "Yeah, that's a good one, huh?"

After a moment to reconstruct the sequence involved with responding to another voice, I turned around slowly, saying, "You know this tree?"

For an electrifying moment I thought I was talking to a grizzly bear. The next moment allowed me to see—with intense relief—a man who might be a bear's first cousin, but still a man. Better still, not a grizzly bear at all: more like a black bear. Someone to treat with respect, certainly, but not necessarily a source of terror.

I thought he could easily be six and a half feet tall. His head was fully framed with long, shaggy brown hair and medium length beard. He wore a faded denim work shirt with the sleeves rolled up under a worn, brown pair of overalls, and his hiking boots seemed enormous. I wasn't sure about his intentions, except that I could have sworn his eyes were smiling.

He was sizing me up as intently as I was him, and took his time in answering. "Known it these seven years now. Has that rare tenacity, you see. I help it along in little ways, but it deserves all the credit."

I turned back to regard the willow again. A part of its root system had wrapped itself around a large stone half-embedded in the river gravel, and then headed straight down. Turning back to him I said, "How far down do you figure those roots go?"

His beard shifted as he grinned. It was a friendly grin, clearly meant to put me at ease. "Why don't you ask it?"

"I haven't had much luck so far getting started with this one."

In an instant the thought seized me in a grip that almost squeezed the air out of me: this guy was talking to me about *talking to trees*, as if it was the most natural thing in the world for a couple of complete strangers to be discussing. The first thing I felt after the shock was a bolt of fear; was this guy playing with me? I looked at him again, and it just didn't seem possible. The fear died down enough for me to consider going with this—extremely carefully—for another few moments.

I said, "How about you—ever get one to answer a question?"

He chuckled. "Nah, Bringers don't have the knack for talkin' to tree people like that."

"What's a Bringer?"

A look of consternation crossed his face, and then smoothed itself out. "Maybe we can talk about that sometime." He seemed to consider something seriously for a moment. Then, "I'm known as Hucklebark," he said.

"Just Hucklebark?"

"That's right."

"I seem to be meeting an unusual number of one-named folks these days."

Hucklebark smiled. "Is it all that amazin'? Who else you met with one name—anybody 'round here?"

"No, just a guy in Seattle—Pioneer Square. He's a pretty strange character, and just calls himself Henry."

His shaggy, dark brown eyebrows rose at that. "Huh. Well, that's interestin.' Might I presume that you have a name?"

"Oh, sorry. Mine's Ray Holdman."

"Ray. Well, I'm glad and interested to meet you. Where you stayin' tonight?"

I waved a hand vaguely towards the Fairfax Preserve, eastwards. "I figure there's room here somewhere."

Hucklebark laughed, a relaxed, pleased kind of laugh. "You got that right. I got a nice spot about a mile north of here. If you want, you can set up there for the night 'n we can pass a pleasant evening swappin' lies and enlightenin' each other."

Gambling comes in many forms and styles, but it's always there solely because it fills—or seems to fill—a need. My mind took another, half second peek at Hucklebark and rolled its personal pair of dice. No wheedling, no aggressiveness, no slippery come-on. So far. Despite a lifetime of bad experience, but in the absence of any kind of evidence like that, it chose to take a chance.

"Sure."

"Good. We have about twenty minutes of light left—that's plenty." He turned and started back to the embankment leading to the Fairfax road, going slowly so I could hoist my pack and follow.

Chapter 3

Hucklebark's campfire was compact and discreet. Whether that was because he didn't want to be noticed, or because he was naturally scrupulous in all he did, was something I had no way of knowing. His fire was exactly the size needed to hook one small cook- or coffee pot over it by way of a piece of wrought iron jammed into the ground. It was a cheerful little thing, and it lifted my spirits to be near it. His conversation, which was compact and discreet too, didn't amount to much until we had both pulled out supper offerings, cooked and shared them. I don't normally drink coffee at night, but it smelled so good and the prospect of declining seemed so disappointing that I joined him.

He slurped a half cup of coffee from his huge enameled metal mug and set it down carefully. "So—if you don't mind my askin'—what brings you out here, Ray?"

I laughed. "One of my favorite chestnuts is, 'Ask me anything you want—just don't expect an answer.'"

With a smile, he said, "That's all right. I don't want to pry. Some people think I'm too forward. I prefer to think I just want to get to the good parts of a conversation without all the formalities, but I do understand."

I shifted to a more comfortable sit, and thought for a minute. There was something so unthreatening about this Hucklebark, something that promised a few minutes or hours of unjudged relief from my normal human experience, that it pushed me to ignore all the complex, cautionary behavior I'd built up over a lifetime of living in hostile environments. Why should I tell this person anything? Because I am a human, and humans need to tell things to each other. It's that simple, and ultimately, that intractable.

"Actually, though I don't exactly know why, I think I'm willing to talk about that. I'm here because I don't know where else to go; I'm out of options."

His eyes came up from the campfire to mine. "I could see how a life might run out of options if you was mortally sick or injured, or rotting in a prison cell somewhere. But you look healthy, intelligent and able to me. Care to say more on that?"

"There's more to life than a brain that works—at least part of the time—and a reasonably functional body," I said. "There are things like balance between all the different parts of a being. Things like never being able to fit in, never having the slightest chance at settling somewhere. Things like living a life of uselessness, of—of pointless movement that can never stop, things like—like never being able to understand what's required of you, like an emptiness that refuses filling."

He put his coffee cup down, picked up a stick and carefully adjusted the coals in the fire, eventually snuggling the stick among the coals. Reaching to his right for more wood, he said, "All right. It was wrong of me to throw the smug and simple at you— hope you'll forgive it. I know my share about what you're saying. It takes a different shape for each of us, though. What's after you, and what's it look like?"

That led to a long silence. Hucklebark kept it while I considered not only how to answer him, but whether or not to answer at all. This meeting had suddenly become something much more than "swappin' lies and enlightenin' each other." Once again the chance-taker inside told me to go just one step further, while the rest of my internal Babel was screaming at me to close up and leave. What was making me want to open up to this stranger, to hand over everything I'd spent my life so ferociously clutching to my chest? It almost felt like this Hucklebark was a tree who had invited me in, and nothing I thought or tried would allow me to refuse him. A fear began to rise in me, and the urge to grab my pack and flee into the darkness was strong. And yet I still sat there. My mind, which was hard to control at the best of times, took a step to the side, ignoring the mounting anger at the too-familiar feeling of powerlessness, and considered a response instead. The words were forced from me, halting and yet determined, and I heard them with astonishment.

"There—there's no fire-breathing, slobbering, mythical monster on my trail. I almost wish there was, so I could turn and fight and get it over with, one way or the other. What's after me is people—human people. I scare them. They think I'm crazy, they think I'm dangerous. They run me out every time I stop somewhere for more than a few days, because they can't accept the fact that the trees talk to me, and—and what the trees have to say is more important than what humans say. There's no rest, no safety, no friendship, nothing but fear and hating and fleeing and running. And the—the trees keep trying to take me to places, to ways—ways of seeing and feeling that don't make any sense to me. It's—I don't know, it's been going on for so long, and I'm tired, and I'm sick of the whole thing, and there's no way out of it."

Hucklebark's eyebrows had risen a couple of notches when I said *the trees talk to me*—even though he had found me trying to do just that—and I was filled with dread that I had made a spectacularly stupid mistake, and would spend the rest of the night running. What he said next was the last thing in the world I expected.

Quietly, he said, "What the trees have to tell us usually *is* more important than that endless human jawing. Like I already told you, I can't hear 'em, and more's the pity."

He looked down at the fire, muttering to himself. I thought I heard something like, '...always louse it up with speakers...' He looked back up at me.

"So, are you crazy? You dangerous?"

All the fear and uncertainty twisting inside suddenly rose up into a hot, tight ball that almost closed my throat, and I flushed with anger. "Yes, of course I'm crazy! And no, I'm not crazy at all. And I'm only dangerous if you have a mind that runs howling like a dog that stuck its tail in the fire, every time you hear or see something that doesn't fit into a neat little pill you've swallowed a thousand times already. That answer work for you?"

He surprised me again, this time by not getting angry, not even reacting to my outburst.

"Yeah, Ray, that answer works. Well, I'm not known for my instant, penetratin' insight." The fire had started smoking a little, and he adjusted it to burn with perfect clarity again. "You said you'd run out of options, so you came here. How'd that come about?"

"It was this guy Henry. I don't even know exactly what he said to make me think there's something here. But once he started talking about coming to The Mountain to ask people things, I had to." I looked over at the battered pack and sleeping bag that held everything I had owned since it was possible for me to own anything. I thought again about picking them up and leaving, getting away from this baffling, unruffled puzzle of a man. And again, I simply remained sitting there, wondering why I did so.

Hucklebark drained his coffee cup and rinsed it from a pan of water near the fire. "Sounds to me like enough talk for one night. Look, Ray—you can go or stay tonight, I got no agenda here. But if you want to stick around, we might find something of interest tomorrow."

"What would that be?"

He got up and went over to his gear, pulling out his sleeping bag. "What say we let it rest 'til morning."

"All right, then. Suit yourself," I said. Hucklebark set down an old saddle blanket and then his bag a few feet from the fire. He was no more than eight feet away from me, but I could feel that he was leaving me completely alone. It was oddly comforting. When he had gotten into the bag and been still for a bit, I set up my own bag on the other side of the fire. I lay on my back, hands under my head, and contemplated the night sky.

The south was filled with a thick cloud layer, but overhead and to the north it was clear. When I was a kid I used to make up constellations in the sky, when the city lights didn't hide them. I had cats, cars, trees, bicycles. But ever since I'd read the myth of Prometheus fifteen years before, that's all I had been able to see. Everywhere I looked in the sky, I saw a man chained to a boulder, with a huge eagle pecking out his insides. But Prometheus was lucky, because he knew every day what was coming for him and why. And *he* got rescued—conveniently and completely—by no less a personage than Hercules. Those of us lowly humans who live out our lives as demon food have nothing like that to hope for.

My mind ran, as it had for years, in a mortally tiresome circle, touching and then recoiling from humans, memories, times and places that were like wounds that would never heal. It was, like all of me, exhausted from endless movement, and terrified of being still.

Most of the time if I don't remember my dreams, sleep helps with all of this. I said a short mantra to ward off dreaming, and went to work on becoming unconscious.

Chapter 4

I put a great deal of stock in what I see when I first awaken in the morning. Whether superstition, or habit, or something even less respectable, it is important to me, and I don't quarrel with the notion. Even with its stupendous disadvantages, there's something that must be said about the Promethean life: the sunrises are incredible. If, when I wake up in the morning, I see something I can identify as beautiful, or that catches my interest, I know that something has already happened to make the day worth engaging in.

This morning there were multiple things of beauty and interest, an auspicious beginning. The eastern sky, clear as the world's first day must have been, was washed with a dusty rose hue that could be nothing but a benediction. The small stones that hemmed in the cold campfire, the ash inside their circle, the fireweed reaching up to the sky in its light blanket of dew—everything shone with an insistent, piercing clarity. Across the campfire from me, the man/bear who called himself Hucklebark sat cross-legged on top of his rumpled sleeping bag. His huge hands were draped like lounging cats in his lap, and his eyes were hooded. I counted four of my own breaths before I saw his chest expand slightly.

Quietly as I could manage, I got disentangled from my own bag and stood. Hucklebark appeared to be utterly unaware I was there, which was fine with me for the moment. I turned and walked softly away from the campsite to look for a place to relieve myself.

The night before, I'd seen very little of this hillside nook that Hucklebark had claimed, for we'd arrived in the last moments of dusk. This morning I saw that it was in the midst of a huge clear cut. The stumps lurched across the landscape like broken teeth, and it hurt like that to look at them. The area hadn't been replanted yet; all the vegetation to see on this slope was some scraggly bunchgrass, and the fireweed. But oh, the fireweed!

It grew in thickets, in carpets, in groves. In this early August weather its long, upright rods made four-foot cones of color with their tiny blossoms. The bumblebees were already on the job; even here, where the altitude is only about 3500 feet, their deadline is hard and short. The fireweed stretched up the hillside to the north, and far to the east and west. Off beyond this enormous patch the ragged line of fir seedling replants took over.

I walked a hundred yards up the torn slope, hopping bulldozer ruts and skirting slash piles, and sat down facing the valley. The fireweed stretched out before and behind me, making a deep carpet of color that ranged from light plum to violet wherever the soil chemistry changed. The river from here was a benign gray snake at canyon's bottom, waiting for the sun to surmount the ridge so it could bask in it. Across the valley to the south and west—the direction from which I had come—there were patches of adult fir that had escaped the chainsaw by virtue of their inaccessibility. I sat as quietly as I could, trying to empty my mind to make room for this remarkable, haunting place and its feel.

My mind was not in the mood for making room. It wanted to run, its perpetual squirrel cage squeaking with each revolution. I thought about Henry, and what he might have been talking about—if anything. I thought about Hucklebark, and wondered if I was a fool to have anything to do with him. I doubted my ability to know if I was adventurous and open, or stupid and self-destructive. I looked hard at the reasons I'd recited to myself for coming here, as if examining the motives of a character in a deservedly forgotten soap opera. When I started to doubt that I was capable of actually perceiving things of beauty and interest, I knew my mind would not let me just enjoy this place and the moment. I got up, dusted off my pants and with a sigh of resignation slowly headed back to Hucklebark's campsite.

Hucklebark had a small fire going with his coffee pot hanging over it. He looked up at my approach with a puzzling mixture of friendliness and reserve. "Morning. Got any coffee with you? I'm running low."

I went over to my pack and started rummaging. "Yeah, some really nice French roast. I hope I didn't disturb you earlier."

That seemed to help some. Hucklebark relaxed visibly. "Nah, no problem at all. I don't notice much at that point. You probably could have hollered bloody murder and I wouldn't have had a clue."

I smiled. "I thought about that. If you don't mind my asking, what kind of meditation discipline do you use?"

He hesitated. "I don't even think of it that way, tell you the truth. To me it's more like—well, inventory, I guess."

"Inventory. I have to think about that for a bit."

Hucklebark chuckled, a low near-growl that still managed to be friendly. "Don't break anything. If it's me doing somethin', you can depend on it not bein' too deep."

I wasn't at all sure of that, but didn't answer. With the coffee grounds safely dumped into the pot, we sat back and waited in a silence that approached comfortable. My outburst the night before wasn't forgotten, but it seemed like perhaps it was forgiven. I was willing to assume it resolved, and see about letting it flow on downstream to be a useful memory without being too painful. My gratitude to people who let that happen is almost pathetic. To cover that up, I moved on to what I hoped was a safe subject.

"You mentioned something interesting today. Ready to tell all?"

He grinned. "Coffee first, then work. A rule I live by."

I laughed. "I can handle that."

Hucklebark gingerly lifted the hot lid from the kettle and gave the coffee a gentle stir with a long-shank screwdriver he pulled from a jacket pocket. "Ready in about two minutes."

"Is that a Swiss Army kitchen utensil, or the first thing that came to hand?" I said, smiling.

"Ah. We'll get to that. Anyway, the answer is pretty much Yes."

The coffee pot started to make the light crackle they do when the water begins to get good and hot, but not yet boiling. I thought about the Fairfax Preserve road, only a mile away, and the Carbon River Road another mile beyond. In this incredible quiet, we would easily hear a car or truck from that distance, and it would intrude on the landscape for ten minutes or more. But there was no car or truck now, and in the still air the silence was so profound that the Carbon River's distant murmur was the only backdrop to the small snap of the fire and the pot, which soon began to bubble.

The sun wouldn't be making an appearance over the eastward peaks of the Cascade Range for another hour or more, but the light grew, and the knife-like clarity of dawn softened into early morning as Hucklebark lifted the coffee pot from the iron stake with his screwdriver, setting it down gently. A battered dish towel served as potholder so he could pour into our cups. The smell of the coffee, mixed with the sweet smell of the cleanly burning wood, made me wonder what more was necessary in life—even as my mind reminded me of the hunger for something I couldn't even properly identify, a hunger that gnawed at me without letup.

A cup later, I said, "Okay, out with it. What's up today?"

He put his cup down on the sandy ground and picked up his screwdriver with a curious mix of familiarity and tenderness I'd never seen devoted to something so common. "If you want to, I'll take you on my work rounds today. Before you get into too many questions, I got to say that I'd rather let you spend the day observin', then we'll talk more tonight. That agreeable?"

"Just a couple of questions that have to be answered first. Do you kill things? Will we be running afoul of the law, the rangers, or anyone else? And finally, would my ignorance be a liability to either one of us for any reason?"

Hucklebark chuckled. "Good questions, all. No, most un-likely, and definitely not, as long as you're willin' to stretch your patience farther than it's likely gone before."

I considered while he poured the rest of the coffee. What he proposed was still completely obscure, yet his answers were immediate and concrete. What was it I'd come here for this time, after all? "It sounds fine. I'll do my best to stay out of your way."

"Don't worry too much about that. What I'll show you is outwardly uncomplicated. It's the part that can't be expressed in a bunch of words that'll make for a bit of work."

"I'm good to go," I said. "Ready when you are."

"I don't normally eat much until midday. That gonna work for you?"

"At least today it will," I said.

"All right, let's clean up and get on it."

One thing I liked about Hucklebark's spartan camping style was that it took about three minutes to be ready to go. In that much time we were ambling down slope back towards the Fairfax Preserve road. I had already had a good look at the landscape up above, so I wasn't surprised by the yawning clear cut all around us.

About a quarter mile from the road Hucklebark abruptly turned away from it, heading eastward across the slope at a place that looked like there was absolutely nothing to distinguish it from any other point in the landscape. I decided to make a game of seeing how long I could go without speaking. For some that might be easy, but for me, the sound of my voice interacting with someone else's in a friendly way is a rare comfort. It would be a challenging game. I followed Hucklebark about six feet behind, in silence.

We walked more or less parallel to the Carbon River, and about a mile and a half up slope from it, for a couple of miles. We took almost an hour to walk it, for in many places the slope was steep and the ground rough where it had been savaged by machinery. I felt exposed and vulnerable on this logged-over slope, which seemed funny when I thought it over. I had walked on many thoroughly exposed slopes near the tree- and vegetation lines on The Mountain. But up there, you're supposed to be exposed. Here, there was supposed to be a thick, hundred foot high canopy of fir, and when we were lucky, some cedar.

We approached a raw, new looking creek that had dug its way about six feet into the slope on its way down to the Carbon. Scrambling down into the tiny ravine, Hucklebark turned and began to work his way up it, staying to the side of the creek when he could. It was maybe three feet wide, and not moving very fast this time of year, for there was no snowmelt from the ridges above us. As we hiked upwards, the walls of the ravine grew taller and the climb steeper. A half hour after we'd begun to follow the creek, he stopped and slipped out of his pack. I followed suit, and sat down a few feet away.

Hucklebark surveyed the place intently. The walls of the ravine were about twenty feet tall here, while the bottom, which held the creek, wasn't more than ten feet across. The walls were steep enough that climbing them looked chancy if not out of the question, and there was nothing here I could find that looked any different from what we had seen until then.

He sat down on the ground, about three feet from the little creek, facing the west wall of the ravine. I sat quietly about ten feet to his left, figuring he'd shoo me off if I was in the way. His hands, resting in his lap, began to assume the lounging cat aspect I had seen that morning, which suggested we might be there for a while. His breathing began to slow, but his eyes were wide open, gazing in an unfocused way at the ravine wall.

We sat that way for nearly three hours. I was incapable of actually holding still for that long, though I managed to get through it by moving my legs very slowly, and resisting their movement as I crossed and uncrossed them, stretched them out in front of me, and once assumed a kneeling position. Hucklebark, on the other hand, never seemed to move anything more than his eyes. I wouldn't see him move them—it was more a matter of seeing after some period of time that he was looking in a slightly different direction. The rest of him could have been concrete poured into a vaguely bear-shaped form and left to harden.

When he was done, he unfolded his legs very slowly, stretched them and his arms, yawning. Looking back towards me he grinned and said, "Nicely done, Ray. You want to get a small fire goin', or do you have a stove? I know I could use some coffee."

I chose to use the white gas bottle that powered my tiny cookstove rather than forage for firewood. The coffee pot came out of his pack and, filled with water, perched on the stove. He yanked a plastic bag from his pack, and pulled out a thick slab of something that came with a purplish tinge, and was crumbling at the edges. "You want some? Keep you going for days on end."

I did my best to be mannerly, but couldn't quite avoid eyeing it with some suspicion. He waved it in my direction.

"It's vegetarian pemmican. Berries, a few pinches of various roots and barks, and peanut butter instead of bear fat or fish oil."

I extended my hand to receive a hunk of the stuff.

"Thanks, I'll give it a try."

It tasted much better than it looked, though the roots would take a little getting used to.

We ate in silence, the tinkling of the tiny creek making up for our lack of conversation. When the coffee pot had made its bubbling announcement and we had gone through a first cup, Hucklebark seemed to decide I'd waited long enough.

"I imagine you're pretty curious about starin' at a ravine wall for three hours, and callin' it 'work.'"

I had to smile. "The thought crossed my mind, I'll admit."

Hucklebark stared at the ground, concentrating. "It's really hard to know where to begin. But I bet you know at least a bit of geology, natural history, stuff like that."

I looked around me at the creek, the ravine, the few scrub bushes that grew there after the devastation of the clear cut. My eye caught a patch of fireweed at the lip of the ravine well above me, with its glinting, violet blossoms waving lazily in the early afternoon breeze.

"Not what you'd call disciplined education, no. But I read all the time, I have since I was five, and you can pick up a lot that way."

I smiled with a trace of bitterness. "Books will keep you company when nobody else will."

"But you know at least a bit about how wind 'n water and time shape a land and everybody that lives on it, and maybe an idea or two about what lies beneath the surface, yeah?"

"Sure, a little," I said. "I've spent some time in interpretive centers around here, read a good bit about volcanoes, glaciers, and all that. I'm no specialist."

He laughed. "No problem there. But look here, Ray." He leaned forward. "Change is something that never stops. We all do it, we're all a part of it, and we're all responsible for it. Make sense?"

I left the question in the air for a moment. "Yeah, it makes sense on an intellectual kind of level. But do I feel that in my gut? I'm not sure."

"Still not a problem," he said. "If you're willin' to be open to that, and to be open to some new ideas, you'll find what I do real interestin'. Right now, though, it's time to get back to it. Just so you know, I don't work for three days at a time or anything."

"Good thing. I don't have that kind of stamina," I replied.

Hucklebark hoisted himself to his feet and returned to the spot near the creek where he had sat before. As he settled himself in, I moved to a different place farther behind him for a change of perspective. The ravine wall I was nearly backed up to wasn't vertical enough to lean against, but it still felt like I was right next to something solid and reassuring. When I sat down, I immediately felt a rock. Lifting my backside to pull it away, I saw that the rock was shaped like a small fist with the first two fingers pointing out. Turning it over in my hand, I thought briefly about how wind, water and time sculpt these things, and if one might ever find real meaning in the sculpture, instead of a simple "oh, this looks like that." I set the rock down beside me, thinking if I ever did find an answer, it wouldn't likely be today.

Hucklebark had resumed his original stance, gazing intently at the ravine wall. I tried to settle in for another multi-hour wait, hoping to keep some semblance of watchfulness. What was all this business about change? I was willing to agree that no other living things have changed the world in so short a time as humans have—who would argue with that? And any thinking person would concur that it's our responsibility—not only to ourselves, but to all things living—to make at least some attempt at intelligent use instead of wasteful stupidity. But it seemed like Hucklebark was trying to tell me something more and I couldn't get to it. I felt a lot more like a piece of human flotsam being carried along a raging river of change than like some steward of it. I had very little faith in my own abilities to be a useful or important influence in the world, and not much more in humanity in general.

Shift legs. Think. Shift hips. Think. Whatever Hucklebark was doing, I didn't expect to master it any time soon—if that was even what this was about. I couldn't sit still for more than a few minutes, and my mind would not stop gnawing on everything within its reach.

It was then that Hucklebark surprised me again. We had only been sitting this time for a half hour or so when he uncoiled himself from the ground, stepped over the tiny creek and strode over to the ravine wall on the other side. I would never have thought anyone could climb it, let alone someone as massive as him, but climb it he did—slowly, without tension or excitement. He placed his feet and hands with ponderous deliberation, making his way up the nearly vertical wall. About fifteen feet off the ground he stopped and replanted his feet. The Swiss Army kitchen utensil—the long-shank, flat bladed screwdriver—emerged from a pocket somewhere. Held in his right hand, it hovered for a moment over the rocky dirt of the wall. Then he gouged a pockmark in the wall; the displaced dirt fit comfortably in his palm. Sliding the dirt into a vest pocket, Hucklebark began backing slowly down the wall. He used ten minutes to make his way down. At the creek bank again, he gently dusted off his hands and looked in my direction. "That's it for this place. There's another spot about a quarter mile up slope to work with today."

Watching him do all this, I'd forgotten to be restless. Now I could feel a cramp waiting to pounce on my left foot. "I don't mean to be flip, but that handful of dirt you put in your pocket—

does that represent four-plus hours of work?" I said, yanking at my boot to forestall the cramp.

He grunted. "No. More like a week. Come on, I want to get this done before dark." He shrugged into his pack and stalked down slope, and I scrambled to keep up. Soon we turned to the ravine wall and began to climb out. I had the feeling we had only come this far down so Hucklebark could find a place where I could climb out too. Sure enough, once I managed to scrabble my way to the top we turned back up slope, heading across the rough ground in an easterly direction. About twenty minutes of hard walking left me well winded. Hucklebark stopped abruptly at the base of a stone outcrop about ten feet across. It rose no more than three feet into the air, its flat top making a rock platform of sixty square feet. He pointed to a spot about ten feet from the outcrop, indicating I should sit. Then, having slipped out of his pack again, he took up a standing position facing the outcrop and planted his feet firmly.

He had been standing like this for no more than about ten minutes when I realized that if the light had been different, I might have mistaken him for a tree. He looked so completely *rooted* it was easy to imagine I'd have to find some way to pull his feet up or leave him there. The sun had dropped behind the ridges to the southwest of us while we were walking, and the light was fading now. Hucklebark stirred, and slowly moved a foot to his left, again planting himself firmly on the ground.

I was less worried about my own restlessness now, knowing that we'd be done soon with whatever it was we were doing. I almost missed the small movement of retrieving the screwdriver; Hucklebark stood with it in his hand for several minutes, then suddenly swooped down and drove it into the ground a few inches from the rock face. He levered the screwdriver back and forth several times, and pulled it from the ground. His left hand delicately scooped dirt from the hole he'd punched, pulling it gently away from the rock to make a fist-sized V-shape in the ground at the rock face. Then he stood again, pocketed the screwdriver, and went to retrieve his pack. "That's it for today. Man, I'm hungry. What say we get back to camp and eat ourselves out of house and home?"

I laughed. "Yeah, I know. This sitting quietly for hours on end is the most hellacious hard work. Whatever it's about, I'm with you—let's go."

The walk back was mostly silent as we concentrated on keeping our way in the failing light. By the time we got back to his camp site, the stars overhead were appearing. We indulged in some more silence while a fire was started and food prepared. But when the rice was still twenty minutes from being done, and I had another chunk of Hucklebark's pemmican inside me, I decided I'd had enough silence.

"Hucklebark. I've shut up for a long time, at least by my standards. But I'm not a disciple, I've never been one, and I wish you'd just tell me what in the world you did today."

He laughed, a deep slow rumble that alternated between comforting with its own comfort and infuriating in its refusal to hurry. "You've done way better than I have a right to ask for, Ray. I'm gonna try and keep you from any more suspense." His gaze shifted to the fire, and he gently adjusted it with that precision I was coming to admire deeply. "Never thought of myself as a teacher. In fact, I've usually thought of myself as a pretty poor student, let alone capable of teaching anyone else. So all of a sudden, here I am in the position of tryin' to introduce you to something that I'm prepared to say is unteachable."

"Wait a minute. You'll forgive my memory, but I can't recall sitting at the gates of your temple and begging for admission. Since when did I ask for a teacher, or to be introduced to anything?"

He looked up from the fire. "When I first ran into you, you were makin' a noble but misguided attempt at being taught by a willow tree."

"Misguided?" I said. "So you know more about this kind of thing than I do, maybe. But I still don't remember walking up to you and saying 'Good day, whoever you are, would you kindly take me under your wing and show me things I don't know about and haven't imagined yet?'"

That got a smile from him. "You've hit on the important part, whether you know it or not. That's what I like about you, Ray—among other things. Think about it this way. Let's say I've been given something that's really—I mean *really*—important to you, and you don't even know it. Let's also say that I have two choices here: I can say nothing at all to you and depend on dumb luck to bring you to me, or I can pick you up by the scruff of the neck, plop you down somewhere, and bang stuff into your head with a mental nine-pound hammer. How's that work for you?"

"How that works for me is I'm trying hard to not say something I'll regret instantly. I'm also taking a lot of trouble to not stand up, grab my pack and get out of here."

Hucklebark extended his arms in an "okay, okay" gesture. "That's exactly what I would do. Now, let's get past the stupid part as quick as possible. Let's say instead there's a huge territory between those two useless ways. Say it's a territory that has lots more room for spectacular mistakes and spectacular success than either end. Done that way, there's time and—and some kind of structure where we can get to know each other, decide if each even makes sense to the other. I can test my gut feeling that you need what I can offer; you can hear some of my clumsy explanations and make a reasoned choice."

"You're the second one in recent memory to decide you know more about me than I do," I said. "While I suppose I'm honored to be so interesting, I have to say it could get tiresome real soon."

He grimaced. "Yeah. You're referring to Henry. Look at it this way, Ray." He leaned forward. "Henry and I don't exist for most people. At least, we don't exist in the sense of who we really are, what we really do. Now it's not easy to offer something to someone if they don't suspect its existence. I'm willing to be sorry about being pushy, but give me a little credit for tryin' not to be."

The lid to the rice pot was rattling, so I nudged it back into place. The pot burbled happily, and I heaved a noisy sigh. "Okay, you have a point about trying to talk to people about what they don't suspect is there—I know a great deal about that. But before going into it, tell me this—why? Why me, why you, why anybody? Are you some kind of recruiter? I got that impression with Henry."

He snorted. "Henry and I respect each other, but we don't always agree and sometimes we have to work to get along. Lucky for both of us our work leaves us with plenty of elbow room. But as for you—sure, we can always use help. The work I'll tell you about has room for as many folks as want to do it. I found you doin' somethin' I've never seen anyone I didn't already know out here do, except once or twice a long time ago. That makes you interestin', Ray—interestin' to such as us. If you'll put up with my bad teachin' style for tonight, at least, I won't ask you for another minute if you don't want to spare it."

I picked up a twig and adjusted a brand in the fire, wondering if it was Hucklebark's job and I was trespassing. But he smiled and said without demonstrating, "They smoke less if you cross 'em a little looser."

Still playing with the brand, I said, "I guess the whole thing has me tangled up hard. I come up here on the word of a strange but convincing guy, looking for a chance to find the way out of a life that doesn't work and can't keep going like it has been. But I come, thinking I'll just listen to people and something will either reveal itself or not. But the first one I run into—I haven't even walked into the park yet!—starts in with teaching me things I didn't ask for and that make no sense whatever. I guess I was hoping for something a little less obscure." A small, pinched laugh, and I added, "Though why I should expect something reasonable is a good one. Crazy people shouldn't be so fussy, huh?"

I put down the twig. "Okay. I keep circling around to the fact that for me there's nothing to lose. I may not look like I have nowhere else to go, but looks are both more and less than they seem," I smiled, "especially to someone who looks at a dirt wall for four hours at a stretch."

He laughed. "Yeah, you might think that. Well, good, then. Here's my proposition. You spend a few minutes seeing what you can work out for yourself about what got done today, and ask me whatever you want. Then I tell you a story, and we sleep on it. Does that work better than the brushoff or the nine pound hammer?"

"Sure. As long as we get to eat."

Hucklebark started. "Oh, man! I almost burned it to death!" He snatched the pot from the fire, setting it down and sucking on his fingers. The rice was just beginning to smell nutty, but he'd caught it a minute away from scorching. "Ha. Lucky again. Let me get a can of beans in here, some flavor, and it's dinner." I turned back to my own pack, rummaged until I found and offered a small canister of chili powder. He accepted it with a nod, opened the can and sniffed, and raised his eyebrows appraisingly.

"So. Industrial Strength. How much?"

I shrugged. "A teaspoon if you're brave, a tablespoon if you're a madman, a couple of pinches if you're normal. It's pain medicine."

He eyed the can with suspicion. "Does it relieve pain, or cause it? Well, whatever you call it, I'll go against my nature and try 'normal'." He took out three pinches, just to be (I thought) not *too* normal, and divided the stew into our bowls. "Ready when you are, Ray."

I ate for a couple of minutes, thinking about how to think about the day's "work." Hard as I tried, nothing really presented itself. "I'm drawing a blank, Hucklebark. We sat, you dug a couple of little holes in odd places, and that was it. How am I supposed to get anything from that?"

"Come on, Ray, you can do better than that. What did it look like I was doing?"

I heaved another sigh. "Okay, it looked like you were watching television. Though your eyes weren't vacant enough; in fact, they weren't vacant at all."

"That's great!" he said. "So if I didn't look like I'd left my mind in my backpack, what else might I have been doing?"

"Hm. Maybe you were reading a book."

"Beautiful! You're closer than you think. Where were we?"

"I'm staying patient, Hucklebark, notice that. We were in a small ravine."

"And in the ravine was…"

"A little bit of running water." I started to get a strange idea. "Wait a minute. You trying to tell me you're doing some crazy kind of drainage work?"

Hucklebark lightly slapped his knee. "Close enough for horseshoes, Ray. And by the way, the book is three dimensional, anywhere from a couple hundred yards to miles deep, and the deadline for the work is "someday." Want to give the brain a break and hear a story instead?"

"I thought you'd never get to it."

"Okay," he said, "This is a story about a person I know. It's not too old, and it'll be obvious I got a lot of help with the words. Been practicin' it since a little while after it happened, so you get to listen to my version of high-falutin' oral-history-slash-literature."

I settled back against my pack. "Off you go, mate, I've got all night." Hucklebark began to speak, in a completely different tone of voice, as if he was reciting an ancient, epic adventure.

Chapter 5

A trail of boot prints in the mid-May snow makes a line up the northern slope of a mountain. Here above the timberline the landscape seems barren. The sparse, tough grasses and patches of low, fleshy-leafed stonecrop are covered by a deep layer of snow that leaves only the rocky prominences visible, and the wildflowers still sleep under the coarse, sandy earth.

At the end of the boot tracks Mad Lupine stands alert and still, facing the slope. The legs of her faded blue jeans are crusted with snow. A battered parka rests on her shoulders.

Lupine stands quiet. Her stance is like a younger and softer version of the dwarf fir and spruce that live out their centuries fifteen hundred feet below. She has stood here for hours, listening with feet and legs, belly, heart and ears. She doesn't think about the years she has come up this slope to listen and feel. Her work consumes her—the trembling ground, the tiny differences of temperature expressed in the snow's density and moisture from spot to spot. The rumble of movement beneath is a sound so deep and slow the ears don't sense it. Her young looking face and trim body belie the long, long time she has come here—to hear, to sense, read and taste a puzzle of power and complexity beyond reckoning. Mad Lupine is a Change Bringer, one of the many Speakers for the Earth.

Each place in the world has its Change Bringers, though they are not always human. They are people whose work is to help keep and handle the tension, the energy that shapes and maintains those places. They aren't mythological creatures, though sometimes mythology builds up around them. Of course they're human, but drawing lines between human and not-human in the ordinary way doesn't always work. Flesh, bone, spirit and energy come together in ways that don't always allow that easy distinction, in order to see and meet everyone that's out there. If the question must be asked, set it aside for now and return to it later.

There is a man in this part of the world known as He Works, who was responsible for finding the right one to help bring about this coming change. No one really thought there was any decision to be made. This was work for a master, and there was little doubt it would end up being her. All who knew her knew well that Mad Lupine was daring without being reckless, wise without being too serious, just slightly crazy without being in any way insane. She was perfect for a mountain trembling with unimaginable power—like this one.

Lupine tried to gracefully put him off when He Works had met with her years before, to assign the task. Usually in these cases a short game is played out, a game of polite refusal and honorary rebuttal. This time He Works gently but firmly refused the game, and stayed uncharacteristically to the point. Lupine began to understand, then, the responsibility that was being laid upon her.

Now, on this morning of change, the cloud cover is high and gray and the air is hazy. Lupine's straight, dark, shoulder length hair ruffles in the chilly breeze as the ground continues to growl and vibrate underfoot. Great wafts of steam curl into the sky around the bend of the mountain, but Lupine doesn't notice them; she is reading, sensing The Mountain's muscles as they clench below.

There is a sound like underground thunder, slow and huge. It comes up through her feet, a physical wave moving up the length of her body. Lupine stirs as if from sleep; she raises her boots from the depressions her body heat has eaten into the snow, and begins to walk slowly in a wide, clockwise circle.

The sound rises an octave. Her circle is about a hundred yards across. Her body is listening so intently it crackles with the energy starting to roil around her. Her steps quicken, and the circle tightens with each revolution. Four, then eight, then twelve turns and the circle is ten feet wide, and her steps have become a quick, nervous dance. When the circle is six feet wide she breaks the pattern, turning inward to a spot in the snow a foot or so off center. A small smile is born on her face. Dropping to her knees, Lupine pushes aside some of the snow. It lies a little more than three feet deep here; soon she is back on her feet bent over, digging the snow out and flinging it through her legs in a constant spray. Ice crystals dig tiny cuts into the flesh of her hands.

In a few minutes there is a circular patch of bare ground, just enough for Lupine to kneel into. She blows on her hands, rubs them hard for feeling. The earth beneath her is quivering, held in check by the slimmest mass—a mass enclosed in a tiny space. A long, still look at the bare spot to listen and feel for a few last moments, and then Lupine brings out a battered, dull gray tablespoon from her parka. The ground is frozen so that she must jab and dig at the soil to chip out the small pieces of a spoonful. She digs out about a cup of soil, places the frozen clumps in the parka's pocket, and rises to her feet.

The ground's growling has risen in pitch again. As Lupine stands over the tiny hole, gazing at her finished work, the coming loss crashes down upon her. She can hear every cry of terror that will be cut short today. Her gut is wrenched in advance by each wave of panic that will rise and be abruptly extinguished. She is suffocated, drops heavily to her knees, borne down. Tears pour from her to the frozen ground. The time for all this death has finally come; all her foreknowledge of this day, all the girding of her heart against this responsibility, is swept away. Her broken sobs are carried away on rising clouds of steam.

Slowly, over minutes, Lupine's breath comes to rest and her mind and sight return to The Mountainside. Though time is now short, Lupine says a long, silent prayer for everyone and everything in this landscape. Then she turns and with long, fierce strides lopes down the mountainside.

Thirty minutes later she is nearly three miles away and three thousand feet lower, crawling into a small cave hidden in the dense forest on a ridge facing away from the mountain, across the river valley that drains the mountain's north-facing glaciers. Lupine is not surprised to find the cave already almost full of hiders—raccoons, coyote, rabbits, deer mice, voles, martens, fishers, salamanders and frogs—none of them fighting or trying to eat each other. She moves ten feet in towards the back and they make way for her, moving back in to fill up the space as she passes.

The waiting is done. As Lupine sits cross-legged, the earth rears up and a great fist of sound clubs her. The cave floor leaps, then plunges. Lupine sees the landslide in her mind's eye: half a mountain rising up and then simply slipping away to crash into the valley below. It makes a five hundred foot high breaking wave of earth, ice, and perishing life.

Inside the cave, small chunks of rock knocked loose from the roof pelt them; Lupine is flung first against the ceiling, then to the floor, for she has nothing to hold on to. At times she lands on something soft and quickly rolls away. Sometimes hair- or fur-covered shapes collide with her. She and all of them are terrified to silence, desperately riding.

A tearing, whistling sound comes from outside the cave's mouth. The air is abruptly yanked from their lungs and pulled through the opening, and all are gasping, on the edge of panic. For an agonizing time the air is ripped screaming away from the ridge, and there is nothing to breathe. Almost a minute later the shrieking dies away and a little air limps back into the cave. They suck it in like drowned things brought back to life.

Through the long, night-dark morning and into the still darker afternoon, Lupine sits quietly in the cave, keeping company with the tiny band of survivors. The spasms go on outside—whole mountain slopes, whole lakes that had been flung up the sides of nearby ridges take their time sliding back down to the new valley floor.

Afternoon becomes evening without the darkness growing deeper. The torn, roiling land settles towards an exhausted quiet.

Lupine waits on in the cave, listening to the cracking and settling of ashen new rock onto beds of old rock on the other side of the ridge. It is mostly done; the terror ebbs away, and there is time to think.

In the quiet, Lupine hears the soft dry sound of claws scraping against the rocky floor as an animal shifts in its place. Her eyes brighten with new tears as the day's devastation drives itself hard into her again. The ones in here that survived—how will they live in a wasteland? Did Lupine do her work rightly, or have millions of lives been wasted today in a botched job? Why does change carry this horrific price?

The life of a Bringer is always marked by loss and gain, but the loss is seldom so deep and terrible as this. Lupine wonders why she ever wanted to do this work, live this way, be a vehicle of this wrenching energy. She stares into the face of the mystery, and wills herself not to blink or to waver. Her senses reach out, first to torn and bubbling earth, then to a vaporized forest, and finally to the lands and lives beyond. Everything depends on change, on the tension and release of the great energies that drive the world. Lupine long ago gave up looking for final answers to the mystery. Now she faces her harshest test—confronting that mystery, and continuing to serve it.

In the deepest time of the night she rises, stiff and bruised, and walks alone to the cave's mouth. She steps into naked havoc. Trunks, four and five feet across, stripped of foliage, limbs, even bark, all lie flat, each pointing directly away from what was the top of The Mountain. There is nothing else—nothing at all. The thin layer of topsoil laboriously laid down since the last ice age is gone, swept away. The busy, leafy understory, the birds, all the teeming life of the forest—gone like dry ice fog from a darkened stage. Lupine walks to the top of the ridge, and heads down into the wrecked river valley. There is a three hundred foot layer of hot mud there now. On top of that is a jumbled, fifty-foot layer of cooling rock. That's all. It is hot underfoot; she has to keep moving to keep her feet from burning, and she must move carefully to avoid sinkholes of still soft rock.

Smoke, ash and water vapor shadow the moon. She moves by feel, her whole body sensing the hot earth; it tells her where to place her feet. She comes to the center of the valley, finds a long flat table of pumice quickly cooling to the night sky. She climbs up, walks the table's perimeter then stands still, looking towards the wreckage of The Mountain. In the aftermath of rock, fire and water there is still an overwhelming flow of energy upwards into the sky, a great river of mineral heat from the deepest, secret center that now spreads out over the world. Lupine knows that the next time she is asked to lay her own life on the line to bring change into the world, she will say *yes*. Standing on the crackling pumice table, her feet begin to move, and her body follows them. Lupine begins to dance, very slowly at first, toe pointing down to ground, then up to sky, then all of her twirling, arms gyring. Without knowing it will be so, her throat opens, her voice tumbles out. How can you, in a single breath, sing for twenty thousand million deaths—a cry of pain, a wild and sweet song of rebirth—both and more than that, all at once? Lupine didn't know before, and she may never again, but in this moment her heart and throat know how it is said.

She dances around the pumice table, stamping, then caressing the crackling stone with her feet, voice skirling upward in grief and joy, madness and resignation and calm, all of a piece. She leaps from the table and sinks halfway to her knees in cooling rock, but moving so fast she is free in an instant. Lupine careens across the valley, a trail of glowing footprints behind, keening a wild laughter whose roots reach down to the very furnaces of the earth, until she reaches a place that stops it—settling into hot stillness—a flight dropped to earth in a single heartbeat.

Mad Lupine looks to the ground. A tiny circle of stones, pebbles really, somehow fallen around an empty space a few inches across. She reaches into her parka; hand comes out filled with soil. She bends down, places the soil there, letting it be held by the pebbles.

Lupine turns towards the surviving forest, twelve miles away. She walks quickly, singing under her breath.

Chapter 6

Hucklebark looked at me expectantly. "What do you think, Ray?"

I wasn't looking anywhere in particular, though I think my eyes were aimed at the ground in front of me. Having that story end was almost more than I could bear. I was frightened, angry, exhilarated, sad beyond expressing, and a host of other things I couldn't identify.

"I don't know how I feel. There's too much right now for me to sort out. But I can tell you, that's a story to remember."

"Glad to hear it," he said with a smile. "I imagine there might be a thing or two you wanted to ask about it. But it's getting on, and I need to sleep some. Want to talk about it more tomorrow?"

"I don't even know what to ask, or why I feel the way I do. Tomorrow's fine."

"All right then, I'll see you in the morning." With his characteristic dispatch, Hucklebark had put food and utensils away, and was inside his sleeping bag before it registered on me I should do something like that too. I moved a lot more slowly than he did. Or perhaps it was a lot less efficiently. At the moment, I wasn't in a position to think about that either.

I lay back facing the stars, as I had the night before. Tonight, though, I barely saw them. What was Hucklebark playing at, telling a story like that? Could this possibly be about someone he had met, or was it nothing more than a particularly vivid fantasy?

I could feel my chest begin to tighten, a sure sign that something I had seen or heard had hit a nerve I didn't want hit.

Maybe I wanted to be like Mad Lupine. Maybe I wanted it more than anything I'd ever wanted. I never dared to identify what it was I wanted that badly, because my life had taught me I'd never find it. Better to let it stay unnamed and unknown rather than have to constantly see what can never be reached. But whatever the nature of the aching emptiness in my heart and mind—the yawning void I lacked the courage to confront—Hucklebark's story had named it, stood it on its feet and shoved it into my face, and that was intolerable.

Whether I tried every trick I knew to become calm, or didn't bother at all, there would be no sleep for me tonight. I would hear that story in my mind over and over again, and know that it just wasn't possible…

The sun was still well behind the eastern mountains when it began throwing light into the sky, to sift down from there onto a couple of lumpy sleeping bags separated by a small, cold bed of ash. The broken ground of the dell we lay in, the jagged tree stumps and shaggy cones of fireweed were still washed in shadow. A tiny, amorphous shape darted across my field of vision, where I lay on my side; too small and too fast even to be a mouse, it must have been a shrew—one of the few who could still make a living, however modest, in this wasteland.

I felt shrewish too. I was raw from a night of fruitless rumination and endless cycles of hope and despair. My body—which by rights should have been vigorous and well rested—was exhausted, stiff and sore. Sitting up made my head spin, but if I didn't do it my back would seize up, which was worse. I rested my elbows on my thighs, and my head in my hands, eyes closed to shut out the growing dawn. I thought about how much beauty I had seen the previous morning, and how it had seemed to bode well for another day of life. This morning it all seemed like a cruel hoax, and working through the day would be an epic, drawn out ordeal.

A rustling across the fire told me that Hucklebark had wakened and was moving about. I couldn't summon the energy to lift my head, or to say anything. Why did he have to tell me that story? I heard him take the four steps around the fire ring towards me.

"Morning, Ray."

I couldn't answer. Couldn't move. After a moment, I heard him step quietly away. His pack rustled quietly, and his steps diminished into the distance. The air was thick and sweet with the coming morning, but it felt to me like a flatiron in my lungs.

Sometime later I heard Hucklebark return. Wood clattered lightly to the ground by the fire ring. In the following moment of silence, I could hear the blood coursing through my temples. Off to the south I heard the raucous, deep croak of a raven. Miles away, the nasal snarl of a pickup truck making its way back towards the Pioneer Highway.

"Ray."

Water was sluicing into the coffee kettle. I heard the rasp of a match, and the first tender crackling of the dried moss and tinder he'd found.

"I won't make you move, or do anything. But I can't recommend paralysis, it's bad for the muscles. If you decide you want to do any talking, I'll be listenin'."

The small, light clop of dry wood being dropped onto the kindling, and the crackle that started so modestly and gained bravado moment by moment. Usually a deeply comforting sound—this morning it scraped across my mind, making nerves misfire all the way up my spine and into my head. It wasn't going to get any better, so I lifted my head slowly to look at Hucklebark.

"Why'd you tell me that story?"

The question startled him, I could tell. I didn't care.

"I thought—hoped, I guess—you'd find it interestin', and it'd be a good way to give you some idea what I was doin' yesterday."

"Why do you care if I'm interested, or if I understand? How can I believe something that beautiful, that terrible?"

Hucklebark stared into the fire for several breaths, obviously trying to sort out what might have gone wrong here.

"I told you the other day, Ray, you're interestin' yourself. I don't think you'd be here at all right now if Henry hadn't found you interestin' too, and whatever else, he's a shrewd judge of character."

"You know what it feels like?" I wanted to be angry, to yell at him, but I was too tired. Besides, it hurt just to put thoughts together, let alone make them into words. "It feels like you offered me some kind of joy, some fulfillment, maybe, knowing full well I'll never see it, or even get close to it. Even if there was a Mad Lupine, how could I ever even get near it, or her, or whatever, let alone even dream of a life like that?"

Hucklebark's voice was low and even. "I said last night, Ray, I count Lupine as one of my teachers. And whether I said it or not, I also count her as a deep friend. You want to tell me what this is all about, or do I have to keep guessin'?"

"Don't you see? I hardly even know who you are, let alone what you really do out here. But I'd already give anything I have to be doing it too. How many times in this stinking life do you figure I can stand to see other lives that make some kind of *sense*, people doing things to be proud and happy about, when I can't even crawl out from the mess I've made of my own mind?"

The water in the coffee pot was demanding that Hucklebark put coffee in there, so he did, thinking as hard as he could all the time.

"I wouldn't have told you that story, Ray, if I thought I was offerin' something beyond your reach. I gotta ask you again— what are you drivin' at?"

"Hucklebark, I'm lost, I'm tired beyond endurance, and I'm sick to death of all of it. I was born with a mind that doesn't know anything about being anything *but* lost. Nothing has ever seemed to help me, and for a long time now, I haven't seen a rope to be at the end of."

"Ah."

A long, slow stirring of the coffee, and the pot lid replaced with tender precision.

"I don't have any of the words that'll take that away, even for a bit. So I'm gonna have to limp along with the ones I do have. But I'm slow, Ray, when it comes to things like this. I got to think it over, understand how to say things when they're this important. So wait. Hold yourself together in whatever way you can, and wait for me."

We drank our coffee in silence, with the early morning breeze and the waking insects making sound for us. It's happened before to me, after a night like that; the one thing I'd think would be the wrong thing—a cup of coffee—is what forces me down from the peak of fear, and rage, and confusion. I set my cup down, eyes drooping.

Hucklebark got to his feet, hefting the coffee pot off its wrought iron spike.

"You look like you could use a day off, Ray. Take it easy, get some rest. I got some things to do. But stick around, okay?"

My head was already on its way to the soft spot at the end of the sleeping bag.

"Yeah, okay."

I didn't notice what direction he headed off in.

The sun was well into the west when Hucklebark returned. I was sitting next to the fire ring, staring absently at the mound of ash in the middle. Four hours of dreamless sleep had done a power of work on me, and I felt again like tomorrow was at least something that could be faced. I think I might have slept for two days, but for the bodily organ that is the alarm clock of much of the living world: the bladder. It had done its job again today, waking me when I had rested just enough, and forcing me to move. My gear was neatly packed and ready for travel. Hucklebark's glance took it in, and he raised an eyebrow.

"Glad to see you lookin' a little better, Ray. What's the plan?"

"The plan, such as it is, is for some more talk first. Then I need to move on, Hucklebark. I'm too restless to stay still any more."

He gently dropped his pack on the ground and settled down across the fire ring from me.

"Tired of clumsy talk and clumsier teachin', huh?"

"No. Don't think of it that way, Hucklebark. It's a mistake to blame yourself for having a tough time working with a crazy man. I'll agree that even if I could think clearly for more than a few moments at a time, I'd have a big job sorting through what you've offered so far. But that doesn't have to mean the fault lies with the teller, or even the listener for that matter. I'm hoping we can agree to bump into one another sometime in the future and take a few more steps into this work of yours."

"That's all right with me, Ray," he said. "You know, you're the first person I've tried to talk to about this way of livin' in a really long time. Except for all the folks who've taught me, and the others who live pretty much the same way. I already have some regrets about how I've gone about it. Be happy to try again sometime—I expect we may bump into each other, as you say, sooner than later."

"That'll be fine. But for now, will you try and answer a few things?"

"Sure I will," he said. "Whatever I can do, as long as it doesn't confuse things any further."

"I need to hear some things flat, clear and straight, but I also need you to know I'm not trying to piss you off. Do you really know someone called Mad Lupine?"

"Yes. Flat enough?"

I laughed. "You know, no matter how messed up my mind gets, and no matter how confused and scared I get, it's impossible not to like you."

"That's a good start, Ray," he smiled. "I'm glad to hear you talk that way. Okay, look. Lupine has been around here for a long time, much longer than me. She hasn't told me her whole history going back to whenever, and I haven't asked for it. But she's told me a lot, showed me a lot, and helped me to find new ways to do the work I want to do. She's important to me, and if you're very lucky, she'll be important to you too."

"She's already important to me, Hucklebark. That's why it matters that you're not telling me fairy tales. Did the story you told me happen here, on this mountain?"

"No, she's not quite that old," he laughed. "If it'd been right here, it would've had to be at least a couple thousand years ago. I figured you'd guess it was on what people think of as Mt. St. Helens, and it wasn't that long ago at all. She covers a good bit of territory, you see."

I let that sink in for a few minutes. Hucklebark sat quietly, watching the sun make its way towards The Mountain, waiting for me, until I stirred and looked up at him.

"What about you? I mean, you tell me about Change Bringers, you imply that you are one, but that makes for a lot more mystery than it solves. Who tells you how to go about it? And why? How did you get here? And why does a volcano need someone to help it blow its top off?"

"If I could give you all of that, flat, clear and straight, I'd be a whole lot smarter than I am," he said. "But I'll do what I can with the parts I can handle, starting from the last. A volcano doesn't necessarily need anyone's help to blow its top off, naturally enough. But volcanoes are like everyone and everything else in the world—they don't live in some kind of total isolation. Like everybody else, they benefit from someone dropping by to lend a hand. As for who and how, I can't give you that. Not because I don't want to, but because it isn't mine to give. My who and how could be different from your own, maybe totally different. You'll either discover these things for yourself, or they won't be discovered. And from what I've seen of you so far, you'll discover them, all right. You just keep on going, and you'll get there."

"Okay," I said, "I'm going to try for that. But what about the why? Why do you go around tinkering with watershed drainages? Why did Mad Lupine 'direct' the destruction of The Mountain?"

"Try thinkin' of it this way," he said. "Consider it a magnificent gift, maybe a privilege, to be able to take part in all this.

Think about how good it might feel to be *useful* in this way. If you stay up here a while, and keep your eyes—and the rest of you—open, you'll be approachin' a whole bucket of mysteries. Approach 'em with some respect, and be willin' to think in ways you haven't done before, and interestin' things will happen, no doubt of that."

"It'll take a while to get comfortable with all this," I said, "if I ever do. It feels like I need to be moving to work on it, so I'm heading into the Park."

"Tonight?"

"Yes. I can't sit still, Hucklebark, I have to get going. Before I go, there's something I really want, but I don't know exactly what it is. You ever feel that way?"

"Never more than three or four times a day," he laughed. "Since you mention it, maybe it's somethin' to do with me. Is that it?"

"I think so. Well, yes, of course it is, but I don't feel clear about it. It's something about wanting to be friends, or wanting you to think well of me even though I'm crazy, or... I don't know what I mean."

Hucklebark leaned across the fire ring. "Don't worry about it, Ray. I mean it—let it go. I already told you I like you, and I don't make those decisions lightly. I don't doubt for a second that we'll run into each other again. Maybe by then I'll have figured out how to answer questions better."

I stood up to hoist my pack onto my back, and Hucklebark lumbered to his feet. The sun was about fifteen minutes above The Mountain and I'd be walking in darkness by the time I got back to the Carbon River Road.

It felt ridiculous at first, but something made me stick out my hand to Hucklebark. He grasped it without hesitation, his great paw dwarfing mine. We held ourselves that way, in some unspoken agreement: enough talk for now, more later. Then I turned and climbed out of the little dell, heading down towards the river.

Part Two

Mother Mountain

*Wandering is not really about movement from place to place,
whether by accident or intent. It is actually about being awake.
Nothing happens without movement, of course, but without wake-
fulness, nothing useful happens at all.
It only matters where I end up insofar as I can find ways to keep
from starving, freezing, or falling victim to predators, human
and not-human alike. Beyond that, what matters is being alert to
everything around me. It would be so easy to fall into one dream or
another, and never emerge.
How am I to stay awake? The trees draw me into one way of being,
humans try to push me into another, totally different way of being,
and neither one makes any sense to me. It is a perpetual struggle to
resist the numbing apathy that drops down like a cold, musty blanket, to resist it and be awake, to see, to think clearly, to feel things
other than confusion, anger, fear, and resentment.*

(San Luis Obispo, Jan. 1998)

Chapter 7

By the time I had crossed the bridge back over the Carbon River and reached the road, it was fully dark. The moon, just beginning its first quarter, would not rise for some time, and even then would have little light to offer. On this side of the river the forest was mostly intact; the dense canopy of fir and hemlock overhead shut out even the starlight, and I walked slowly to avoid turning an ankle in the numerous potholes. I wasn't in any particular hurry; there were still several level, riverside miles to go before reaching the park entrance, but I had all night.

The road at this point is only a few hundred feet from the riverbed. It is overlaid with a thick layer of dust, which during the day is kicked up into great clouds by passing cars. All of the plants that have the misfortune to find themselves at the roadside—the vine maple, devil's club, huckleberry and salmonberry—are covered with it from June or July to September at least, and only the fall rains free them of it. It seems to me that this isn't ordinary dust; maybe it is left here when the river roars over its fair weather banks and washes over everything within a quarter mile. Perhaps all dust can be considered rock flour, but this dust is so close to the source it still has the consistency of flour. It sticks to you, as it sticks to anything it touches. Although I couldn't see the little clouds that puffed up from my feet with every step, it was easy enough to imagine them. My muffled footfalls barely registered against the hush of the woods, and the occasional creak of my pack sounded like an intrusion on the night.

I wondered, as I walked along this road, how it might feel to really belong here. I wondered how it would feel to belong anywhere at all. There was no earthly reason why I should not be there, walking quietly, minding my own business, yet I felt like a trespasser. I have always felt like a trespasser—like someone who had no business being at all, let alone being somewhere in particular. Why should I feel that way? Being alone—being an eternal outsider—was a way of life I knew well, but I still didn't understand it at all. I found to my surprise that I already missed Hucklebark. Looking back on the last two days' time, it began to feel as if I had known him forever, and had simply been waiting for him to show up by the river to tell me about his friend the willow, the tenacious one. And to tell me about other things of which I was grievously unaware. What was it that Hucklebark was trying to offer me, and why so impossible to talk about it in plain language?

These ruminations occupied me for a long time, while my feet found their own way along the dusty road, until I was startled out of my reverie by a large blob of darker-than darkness in the middle of the road. After the panicky moment it took to hook myself back up to the world, I could see that I was approaching the park entrance kiosk, where I would have—if I was driving a car in the daylight—rolled down the window, exchanged a few words and some money with a ranger, and driven on into the park. At this time of night the kiosk was dark and shuttered, as was the rangers' office a little ways beyond, though a small light shone down from above the door.

I walked off the road to the office. Next to the door was a stand with a slotted metal box on top, for people to register and pay their park fees when the kiosk and office weren't staffed. Against the wall of the office, I found a wooden box with the little envelopes for registering.

My plan, vague and undecided as it was, was to avoid the main trails whenever possible, and to grant myself an unlimited Back Country Permit. In the time I had spent on the Mountain before now, I had never once come across someone like Hucklebark, and it seemed unlikely I'd find anyone else like that by staying on the trails. That didn't mean I was unwilling to pay my share, though—the Park Service gets little enough support as it is. The door's light was more than sufficient for using the gnawed-down pencil stub on its string to fill out the information on the envelope:

> *NAME: Woeford B. Gonesome*
>
> *ADDRESS: Wish I Was Here*
>
> *DATES OF VISIT: Tonight   TO: No Telling*
>
> *ENCLOSED FEE: $ 10*
>
> *COMMENTS: Thanks, and keep up the good work!*

I had twenty seven dollars and some change with me. I briefly considered putting it all in the envelope, but settled for putting in only the ten dollar fee. I supposed I wasn't ready for that kind of freedom yet.

Leaving the little pool of light by the office door—made by humans, to be appreciated by humans—seemed like it should be some great symbolic event. As it happened, though, it simply went back to being very, very dark on the road as I made my way east towards the Ipsut Creek Campground. The campground coincided with the end of the road and the joining of Ipsut Creek with the Carbon River, and was still about four miles away.

About a mile from the rangers' office it occurred to me that it would be good to have a plan that was a little more detailed than simply staying off the main trails. There is a lot of territory here, and the scratched-together food I had would last for a week at best. I shuffled to the side of the road where the darkness was deeper still, and then moved under the canopy of the trees, where it was complete. I rummaged by feel in my pack until I found my map and flashlight, and sat down with them. When I turned on the flashlight its harsh glare exploded among the trees and undergrowth, so bright I could almost hear it shouting and spewing light. I quickly shut it off, and rummaged some more until I found a washcloth in the pack. With this folded over the flashlight's muzzle, I had enough light to see but without the blinding fury. I opened up the map and folded it so the top left hand corner—the northwest corner of the park—was exposed.

There are three creeks that cross the Carbon River Road within the park, on their way down to the river. I didn't recall them as being very large, though mountain creeks are nothing if not changeable. I was pretty sure I had passed over the first one—June Creek—already, though I hadn't been paying much attention to what little I could see and hear in the darkness. About a mile farther on Falls Creek would cross, and a mile or so past that Ranger Creek would do the same. Another mile after that would land me at Ipsut Creek Campground, where I didn't particularly want to land tonight. Shortly before Ranger Creek crossed the road there was a trail that headed in a southerly direction towards the Mountain. It ran for about a mile before dead-ending at the not-very-originally-named Green Lake. The landscape between Ranger Creek and Ipsut Creek Campground, where the cars all camped while their masters day hiked or set out for longer excursions, was more interesting. It sloped upwards from the river in a great curve towards Gove Peak, which is a small mountain (for these parts), not quite reaching 6,000 feet in elevation. On the far side of the curve I could descend cross-country into the canyon carved by Ipsut Creek, crossing the Wonderland Trail there. As I looked beyond the curving sides of Gove Peak and the Ipsut, Mother Mountain leaped out at me from the map.

I have never heard or read how Mother Mountain got its name. Almost anywhere else it would be big, with a top ridge almost two miles long, ranging from 6,000 to 6,500 feet high. It is a massive, jagged, young looking mountain with alpine meadows dotting its middle flanks. Above them is only rock, for the vegetation line—not just the timberline, but the place beyond which nothing grows but scattered, stubborn lichens—is lower on the northern side of the Mountain than on the southern side, where the line in places reaches up beyond 7,000 feet. Well, I was here to travel off the beaten path; Mother Mountain called to me to be a starting point, and according to the map, it was completely free of paths. I wondered what I expected to find on Mother Mountain, and then wondered why I wondered at all. Nothing had made sense to me for a long time now, and there didn't seem to be a reason why it should make sense now.

I thought of Hucklebark again as I shoved map, washcloth and flashlight back into my pack. I wondered if he had a flashlight at all, or if he simply didn't need one. It seemed unthinkable to be out here with no source of artificial light, but then Hucklebark had started me thinking about how very many things I didn't know.

Back on the pitch dark road, shuffling through the dry dust-flour that by the earth's reckoning had very recently been part of its molten under-crust, I tried to gauge how fast I was moving, and to chart my way towards Falls Creek. After about ten minutes of that I gave it up as a lost cause; I wasn't interested in counting thousands of steps, and if I assumed that Falls Creek still actually crossed the road—which it must to keep its rendezvous with the Carbon River—I would either recognize it or not. In fact, I reminded myself, I would either go to Mother Mountain or some obstacle would prevent me—at the moment, there wasn't much else to know. But it seemed, now that I had seen it on the map and it had called to me from that piece of plasticized paper, that it was of great importance for me to be there. Why, what or even how were relegated to issues of little importance. So walking was the only answer, though I wished it were more comforting to have only one option to consider.

A delicate crescent moon had risen, throwing faint beams through the forest canopy, when I heard the sound of running water ahead. A moment later the road dipped sharply downward, and I heard rather than saw that there was no bridge here, just the road dipping through the creek. Moving to the right side of the road I nearly bumped into the wooden sign that almost certainly said "Falls Creek," though I didn't bother with the flashlight. I also didn't bother with trying to find a place to ford the creek dry-shod. I figured that the near future might hold a good bit of wet and muddy for me anyway, so I could as well get used to it now. I hadn't planned on each foot carrying an extra couple of pounds of wet rock flour once I got back to the road's dusty bed, but that too would take care of itself in time.

Now, with at least a mile of trudging to move along the rough, dusty road in almost total darkness, I settled into a deliberate, feeling-with-my-feet way of walking. I tried to stay in the middle of the road; amazing how it felt wrong to be walking in the middle of an utterly deserted road, where I would have a half mile's notice if anyone miraculously passed by. It only took a few moments to fall into a pattern of movement that required hardly any thought, even though I could see almost nothing. The upper part of my mind was left free to saunter, stride or gallop through whatever obscure regions it might come across—not necessarily a good thing, but something I had never learned to control.

I began going over all the conversations with Hucklebark I could remember: a strange and powerful woman called Mad Lupine, the gift of being useful in the world, what it might mean to stare at a ravine wall for hours on end, how and why one might "help" water to move from one part of the land to another. But replaying them, as best as I could recall, was no better than listening to a piece of music that I just plain didn't understand, and would not understand without some serious help from somewhere or someone else. Yet the problem of who he was, what he did, and the why and how of it filled me with an aching longing if I allowed it too much freedom.

I managed to lose track of time without much difficulty, until I suddenly stopped in the middle of the road and wondered where exactly I was. Somewhere between Falls Creek and Ranger Creek, of course, but where? And where would be the proper place to turn off the trail and start moving upslope around the curve of Gove Peak towards Mother Mountain? That seemed like an insoluble problem until I realized something important: I would be moving cross-country. Maps help with that, but no matter how you try to scope it out, moving that way involves adapting to whatever the landscape presents. If I had suddenly thought to stop right here, this was as good a place as any to leave the relative comfort of the road, and move into the true land.

It took all of a dozen steps from the road to realize that in the darkness, I'd never make a mile if I took the rest of the night. The flashlight with its washcloth muffler came back out, and aimed almost straight at the ground kept me from walking into trees or boulders without blinding me completely. The land sloped upwards gently, and with my dim light I made as much time as I had shuffling along the road. The undergrowth was mostly low growing salal with some taller mountain dogwood scattered here and there. It was enough to make the ground complicated, but easy enough to travel through. I made about as much noise as a deer would make, which is to say I did my fair share of crackling, rustling and crashing.

When the land began to slope more sharply upwards, I started thinking maybe I'd had enough for one night. I found a clump of vine maple neighboring with some salal, and gently cleared a small space on the upslope side of the clump. The night was dry, just as the last two had been, so unrolling the sleeping bag and pulling off my boots was the extent of getting ready for sleep.

I switched off the muffled flashlight and sat down on top of the sleeping bag, with the sudden feeling that I had been moving for a long time. It felt good to be still. The unseen maple grove surrounded me with a comforting presence in the darkness. Free of the noise of my own movement, the hush of deep night was soft and intense. All the tiny, unidentifiable sounds I had covered with my walking emerged from the silence: small rustlings and scrapings to remind me that there was a world of not-humans for whom this was daytime. I lay down, breathing in the soft, night air, and fell asleep instantly.

Some time later, my eyes opened to a pearlescent glow. Dawn seemed only a few moments away, but it wasn't there yet. The light was a palpable silver dimness. I sat up slowly, feeling like I was not alone. But for a reason well beyond my understanding, there was no alarm in that. I turned to my right to see someone sitting very near, and still there was no fright; some part of me was trying its best to be scared and startled, and something was keeping it cooled, like stroking and gentling a nervous horse.

As I got more accustomed to the dim light, I saw that the one sitting next to me was an old, old man. He was slight, somewhat frail looking, yet there was a feeling of power emanating from him that should have scared me by itself. He turned slightly, and smiled. The wrinkles on his face and hands told uncountable stories that I felt I could almost hear. His long, silver hair hung gracefully over his shoulders and down his back. His clothing was dark, plain and old-fashioned.

When he smiled, the air around me became clear and clean in a way I had never experienced. I could see everything around me with a clarity that made me want to shout with joy. I looked back at this man, and his eyes took me in, found my soul, and patted it on the shoulder in encouragement. I wanted to talk to him, ask him a million questions, but without knowing why I said nothing. Instead, I accepted this exquisite clarity of vision, in this soft and piercingly clear air, and looked into my own body and mind. I looked fearlessly, dispassionately, as if I was examining someone or something not of myself. I saw disarray and disorder, certainly—a damaged, fragmented landscape. But I saw that there was *nothing fundamentally wrong* with the landscape. The stump in the clear-cut had told me we both have regenerative abilities; what I saw was simply a damaged life, awaiting repair. I would have guessed that that too would make me shout with joy. Instead what I felt was a warm acceptance, as if I'd always known this and had simply seen it proved.

I looked back at the old man again. It occurred to me that I should remember this encounter—every detail, every sensation, thought, every feeling—and I resolved to do so, knowing that it would be like trying to remember the exact nature of a rainbow arcing over the land, seen from across a great canyon. He looked back at me and arched an eyebrow, and I was overcome with sleepiness. I lay slowly back down, and slept.

When I woke there were shafts of sunlight slanting down through the forest canopy. For a moment I felt warm and contented, basking in the afterglow of a lovely dream. But was it a dream? Or had an ancient and powerful man sat next to me in an anonymous grove of vine maple in the hour before dawn?

It seemed there was no way to make the distinction between dream and life. I gave it up for the moment, and then remembered where I was, and where I wished to be. I pulled out my map and pored over the topographic features of the area while gobbling the first edible thing I could find in my pack.

If I faced upslope and then turned to my left, walking more or less at the same elevation, I should easily move round the curve of Gove Peak. When I got to where I was facing southwest, it would be time to head straight down slope (assuming that was possible), in order to cross Ipsut Creek and then the Wonderland Trail. On the other side of the trail, I would be ascending the slope of Mother Mountain. The map made it clear that there was a band of very steep climbing that ran around most of the mountain. I knew from viewing the mountain from other places in the park that much of that band was the upthrust of a thick, nearly vertical layer of granite; if no way up presented itself, I would walk several miles south and west to the far curve of the mountain, where the map promised an easier way up. Recalling past experiences, I reflected on how good maps are at promises, and that they are better still at concealing surprises.

I was impatient to be going. A scant moment to pack all away (Hucklebark would be pleased), and I was ready. As I stood to lift my pack, something about one of the vine maple trees caught my attention. Perhaps it was the slightly odd way the branches moved in the almost non-existent breeze, but I wasn't sure. In my mind, the tree spoke.

We thank you for bringing about the blessing of last night. Journey in strength, and farewell.

I sat back down suddenly. I tried to frame an appropriate reply, but I was so astonished all I could think of sounded lame and clumsy.

The pleasure was mine, and thanks for being who you are.

There was no reply, and I was left to ponder the mysteries of ancient men, the line (if there is one) between certain dreams and certain realities, and how these things might bear on a small grove of vine maple. Figuring I could ponder just as well walking as sitting on the ground, I got back up, shrugged into my pack, and began to make my way around the slope of Gove Peak.

Chapter 8

A half hour's walking went by pleasantly. The undergrowth was sparser on the slopes than down lower and nearer water, which made moving laterally along the curve of the mountain relatively easy. I got my compass out from the pack and left it in my pocket, checking once in a while to see just which way I was heading. I wouldn't necessarily know when the sun had cleared the mountains to the east of me, as I was moving away from it around the shoulder of Gove Peak, and the forest canopy here was thick enough to leave me in perpetual shade. At length the compass showed me that I was heading southwest, and it was time to head downslope.

I crossed Ipsut Creek without getting wet on a short series of boulders laid in the creek by last year's ferocious flooding, filled a couple of water bottles while I was there, and made my way across the Wonderland Trail above the creek without encountering anyone. The late morning was quiet and warm. The undergrowth was heavy near the creek, but as I moved up slope it thinned out again.

As I gained altitude—acquiring a heavy layer of sweat along the way—the landscape began to change. In this region, it's possible to traverse four distinct ecosystems—foresters and naturalists call them "life zones"—in a few miles of rigorous, uphill hiking. Down at Ipsut Creek, where the elevation is around 2500 feet, I was still in what's called the Transition Zone—the land that expresses the change from sea level to the lower mountain elevations. The next higher zone, which I had just passed through toiling up the side of Mother Mountain, is called the Canadian Zone, and that is followed, at around 4500 feet, by the Hudsonian Zone. The dominant tree species change, as does much of the undergrowth and to some degree the animal life. The changes I had seen so far were minor—fewer of the huge Douglas Fir, more of the shorter, droopy-topped Western Hemlock—but I was somewhere within the meeting place of the two middle zones. When I got close to 6000 feet, I knew I'd be entering another world: the Arctic-Alpine Zone, where what life there is works harder than anyone anywhere else, just to exist.

Well before reaching that elevation the slope increased sharply and the undergrowth disappeared almost entirely. The trees were smaller still, and the ground around them was sparsely clad in low growing Oregon grape and salal. Soon I was wending my way slowly upwards through the short brush thickets and around the trees, bent over almost double on the slope. When I stopped to rest, I looked ahead and saw a wall of granite rising up about fifty yards in front of me. It wasn't vertical, but it was close enough that I had no intention of going straight up it. A short map consultation indicated that I was at one of two places in the general area where the wall was nearly vertical, and that by moving to my right along the base of it until I crossed a little waterway called Doe Creek, I might find an easier way up. I set down my pack and sat on the ground for a longer rest.

Because the slope here was so steep and the undergrowth low, I could see down it for a great distance. I had only been sitting for a few moments when a movement far down caught my eye. Something was moving, at what looked like an athletic runner's pace, though I couldn't see clearly. It was coming up the mountainside with remarkable speed, and it was moving directly towards me.

At first I wondered if I was watching a bear, it moved so fast and certain over the steep, uneven slope. But I had never heard of a bear moving in such a straight line, nor of one running so steadily on two legs. Still, I looked nervously around me to be certain there was no bear cub nearby that I was threatening. Of course, there was not. Whatever—or more likely, at this point, whoever—was tearing up the mountainside would be here so quickly there wasn't much point in trying to evade them. Besides, where would I run? I sat quietly next to my pack and waited.

I had never seen a man walk up a forty degree slope as fast as I can run on the level. He was easily a foot taller than me (which made him a shade over six and a half feet tall), rangy and clearly very limber. He was carrying the biggest backpack I had ever seen; it loomed at least a foot above his head, and appeared to be at least two feet thick. I couldn't imagine what it weighed unless it was filled with packing peanuts.

He came to a smooth stop directly before me.

"You Ray Holdman?"

He wasn't even out of breath, and he was looking for me. "Yes, that's me."

He broke into a smile. "Excellent. I have some supplies for you."

I gaped stupidly for a moment; I couldn't help it. "You have supplies—for me."

"Of course. Hucklebark seemed to think you'd be running low soon. Especially since he said he drank half your coffee."

My wits weren't keeping up with this as well as I might have liked. "So you know Hucklebark?"

"Absolutely. Him, and all the rest of the Mountain's Bringers, and a lot of others, too. I keep 'em supplied. And I get my exercise, I can tell you."

"Um—do you have a couple of minutes to talk? Like maybe I could ask you some questions about all this?"

He immediately slipped out of the enormous pack and laid it gently on the slope as if it was a child's day bag. "Yeah, sure. What do you want to know?"

"Well, for starters, you know my name, but I can't say the same for yours."

He bonked his forehead lightly with the heel of a hand. "I always forget. You know, I don't actually meet very many new folks in this line of work. I'm Ev—short for Everett Longhaul."

"Well, pleased to meet you, Ev. You came up that slope in an awesome hurry; you must have a horrific schedule."

"I move fast, but I never hurry," laughed Ev. "There are a lot of folks to take care of, so when I get moving, I move right along. However," he continued, "I wouldn't do this if there weren't time to stop and talk."

"I don't know where to begin, Ev. I want to ask too many questions. Like, who do you work for? How many Bringers do you "supply"? I still don't understand what, exactly, is a Bringer? How do you get to be one, if you want to be? Do you know someone called Mad Lupine? And what—" I was running out of breath—"is this crazy show really about, and could there possibly be a place in it for anyone else?"

Longhaul held up his hands in a 'whoa!' gesture. "I'll do my best, Ray, but let's try and take this a piece at a time. First things first. You want some coffee, water, something? I'm a black tea man myself."

He leaned over to his pack, snapped open a small compartment. A tiny cookstove, water bottle and a smallish kettle emerged. Before I could do any more than think about it, the stove was assembled and lit, and the water was heating. I said black tea was fine with me.

Ev wrapped his long legs into something a bit like a cranefly in a half lotus position, and stared thoughtfully at the ground. "Maybe the easy ones first. Of course I know Lupine, who you've heard referred to as "Mad Lupine." She has to eat, just like everyone else. She's pretty hard to keep up with, though," he said with a chuckle.

"I think I recall that Hucklebark mentioned He Works to you. I'm a pretty independent agent; I know what needs to be done and how to do it. I mainly see Works when there's something I can't solve. Sometimes too, I think he arranges to accidentally run into me once in a while. But to be honest, it's comforting to run into him. We have no bosses, Ray—no managers. I wouldn't say we work *for* anyone at all. We aren't involved with some kind of business here—we're a part of the workings of the world. We work together when it's time to, and we work totally on our own when it's time for that."

"But who *runs* this show, Ev? How is it put together, who *are* you all?"

"You know, Ray, you might not like this answer too much, but when you get down to it we just *are*. Honestly, I think you got more important things to work out first."

I looked up at him abruptly. "Like what?"

"Well," he went on gently, "I expect you don't need me to tell you that, but if you insist—I've heard you think of yourself as all messed up and crazy. Now before you get too wrapped up in becoming *not* crazy, or however you think of it, I'd advise you to put in some work on how you're seeing things."

"That's all? Work on how I see things?"

"That's all, Ray. You may not believe it, but most of us know a lot about not fitting in, or being considered one thing or another, or being kicked out of some place we had come to think of as home. Tell me something. You had any interesting dreams since you got here?"

I waited for a bit, trying to decide what to say. Finally, against my better judgment, I told Longhaul my experience of the previous night with the ancient man, and in a reckless burst of completeness, about the vine maple that spoke at dawn without being spoken to.

Whatever I had expected him to do or say didn't happen. Instead, he stared thoughtfully at the ground for several moments, then straightened up and knocked back the rest of his tea in one breath. "Two things I have to say to that, and then I gotta get going. First, that's one of the sanest stories I've ever heard from someone outside my little circle of folks. And who do you suppose that old fellow might be?"

"Search me. I was hoping you might have an idea."

Everett Longhaul smiled broadly. "Oh yeah, I have some ideas. But I'm also certain that you need to work this one out on your own. The second thing, and my two cents, Ray—concentrate on where you are and who you're with, and set the bad and crazy part aside, if you can."

"Hm. Well, thanks, Ev. Did you say you had some coffee for me?"

"Dang! I almost forgot! Haven't done that since I don't know when, come by with supplies then forget to leave 'em." He was into that giant pack in an instant. "Let's see here, the coffee, here's a pound of rice—wicked hard to cook above 4,000 feet, you know—some rye bread (hang onto that container, they come in handy), pound of cheese (let me know what you like for next time), and a pound of peanut butter, same goes for the container. Hucklebark said to suggest looking for some salmonberries before you get too high up, you could make some pemmican."

I looked in wonder at the pile of food in front of me. "Wow. Thanks, Ev. What do I owe you?"

"Owe me?" he looked up in surprise. "Don't mention it. Anyway, I'll see you around. Oh, and by the way—if you head a couple hundred yards to the right, you'll find a pretty nice cleft in this wall, it's a good way to get up higher. Take care of yourself, Ray."

With that he shrugged into his pack and loped off down the slope, moving with sureness and grace at a rate I couldn't have matched if I'd been rolling end over end.

Everett Longhaul was right about the cleft; it looked like the only reasonable way up—and barely reasonable, at that—as far as I could see in either direction. I wondered if he was right with his other advice too. From the bottom the wall looked to be about a hundred feet high, and as I started up I hoped it wouldn't be any higher. I also decided I would look hard for another way back down when the time came for that.

The last twenty feet were the hardest, as they generally are. Up until then there had been abundant footholds that held firm under my weight, and the one place where there was almost nothing to hold onto had offered an exceptionally tough clump of bunchgrass for balance and encouragement. At every glance the last stretch looked for all the world like a featureless expanse, close enough to vertical that there was no way for someone who knew nothing about rock climbing to go on. But each time I thought there was no next foot- or hand-hold, that the stone in the wall was smooth and without opportunity, my hands or feet came across some small opening that my eyes hadn't found, and I moved once more. With one last heave I brought the top half of my body over a ledge, and into another world.

In the short space of that near hundred feet of altitude, the land and I had moved decisively from the Hudsonian zone to the Arctic-Alpine. Broken rock lay atop coarse, sandy soil dotted only here and there by clumps of tough mountain grasses, thin blankets of low growing heather, and a sprinkling of dwarf lupine. There were no trees to be seen, not even the contorted dwarfs found on the interglacial ridges on other parts of The Mountain. Off to my left about ten feet away, a striped chipmunk perched on a small, flat stone. It had waited, poised for flight, to see what kind of creature might be clambering up the rock wall. Having seen for itself, it turned and vanished in a flicker of red-brown.

The ground here angled gently upwards, increasing in steepness as it approached what appeared to be a ridge several hundred yards above me. I hadn't been certain from the map whether this part of Mother Mountain's top was a shallow caldera or simply a rolling plateau, and I was deeply curious to see for myself. Perhaps what had drawn me here would be up there, for so far—though the landscape was fascinating and austerely beautiful—I still had no idea why exactly I felt so compelled to come. My feet sank into the sand and gravel as I made my way up, admiring the tough, unpretentious plants that lived there and their flowers, so delicate in such a harsh landscape. Rather than zigzag my way up the last stretch of the slope, which would have been easier, curiosity drove me straight up the slope. As usually happens, the climb to the top was much farther than I had thought. When I finally reached the top of the ridge, chest heaving, I stopped in my tracks.

I looked down on a shallow oval bowl, a quarter mile long, two hundred yards across, and perhaps a hundred feet deep. I would not have been surprised to see an ancient god striding across the depression on some celestial business, or a bodhisattva sitting still as a stone, deep in a centuries-long meditation. There was no one of that elevated company, of course. But the floor of the bowl was richly covered in wildflowers and grasses, all stretched to the limits of their height reaching for the warmth and energy of the summer sun. There were a few remaining avalanche lilies, their white star-shaped blossoms long turned to seed farther down; thick patches of low, blue-tinged mountain phlox, dotted with the crimson blooms of Indian Paintbrush. Somewhat taller than the rest, the lupines reached out to the sunlight with their deep blue flowers. And on the other side of the bowl, a solitary tree.

It was no more than six feet tall; gnarled, slightly lopsided, twisted around by the ferocious winds that swept through even this protected place during the winter storms. I was drawn to it irresistibly. I walked as lightly as I could across the concave meadow, trying not to step on any of the marvelous not-humans who made their home in a place where I couldn't possibly live, making straight as possible for the tree. It was a six-foot mountain spruce. Three thousand feet down hill from this spot, its relatives reached a height of more than a hundred. The seed that had fallen here—whether by the agency of wind, bird, or animal—had found the exactly correct instant of warmth and water, sent up a tiny, tenacious stem, and refused without letup since then to yield to the tearing of the wind, or to the punishing weight of snow and ice on its branches. I knew that at this altitude, this tree was at least a century old, perhaps much older.

When I reached the tree, I set my pack down nearby and sat down close to it. The whorls of needles circling its twigs made endless patterns that led my eyes onward, up and down the length of its branches. I was filled with admiration for someone who could live here. The fact that I was visiting during the one month of the year when the weather could almost be counted on to be benign made it all the more remarkable. Under the tree's branches was a tiny world of fallen needles, thoroughly chewed cones and windblown stuff—a couple of square yards of forest duff on a high alpine meadow.

I reached out to lightly brush my fingers against the rough bark of the trunk, which was about three inches in diameter at the base, and felt something akin to an electric shock. I jerked my hand back to consider. Perhaps it was some kind of high altitude trick of static electricity. Perhaps there was something in the tree's bark that had evolved to ward off creatures that might harm it. But the thought came unbidden to me that it had been a physical shock of recognition, and the harder I tried to dismiss the idea as foolish or random, the more it fixed itself in my mind.

I moved to a position where I directly faced the tree, about three feet from it, and made myself as comfortable as possible on the uneven ground. The afternoon sun poured down on us both, and the faint breeze barely registered on my skin. I gazed at the tree, taking in more and more; the delicate infinity of patterns in its bark, its needles; the mysterious asymmetry of its branches that expressed an incomprehensibly complex response to the weather of this place. The more I gazed at it, the more I saw. Even the minute, chaotic jumble of tiny detritus at its base began to take on patterns fraught with a meaning I could not uncover. In my mind I said, *You are remarkable.* In my mind, the tree replied: *Come in.*

Come in? And how would that happen? And *what* would happen?

For lack of any concrete idea how to respond, I tried to relax my mind and body, and not do anything in particular. I thought about breathing, and began to listen to and feel the way I was moving air in and out of myself. My skin began to tingle—very slightly at first, and then more strongly. It slowly dawned on me that I was respiring with every surface of my body. I could feel the air touching my exposed skin, air slyly working its way under my clothing, briefly trapped by denim and cotton but still working its way inside and back out. I was breathing everywhere, and my lungs were simply one part of a vast system that drank in the air and returned it, changed, to the sky. Was this what breathing is like to a mountain spruce?

The ground beneath me began to change. It was still solid, but I could feel innumerable small openings in it; it was becoming something different from what I understood ground to be. The nerves in my legs and backside began to sense things about the ground I hadn't known before: there were ways to move into it, pathways inside of it I could follow and feel. My nerves began to extend themselves, feeling their way into the softer, in-between places in the earth, moving downward, pushing aside the soil that would yield. They wound and looped around buried stone, holding on to it. This was my place, and it was my job to occupy it as best I could.

The strangeness of these sensations diminished as time went by. It was replaced by a slow, deliberate kind of curiosity, and I found the wit to wonder dimly what was going on. While most of me was preoccupied with respiration and roots, a small section of my mind revelled in the notion that this tough, tenacious tree had opened a doorway for me into its soul. I felt honored way beyond my worth, and gratefully accepted the offer. I yielded to the tree, and slipped farther in.

My awareness of the ground continued to move downward, inch by inch. I don't know how deep into the earth I had gone—not very far, I imagined—when I encountered a layer of rock that at first seemed impenetrable. Most of my awareness then began to move laterally through the soil, always seeking least resistance, and always tending downward. A scrap of intention continued to probe the rock layer, looking for a way to force a tendril of myself into it. I found a tiny crack, and began working a part of me into it bit by bit. After going down a short ways the crack closed completely, and leaving that small part of me burrowed tightly in, I moved my attention elsewhere.

I tried to guess how long I had been with this tree, but the notions of time that I had always taken for granted seemed elusive. I found that it wasn't relevant to think about hours or minutes. Days were not really days; those were completely artificial markers that attempted, without success, to divide the indivisible. The wind came, and the wind went; so too light and darkness. I remained as and where I was, responding to it all, without interest in tallying or labeling.

I knew the sun was shining, but I could no longer see it. I knew the moon and stars when they shone, but nothing reached my eyes, because they were no longer relevant. Everything was known through every surface of me, whether above or below ground. I knew when an inquisitive chipmunk climbed nimbly over me, looking for (and finding) food. I knew when the level of Ipsut Creek far below me rose and then fell, responding to the changes in snowmelt and water table at its source high above; not by hearing, seeing or tasting, but by a sense I had never been aware of before. I took all of it in, and remained still.

I sensed movement far down the mountainside from me. It roused that deliberate curiosity that seemed to have become my way of being, and I reached out with my awareness to find out more. Something was moving across the face of the land, at the very limits of my senses. It moved at a pace that seemed familiar, though it took a long, slow sifting through memory to find what I was looking for. It was a human, walking on the Ipsut Creek trail, nearly three thousand feet below me. I gathered in the movement, the tiny changes in the landscape that rippled all the way up the slope to me. I drank it in like water, and realized that maybe I was supposed to be one of those humans, and not a mountain spruce.

A sense of panic welled up, and though I fought to suppress it I could not. Where was *I*? I was gone, that was where—subsumed in a beautiful, courageous but mortally dangerous arctic-alpine spruce that had led me into its life and allowed me to become lost.

As the panic rose inside me, the ability to be still slipped away, and I began to struggle in every way I could. My awareness came galloping back from the world and crawled into the closest, smallest space it could find, kicking and pushing to find its way back to a familiar place. I felt myself pulling against something, pulling as hard as possible. There was nothing more important than getting back to myself; I had forgotten most of what *myself* was, but getting back to it was all that mattered.

I pulled harder. Suddenly I felt something give way; it was like being torn from something that had had me in an iron grip, and the pain was terrible to feel. I thought my body and mind would both be torn apart, but before I could learn whether or not that would happen, I lost consciousness.

Chapter 9

"Ray. Hey, Ray Holdman. Wake up."

A shoving at my shoulder, gentle but insistent. I thought I should open my eyes, but I didn't remember how. Some moments of dire confusion followed as I tried to take inventory of my body and couldn't remember what a body has. Then a piece or two bubbled up to the surface; I had arms, shoulders (one of which was still being prodded), legs, and hands. They all hurt. Then the notion of eyes began to make sense again, and I opened them.

Apparently I was lying more or less on my back, for the first thing I saw was a blaze of stars. The air was so clear they barely twinkled; rather, they were more diamond-like than I could remember ever seeing them before. Even in August, the nights are chilly at this altitude, and I suddenly shivered. The stars were eclipsed by something much darker. It was a face; a woman's face.

"Who are you?"

It was abrupt and rude, and I knew it the moment I said it, but I couldn't remember exactly who or where I was. Perhaps if I knew who the face was, I might remember more. On second thought it was a long shot, but the thing was done.

She was having none of it. "We'll get to that later. First I need to know if you're all right—physically all right, I mean—and how soon you can move."

She clearly knew a lot more about what was going on than I did. At least it seemed that way, and I figured stubbornness wouldn't gain much here.

"I ache everywhere. But so far, nothing appears broken or too thoroughly damaged. Why do I need to move—what's going on?"

Her voice was matter of fact, but there was no mistaking the passion that lay underneath. "You've done some harm here, and your presence makes it hard to recover from that. The sooner we can get you a ways away, the better."

"Harm? What did I do?"

Her patience was wearing thin, but I guess she was willing to wait one more moment, if it would motivate me to move. "You entered into the life of this spruce, and then removed yourself so roughly that the tree is severely injured. It can get on with healing itself if you go away, but not otherwise."

I remembered it all in an instant. The mountain spruce I had loved and admired; it had invited me: *Come in*. And I had come in. And all the things I had felt, sensed and learned came back. And then I had panicked, fearing that I'd never return to humanity. Now I was being told that I had hurt this trusting friend—the very last thing I wanted to do.

"Is this really true? I hurt the tree?"

"You hurt it grievously."

My heart lurched at the thought of this. It was as if a generous, loving stranger had taken me into his home, and in a thoughtless, clumsy moment I had killed him. "Will it live?"

"Possibly. Now will you get up so we can go? Time is important here, Ray Holdman."

I thought perhaps I should refuse to leave, that instead I should be trying to do what I could for the tree. It only took a moment to realize I wasn't even in good enough shape to help myself.

I felt I was learning—maybe rather slowly—that there was no point in arguing with anyone in these parts, so without replying I rolled over on my side and got painfully onto my feet, swaying slightly. I looked right and left.

"I should have a pack around here somewhere."

She nodded to my right and behind. "Back there."

As I shrugged into the pack my shoulders burned inside. Every joint in my body seemed to have been pulled out and hastily shoved back in. But my attention was focused on the mountain spruce, and in my disorientation it took a moment to find it.

In the darkness, illuminated only by starlight, the tree looked no different than when I had first encountered it. I had thought, from this woman's manner, that I would find a few splinters pointing vaguely upward. But here was clearly yet another thing that I did not understand. Perhaps when we got wherever we needed to go, I could learn some more. Better yet, when we got to wherever, maybe I could just go back to sleep for a week or so.

She was already moving. I finished my unsatisfactory contemplation of the mountain spruce and turned to follow. Every muscle in my body shrieked; I was reminded of the fact that there actually are muscles I didn't know I had.

Keeping up was difficult, but I was in no mood or condition to just decide to ignore this woman, and simply wander off somewhere at my own pace. Time was still eluding me for the most part as a concept, but after what seemed like a short stretch of it she slowed down enough for me to catch up with her. Though the stars were out, the moon was nowhere to be seen; whether it hadn't risen yet or was already done for the night was more than I could tell. I stumbled often.

"Not that I'm complaining—at least not yet—but how far do we need to go right now?"

She half turned over her shoulder. "Not much farther. I think having a couple of ridges between us will do until daylight."

She was as good as her word, in that soon we made our way (she with lithe grace, me looking and feeling in need of physical therapy) up and over a low ridge that led us into a small, barren depression about fifty yards across. Moving down into it, my feet told me that it was not so barren as all that; we trod on a carpet of ground hugging grasses, flowers and heathers, to the distress of that part of me that remembered all the warnings about fragile alpine meadows.

Near the bottom of the carpeted bowl the woman stopped. She looked around briefly, and found a spot of mostly bare ground, where she sat down and motioned me to do the same. I slumped down gratefully, letting my pack slip off my back where I sat. I leaned against it, and the plywood box immediately dug itself into my ribs. It hurt so much less than the rest of my body I ignored it.

She looked to be younger than me. But a second glance told less rather than more, and I saw that she could be younger, older, or any place in between. She wore her straight, dark brown hair in a thick braid that reached most of the way down her back. All her gear, from jacket to jeans to boots and pack bore the hallmarks of long, hard use coupled with excellent care. I had thought that when I had a chance to study her face I'd find a hostile set to it, but the lines of her cheekbones and jaw were relaxed, if not smiling. She returned my gaze, studying me in turn, until the silence began to feel awkward to me.

I asked, "What time is it?"

She smiled then—a little. "Better you should ask 'What day is it?' from the look of things."

All the things I had breathed, tasted, sensed and seen in ways that were still mysterious, though I had done and felt them— how long had that taken?

"Maybe you're right. What day is it? Though come to think of it, I don't remember what day it was when I came up here. It didn't seem very important at the time."

"From what the tree has said, I think you've been up here for three days," she said, "and it will be dawn in less than an hour. I hear you have good coffee, you up to making some?"

I hadn't felt like laughing, but she changed that. "I gather you are one of the select millions who know Hucklebark, or maybe Ev Longhaul. Sure, if I don't get to go back to sleep, I can do that." Wait a minute—from what the tree has said? I was in no condition to work through anything new right now. And yet the thought hammered at me: *who are these people?* Still fogged from a mortally intense and painful emergence, and not knowing what else to do, I began to do what this mysterious woman had asked. Rummaging in my pack for the stove, water bottles and supplies was a sharp reminder of how sore I was, and I failed to suppress a grunt of pain.

She looked up at me. "I'm sorry I had to make you move, but it couldn't be helped. If you want, we can get you to some help after sunup."

"I think I'll be all right," I said. "But I feel like I fell out of a tree—" and stopped, amazed and distressed at what I had done, more than what I had said. "As usual, I don't know where to begin, so I guess it doesn't matter where. For reasons not clear to me, there wasn't time for it before, but it seems that you know me, and I don't know you."

"You're right, there wasn't time before. We'll sort that out eventually. My name is Lyla."

"Just Lyla?"

"Not good enough for you?"

"God, there I go again. I'm trying not to say it that way anymore, but I can't help it. Of course it's good enough, Lyla." I shifted on the ground, trying to find a more comfortable position and failing. "I don't have any idea what I did—or might have done—to that tree. Maybe you could start with telling me how you found me, and what you found."

As I adjusted the water pan on my cookstove, she said, "I found you because I was making my way around Mother Mountain, and I sensed a tree somewhere that was in a kind of distress I'd never experienced before. It was a good ways away from me, but I had to find out what was going on. When I got to it, you were flattened on the ground next to it, and the tree was fighting for its life."

"How could I have hurt it so badly?"

"You do know, I imagine—especially after this experience— that trees are *people*, don't you?"

"Of course I do," I replied, perhaps a little testily. "That's something I knew before I ever heard one speak to me. The places where trees are thought of as nothing more than *things* to be consumed are among the many I don't want to live in."

"I can't help you with those places," she said. "But consider how much damage someone could do to you, intentionally or not, if you let them into the deepest part of your being, and they lost control and stamped around in a frenzy, breaking or damaging everything they came into contact with until they could get out."

I thought I could understand that, even though there had never been anyone in my life I might have invited inside me like that. In a low voice I said, "I was afraid. No, not just afraid, I was terrified. It doesn't excuse anything. But I felt like I would never come back, that I might never be human again."

The water was boiling happily, and I threw two handfuls of grounds in the pot. "No eggshells to settle the grounds today, so we'll have to strain it with our teeth."

She smiled again, and it felt good to see her do that. "I figured something like that might have happened. Tell me everything about what happened with you." She hesitated a moment. "Please."

Why did I feel like I should spill my life out to every person I met here? I decided again that I didn't care why. Both the gambler and the fearful one inside were too beaten up to make a problem out of it. I began on the Carbon River Road, where Mother Mountain had leaped at me from the map, and continued through the dream of the ancient man, my meeting with Everett Longhaul, my discovery of this wonderful mountain spruce, its invitation and what happened when I accepted. By the time I was done the dawn had given way to daylight, and we had gone through the first and then a second pot of coffee. She never interrupted me once.

When I was done she simply said, "Thank you," and sat silently, gazing at the ground, thinking hard. I waited as long as I could manage before breaking the silence.

"So now I hope it's your turn. If you can, I really need to know…" what did I need? "I need to know how I can make amends to this spruce. I feel like I don't dare accept another invitation like that again, and now that I think of it, that feels a little bit like dying."

She looked at me searchingly. "I don't think any one of us has ever met someone quite like you, Ray. Of the few humans that are capable of having this kind of relationship with a tree, almost none of them could even survive an encounter like that. There is no living being that lives more intensely than a tree at timberline, or that works harder to just exist. At first I thought this spruce had been mortally foolish to invite you in, but now I'm not so sure."

"What could possibly have changed your mind? I may have killed it!" To say it out loud made me want to weep.

She shifted her position on the ground and gazed up towards the rim of the bowl in which we sat. "They know a lot more about some things than we do. More to the point, I suppose, they know things we don't even suspect." She hesitated. "Did Hucklebark tell you much about some of the different people—human people, I mean—that make their lives here?"

I looked up in surprise and irritation. "You mean you don't know every word of what passed between me and Hucklebark? I thought everyone did."

She could have gotten angry; I would have. Instead, she smiled with a trace of irony. "Two things, Ray: one, we work together here in ways you haven't imagined yet. I suspect you will, in time. Two, my own work keeps me away from human contact for fairly long stretches sometimes. I heard about you meeting Hucklebark from Ev."

The generosity of her reply was enough to make me feel—again—like a complete boor, like a prickly, oblivious fool who blunders into a place of delicate beauty and sees nothing but a shooting gallery. "I'm sorry. No excuses, again, for my bad manners. So Ev supplies you too?"

"Ev supplies anyone who needs it. He spends most of his time wandering into every corner of the Mountain and the country around it, bringing things to people. In between he runs back and forth to the House of Windy Gap."

"Pardon me, the House of What?"

"Windy Gap. It's the name some of us use for a meeting place up on the Mountain."

"What kinds of meetings happen there?"

She stopped and thought a moment. "Sometimes we get together when there's something important to talk about, because it's a very special place. If you consider any part of the land anywhere to be sacred, the House of Windy Gap ranks up near the top. But maybe what's even more important is that sometimes when someone needs something badly—perhaps they don't even know exactly what it is they need—they go there and simply wait. If their need has any chance of being met, the chances are best there."

"House of Windy Gap," I mused. "What kind of house is it?"

Lyla looked up in surprise, and then waved her hand all around us. "You're in it right now, Ray." She smiled. "It's really very roomy. But the place I'm talking about is, I guess, the center of it all, the single most important place where things are learned, and needs are met if they can be met at all."

"I think I need to go there," I said. "I think I *really* need to go there."

"Why?"

"Well, I already had a whole raft of things that I seem to need very badly, but now there's something I need more, and that's how to make amends to a mountain spruce that trusted me."

She looked thoughtfully at the sky, though it was clear she was thinking about something else. Finally, she said, "You can find a place called Windy Gap just by looking on the map. But that won't get you where you need to be, if Windy Gap is what you really need. I won't take you there right away, and I can't make an unbreakable promise. But if the time is better and I can, I'll help you get to it if no one else is around to help.

"There's nothing you can or should do for that tree right now. Maybe in a while, when you know a lot more and you've had the chance to establish ties with some less formidable folks, you should come back here and see what happens."

"Yeah, okay," I said. "At this point, I'm ready to put anything and everything off for some other time." Something very important occurred to me in a rush: I hadn't eaten in three days.

My stomach had finally wakened, and in an instant it took over my whole being. "I just realized I have to eat something. Now. In fact, I have to eat everything that doesn't run away from me. Except you, of course."

"Okay, you eat everything you can find," Lyla laughed. "But if you can do it without taking too long, so much the better." I started ransacking my pack, pulling out the bread, cheese and peanut butter that Ev Longhaul had given me and eating it in hand as she spoke. I noticed there was only one metal bottle with water remaining; I would have to refill the others soon.

"Look, Ray, I have a suggestion. There are some things I have to deal with right away, but I want to help you out. It looks to me like powerful relationships sort of camp out on your doorstep sometimes. Most people get into trouble by looking for it, but when I say I think none of us have met anyone like you, that's part of what I mean. You weren't looking for a timberline tree to talk to, were you?"

"No, not at all. But the spruce attracted me like a moth to a candle. Did I start it? Honestly, I don't know." Trying to talk and eat at the same time was exhausting, so I went back to eating, hoping that Lyla could handle the whole conversation for a few minutes.

"That's what I thought," she said. "So here's the deal, if you're interested. I'll walk with you for a while—in particular, to get you off Mother safely—and maybe you can wait for me somewhere around Moraine Park, wait and rest up for a day or two. When I get back, there are some people there I can introduce you to that will be easier to get to know, and a lot less dangerous. What do you think?"

The intelligent—or at least less stupid—part of my brain had caught up with that part of it that answered to the body, and I had abruptly slowed down my eating. Half the bread was gone, a good third of the cheese, and the peanut butter jar looked like it had been attacked by squirrels. I covered up my need to think by slowly starting to put things away. What did I know about Lyla? In truth, absolutely nothing. Knowing nothing about

Hucklebark hadn't stopped me from trusting his intentions. But I wondered how far I could push my luck with people I didn't know. Unbidden, the question rose up: what does all this have to do with luck? It was starting to feel like luck had nothing to do with any of it. But what *did* have something to do with it all? I thought again about what I had left behind to come up here this time; an empty, baffling life, pointless and disappointing. Why should I not trust her? She seemed to know a great deal about what I had experienced with the mountain spruce, and I was certain I wouldn't find many people that could even talk about that with me. So why would I go any way but forward?

"I think that sounds really good," I finally replied. "But I have a question that maybe you can't answer. It was amazing and wonderful that Everett Longhaul happened by and laid a bunch of food on me, but I'm thinking it wouldn't be wise to depend on that. If I run out of supplies, I'll have to leave The Mountain and figure something else out."

She looked at me in surprise. "Not depend on Ev? Oh, I can answer that one, Ray. First off, once you're on Ev's list, you're on it. Period. Second, he's been keeping us going for a very long time. Third, Ev has never, not once, allowed any of us to go hungry or without something we needed for more than a day. Ever. If nothing else, set your mind at ease on that score."

"But how does he do it?" I protested. "Where does it all come from? How does he know where you all are, what you need, all of that?"

"I prefer to let people speak for themselves, whenever possible," she laughed. "And that goes double for Ev! Trust me, Ray, you'll have lots of chances to ask him anything you want. While you're at it, ask him if you can share what he tells you with anyone, because I'd love to hear it."

I looked in her eyes, and she held her gaze to me without embarrassment or self consciousness. I said, "You know, Lyla, I do trust you. I don't know you, or know why I should, but I do."

She lightly patted my knee, and I managed to suppress the wince that reminded me I still hurt in every inch of my body.

"You're a better judge of character than you give yourself credit for, Ray Holdman," she said. "We need to get down off this mountain now. I promise I'll take it slow. You about ready?"

I nodded my answer, and concentrated on getting back up on my feet. As I rose I heard a long grunt of pain and surprise, and realized it came from me.

Lyla looked at me in concern. "Oh, dear. This is going to be harder than I thought. Well," she sighed, "there's nothing for it but to do our best. There's really only one good way off Mother Mountain—unless you're a goat—and it's not easy. We have to work our way around the northeastern slope and down from there. Whenever you need to stop and rest, sing out, okay?"

"Depend on it. The voice will probably be 'agonoso' *profundo,* I said, suppressing another groan.

The next hours were as hard as any I can remember. Lyla moved on the steep slope, across the slippery talus and around and over boulders as if she were indeed part mountain goat. I lurched, stumbled, and clawed my way along at what was a maddeningly slow pace, even for me. I called for rests often. Most of these rest stops were short and silent, but at one point we sat on a huge flat rock overlooking the Carbon River valley, and she asked me a question I hadn't known I was hoping fervently nobody would ask.

"So Ray—is there anyone in your past that had these relationships with trees? Or with other not-human people?"

I sat still for so long that she finally turned away, convinced I wouldn't answer. I surprised her, and myself in the bargain.

"My father. He talked to them all the time, and he made no secret of it. Not to me, and later on, not to anybody else. Eventually I was separated from him. I went through a bunch of foster homes, and then to an orphanage. I went to see him once, when I was about fourteen, and I didn't recognize him. He died a year later, and I ran away after that."

She sat stock still as I recited all this. When I was done, she said, "Ah." Just that. But into that one sound she put enough sorrow and compassion—without any of the useless pity I would have hated—that I knew she had not only heard, but really felt and understood. I wanted to weep again, but the old taboo against tears held, and I began to feel angry. Not at Lyla—at the moment I felt like I loved her with all my heart, stranger or not. But I was eaten by an anger I knew all too well: a rage with the world, with my father for being magical and foolish and for deserting me, with myself for being different and useless and confused. When I realized I had stopped breathing, I let out a lungful of exhausted air and took in a new one, slow and trembling. The rage and helplessness receded back to their normal, walled-off living space, and I could see around me again. The cliffs, the forest, the valley below, the stones, the sound of the distant river talking its way to Puget Sound miles away all returned. I looked at Lyla and said, "Thank you."

She replied just as simply, and with as much feeling. "You're welcome."

We went down, zigzagging across a slope of tumbled stone so steep that if either one of us fell, we wouldn't stop until we reached the valley floor. My legs tried with every step to refuse to take another, and each time I denied them. My ribs felt like they were several sizes too small for the rest of me, and my breath began to come in wheezing gasps. The pack on my back felt like a small house, and the world contracted into a space about six feet in diameter; all it contained was the next step. With hindsight I can know that this last leg down from Mother Mountain took about two hours—going a distance of about two thirds of a mile—but at the time I was convinced that my life as I knew it was over, and all that remained was an endless, slow motion scrambling and stumbling, always an instant away from falling.

And yet, we reached a place where the ground began to level out. I could hear the river through the trees and knew it was near, though I was too exhausted to even think of how near it was. I sank to my knees without intending to, and after an unsteady moment I slowly toppled over onto my side. I thought, even as it happened, how comically stupid, how contrived it must look, and if I could have prevented it I would have.

I closed my eyes and gave in to ache and exhaustion. Some part of me dimly heard Lyla moving around me, and it slowly registered that she had gently untangled me from the straps of my pack, and laid it down somewhere. I heard other sounds, but could not muster the energy to open my eyes. After a time that may have been five minutes or five hours, I heard her kneel next to me.

"Ray. You need to wake up, just for a few minutes. Come on, now—open up."

I opened my eyes, and was ridiculously proud of the effort it took. She knelt a few feet away, looking anxious. I felt a deep need to please her, to do whatever she asked, and I wondered at it briefly. But there was little room in me for wonder at the moment, so I concentrated instead on hoisting myself into a sitting position. It seemed to take a long time.

"It's clear enough that you can't go any further today. We're off the mountain, and that's what counts. I've made you a place to sleep tonight, and your pack is over there now. I have to leave, but I'm coming back to look for you in a couple of days, if I can. Do you understand me?"

I did indeed feel thick, slow and stupid, but I understood her. "Yes," I said slowly, "I understand. I supposed I need to stand up now."

"Not for long," she smiled. "It's close by. Up we go." She stood and grasped my arm, lifting gently but firmly. I was astonished at her strength. I stood shakily, with her hand still on my elbow, keeping me upright.

She led me like one leads a small child, protective and alert to mistakes, across the small rock field we had stopped on. She led me past a small stand of alder, and around a tangle of vine maple and huckleberry. We entered a tiny clearing, almost completely obscured by the surrounding growth. My pack was tucked into a corner by the flattest spot in the clearing.

"I took the liberty of getting your sleeping bag out, but I didn't do anything else with your stuff," she said. At the moment it wouldn't have mattered to me if she'd thrown it all into the river, as long as I could lie down. She continued, "You should stay here till tomorrow morning. Then you should consider what I said about making your way up to Moraine Park, and waiting for me there. Can you remember that?"

I managed a wan smile. "I imagine I can remember that. I don't want to seem ungrateful, but I can't help wondering why you're going to so much trouble for me."

She looked back at me in surprise. "You really don't understand that?" Lyla thought for a moment, and shook her head. "Maybe I can explain it when I find you." Then, with an ironic smile, "Or maybe you'll have it figured out by then. Either way, I have to go. No one will bother you here, but I suggest you get moving again as soon as you can."

I sank down onto the sleeping bag. It felt like the finest feather bed in creation. "Okay. With a little luck I'll be able to move in the morning. Good luck with wherever you're going."

She smiled again, turned away, and was gone in a few steps. I sank back onto the sleeping bag, and then suddenly ratcheted my body upright again. Fumbling through the pack I found a water bottle and what was left of the food Ev had left me. I inhaled everything I could manage, and in the same near-frantic rush replaced everything in the pack. Apparently my body knew it was important to hurry, for the instant I got the pack buckled shut, I fell back on the sleeping bag and was dead to the world.

When my eyes snapped open, it was to total darkness. I expected to spend some of those awful moments trying to figure out where I was, but instead I calmly listened to the river's conversation with itself a little ways away. There were no small noises, no tiny rustlings or scrapings or creakings of any kind. We are taught by endless stories and movies that this is usually a bad thing; why, then, was I entirely unconcerned about the deep, unnatural silence that lay under the river's muttering?

Slowly I began to put together where I was and how I had gotten there. The hike from hell with Lyla's help, the tiny clearing a hundred yards from a little-visited piece of the Carbon River, and however much blessed sleep I had managed so far. But something had awakened me.

Someone was sitting very near to me. I knew this to be so, even though they sat in complete silence and stillness. There was a short moment of panic, but my body calmed down immediately, as it had during my dream of the old man. My eyes were becoming accustomed to the dark. I went to sit up in the thoughtless, normal way I would—without really thinking about my body—and was forcibly reminded it had been through a lot lately. So more slowly, I sat up in my sleeping bag and turned to face whoever or whatever was in this clearing with me.

It was a woman. It was hard to tell in the darkness, but she looked very old. She sat cross-legged on the ground no more than two feet from me.

Her face appeared composed, though I could see little detail. As my eyes continued to adjust themselves to the darkness, I saw that her hair was twined into two long braids that wound their way down the front of her old fashioned dress and curled themselves in her lap. Her eyes were bright and alert; though she didn't seem to be smiling, her face told eloquently of the smile that lay inside her. She sat lithe and upright, her body and the carriage of it speaking of wisdom and power. Yet I was not afraid.

She made no move to speak, but sat gazing at me with a benign intensity. I returned her gaze with a deep curiosity welling up inside me. I said softly, "Do I know you?"

She did not reply. Instead, she raised her right arm until it was horizontal, the palm of her hand facing upward. In the dim light from stars and moon that made its way through the tangle of trees and brush around us, I could see the lines of her hand; they looked to me like great, world traversing rivers that carried all the world's life in them. Her gaze never wavered as she raised her hand towards me. I sat still, though for an instant my body considered flinching. She brought her hand, palm now facing me, to within an inch of my chest, about level with my heart. She held it there.

The nerves in my body seemed to open themselves up, and I began to feel the world around me in a way that was new and, for a moment, mortally alarming. I could feel the ground beneath me, and I was an open gateway, inviting the ground into me. It came, bringing with it something that made me feel warm and strong. The ground was immense, and connected with all the ground of the world. I could feel the curvature of the earth beneath me; I sensed, beyond all of the fissures, canyons, cracks and holes, how the ground was the same everywhere—there was no separation between me and any place on earth.

The strength of this, the unity of it, came into me. I wanted to shout, to sing as loudly as I could, but the feeling was too intense to break with any self expression, and I sat silent and wondering. The old woman held her hand there, in front of my chest, for a time that seemed to define its own way of being without regard for minutes or seconds. The ground didn't belong to me—I belonged to the ground, and with a shock of recognition I realized what I was experiencing. I *belonged*. I was supposed to be here. Like a child who senses the nearness of a parent, who needs nothing but the safety and security of that parent and whose need beggars anything we feel later in life, I reached for that belonging with all my being. I reached to draw it to me, to hold it, to make sure it couldn't get away from me.

And so it left me. The old woman's hand slowly drew away from my chest, and the earth drew back into itself, leaving me as I was before. It felt like the loss of that feeling would kill me, and that there was nothing to do but let it happen.

My gaze, which had turned totally inward, now returned to her face. She was looking at me searchingly, asking me without words if I understood. My eyes were hot with unshed tears as I said, "No. I don't understand. What is happening to me?"

Her palm went back to facing upwards, to the sky. The rivers in her hand were there again, and I was convinced that I was in one of those rivers, swimming for my life. She brought her hand up and passed it lightly over my eyes, and without protest or murmur I slowly lay back down on my sleeping bag, and slept.

Chapter 10

When I woke again the light was just beginning the subtle change from deep night to predawn. I sat up and remembered— an instant too late— that I should be doing things like that carefully and slowly. But there was no stab of torn or bruised muscles, no ache of creaking, abused bones. With astonishment, I took inventory of my body. I felt like I might feel after a vigorous day of hiking and a good night's sleep—nothing more or less. I wondered how this could be, and then remembered the old woman who had seemed to be there in the night, the way she had placed her palm near my heart, and how the world had come into me. If that was a dream, I could only hope for more of them. And if it wasn't—what then?

I rolled up my sleeping bag and hooked it to my pack. Turning away, I was startled to see a dark colored bundle on the ground, just a few feet from my pack. It appeared to be a canvas bag. Looking closer, I could see that a sheet of paper was placed under the bag, with one corner just sticking out. I gingerly lifted the bag and pulled the paper out from under.

> *Dear Ruy,*
>
> *Here's more of the same, since we haven't had a chance to work out anything else. Most is in bags, since you already have stuff to store it in. Except the peanut butter, har har. Now you have two jars—no problem,*

they come in handy. Hope you're feeling okay.

Regards, Ev.

How did he find me? It occurred to me that if he'd run into Lyla, it wouldn't be a big deal that he had. Then, remembering what little she had told me of Everett Longhaul, along with the amazement of meeting him, I thought he may well not have even seen Lyla.

Come what may, here was food, and high time to eat some of it. I opened the bag, and found—as he had faithfully reported—more of the same bread, cheese, and the ubiquitous peanut butter in its plastic jar. There was no more rice, which was fine—I had never had a chance to cook up what he'd given me before, and if I was going to be spending a lot of time above 4,000 feet, it might not work so well anyway. There were a couple of things I didn't recognize at first. One was a small plastic jar of white powder. Turning it around, I saw it had a blank label pasted to it on which was written "Powdered milk that doesn't suck! Believe it!" along with directions for the water to powder ratio. There was also a bag of something that might have been a kind of muesli, with a label that said, "Hucklebark recommends!"

The thought of Hucklebark made me sit back on my haunches for a moment. I hardly knew him, but I wanted to see him again. Lyla, too. I wanted to meet Mad Lupine in the worst way, though if you had asked me point blank, I couldn't really tell you why. I wanted to know about the old man, and now the old woman too. Who *were* all these people? Was there any chance that all of this fit into some kind of liveable pattern, and that maybe I could join it? It seemed so completely too good to be true that my mind shied away from the thought.

But I remembered again the way it had felt, in that dream or reality, or whatever it was, when the old woman had held her hand up, palm towards my chest. I told myself if I could feel that way every day—for *ten seconds* of every day—my life would be rich enough I'd never need another thing. Then I told myself I was a dreamer, and that nobody should expect such a gift or such a life. But why not? Because, answered some part of me I wanted to deny but couldn't, lives like that are for other people, not for you.

The argument quickly grew tiresome. The cool summer night air was already yielding to the first stirrings of the coming day's light. I shook up a small batch of Ev's powdered milk with the last of my water and tried it with the muesli—by God, it *didn't* suck!—and was ready to start moving. I dug out my map to make some decisions about getting to Moraine Park.

I had to look at the map for some time. Moraine Park was on the other side of the Carbon Glacier from me, and 1500 to 2000 feet higher, for the glacier has carved itself a formidable canyon. Both sides of it range from steep to sheer; the east side of the canyon—where I needed to go—is bounded by the Northern Crags, a set of rugged, nearly vertical peaks that come by their name most honestly. If I wanted to continue to stay clear of the trail that hugged the eastern side of the Carbon's canyon, I had my work cut out for me. I finally decided the best approach was to cross the river below the glacier, and make my way as best I could up the canyon in the narrow, chancy area between the trail and the glacier. It seemed likely that if I was spotted—by either a ranger or a volunteer—I'd just be politely asked to get myself back on the trail, and by the way, which camp was I headed to? Risk notwithstanding, it looked like an adventure I wanted to try. I figured Ev Longhaul had probably run up and down that narrow strip with his monumental pack jouncing along, so I should be able to do it too.

About a quarter mile beyond the snout of the glacier Dick Creek came bounding down the mountainside to join the river. The terrain in that area was incredibly steep, but I wanted to try intersecting the creek and following it up onto the marshy plateau called the Elysian Fields. From there I would be able to take my pick of Moraine Park or Vernal Park, two alpine meadowlands I knew from experience to be exquisitely beautiful. In any event, if it looked like I was going to have trouble, I'd simply double back to the trail and chance it.

I shouldered the pack and was making my way out of the tiny clearing Lyla had found for me when a vine maple caught my eye. It was twisted as if it had endured a long series of raging winds as it grew, though I wouldn't have thought that possible in the depths of the Carbon River Canyon. I regarded it with curiosity and a certain liking for the looping whorls of its slender stem, and it was with only mild surprise that within my mind I heard it say, *Thank you for bringing a blessing here.* I was better prepared this time, and simply thought back, *You're welcome. Live well and strong.*

I left the clearing and headed towards the sound of the river. On its west bank where I was, the trees and undergrowth came to within a hundred feet of the water. I found a tiny, unnamed creek that wended its way down to the river, and stopped for a moment to fill a small pot to rinse my face and hands, and refill my water bottles. I carried a tiny bottle of soap, but rarely used it; sand or gravel clean pots just fine, and the water itself seems enough for most everything else including most daily washing. The creek water was so cold it took my breath away, and I went forward feeling more awake and alive than I had in a long time.

I walked through the tree cover following the course of the river, looking for a safe place to cross. This proved to be much more difficult than I had thought; at this time of summer, the glacier melt is at its greatest, and the river as it rushes out from under the ice is busy, aggressive, and well muscled. I was close enough to the glacier that it soon became clear I'd have to cross somewhere very near where the river emerged, where it was likely to be narrowest.

The dawn was almost come and gone, and the day's light was establishing itself when I saw the glacier's opening ahead. There had been no place even remotely crossable that I could see, so I made my way down to the river's bank, foregoing any kind of concealment. It was a good time of day to be out in the open, for the light was still new and few people would be out hiking just yet.

I stopped fifty feet short of the glacier to consider. The top of the glacier, especially near its terminus, the snout, was covered with a remarkable assortment of loose soil and rock, and in places—unbelievably—shrubs and bushes growing from the deeper deposits. The rocks ranged from pebbles to boulders the size of a car. These tended to come bounding down on top of the glacier as it continuously carved its passage through the canyon; the zone where a glacier meets the earth is a place of great uncertainty, especially where footing is concerned. It's also easy to be squashed by something large and heavy deciding to obey gravity's call just at the moment you're walking at the glacier's edge. I decided that alertness would suffice, and anything else would just be distraction. I also decided, though, that stopping to contemplate the river's emergence from underneath the ice was chancy at best.

Walking along the river's edge as I approached the glacier's opening made it clear that crossing it, at least here outside, was out of the question. The river was about ten feet wide; not all that intimidating, perhaps, in terms of slogging across. But with the glacier melt at its yearly height, the river was running fast, hard and deep. I could hear the angry rumble of stones as they were shoved along the riverbed underwater, and from the sound of them I'd likely be trying to crawl up the other side with two broken legs if I dared it. There was nothing to do but enter the glacier itself, hoping to find a narrow, crossable spot farther up inside.

In the early light of morning, the glacier's opening looked to me like the portal to an ancient, grand and mysterious temple. The lintel of ice that arched overhead was thirty feet above me. Just inside the glacier, there were banks on either side of the river, twenty or more feet wide, of jumbled rock, sand and gravel, the collected detritus of a great monster that chewed the earth and spat it out to someday become soil. I had contemplated this opening from the safety of the Mystic Lake trail above and to my left that led up the east side of the canyon to Moraine Park, and beyond that to the lake. Now, standing near the glacier's mouth, I heard a sound I had only heard from the trail: the raucous clatter of stone, dislodged by some tiny change in the roiled earth and ice beneath it, leaping down from the top of the glacier to crash onto the valley floor. Without waiting to see exactly where the stone was falling, I bolted through the entrance.

I ran for ten yards or so into the glacier over the rough clutter of broken stone. A stumble over a rock I hadn't noticed brought me up short, and my wits began to collect themselves around me. A sense of astonishment grew as I realized I was *inside* the glacier. I had read old accounts of Mount Rainier rangers leading groups of tourists inside the glacier in the 1920's. The accounts had also dutifully reported the occasional death that occurred when an unwary—or perhaps simply unlucky—visitor had been in the wrong place at the wrong time, and been crushed by falling rock, ice, or both. As far as I knew, the guided expeditions into this or any other glacier on the Mountain had ceased long ago, and I was trespassing on the grounds of the occasional scientist, the more adventurous park staff, or more importantly, on the glacier itself.

That last thought sparked another one. While I stood on the threshold of the domain of a huge and powerful force of nature, perhaps it was wise—or at least prudent—to ask permission to be there. No elaborate rituals, perhaps just the simple act of putting the question out there and making a good faith attempt to listen for an answer. What more could you ask of an ignorant human, anyway? So, I stood quietly for a moment and put the question into my mind, and hopefully from there out into this world: *May I come in?* Standing quietly, trying not to project anything, there didn't seem to be an answer. Okay, it's a lot to ask of a glacier. But as I turned and began walking slowly farther in, something came to mind that honestly and clearly felt like it was not from me: *Yes. You're probably safe. But don't make assumptions.* Would I have put it in those terms if I made it up? Who can say? No matter what, it was good advice, and I decided to follow it as best I could.

The point of walking inward was to hunt for a place where the river was narrow enough, shallow enough or slow enough to cross safely. But I forgot all about that for the first few minutes because of the light.

I don't know what I expected, if I expected anything. But being inside the glacier was much like being in a really big tunnel, or perhaps a cave. And the light in this cave may have been dim, but it was suffused with an emerald green that was almost palpable. Perhaps it would be like this inside an emerald, or a beautifully cut piece of jade. The light was warm and cool at the same time, and it glanced off the rocks and the rushing river in waves of deep green. Then I made the mistake—at least in terms of what I thought I was supposed to be doing—of looking upward.

The roof of this cave was carved into a fantastic series of scallops, each of which played with the emerald light in different ways. The depressions in the roof looked to be roughly three feet across, with only a little variation. The central, concave parts of them glowed with a brighter, richer green than their outward-thrusting edges, and the whole taken together was deeply disorienting. Downwards from the ceiling, still nearly twenty feet above me, the ice was sculpted or pushed or faceted in some way into knobs, odd shaped depressions, and occasionally into uneven ribs that ran down the walls of the tunnel. All of them did something different with the light.

I stood still, moving only to turn my head or body to face a different direction, for a long time. I didn't care, of course—I might never have the opportunity to see a place such as this again, and I meant to drink it in until I could remember every last detail. After I'd been at it for a good while, though, the sheer strangeness and the wealth of shape, light and texture made things begin to blur together. I actually shook myself like a dog, trying to break the spell that held me immobile.

Looking back through the dimness towards the glacier's opening, I concluded that I hadn't missed an opportunity to cross the river yet, even though I had paid no attention to that issue. I began to walk further in, unwilling to give up too easily and go back out to try another approach to the problem. The light grew dimmer, but it was still surprisingly easy to see, and I figured that at least a little light was filtering through the ice above me, which at the glacier's snout was relatively thin.

I saw something ahead that looked like an unusually shaped rock. It was larger than most of the rocks I'd seen under the glacier so far, and my curiosity was aroused. It was on the same side of the river as I was. As I got closer, it began to look less and less like a rock, but it was still impossible to make out detail. When I was within twenty feet, my mind refused to believe the starkly mad lie my eyes were telling. The rock was sitting cross-legged on the uneven ground. It was wearing dark pants, and a well-worn but still clean bomber jacket.

"Henry?"

PART THREE

The Snout

*When you have no choice but to move, and the 'no choice' is forced
upon you time after time for years on end, one might think it gets
easier. To some small degree that may be so, but on the whole it
never gets easier.*

*No matter how many times I've had to abruptly move on to
someplace I never saw, and sometimes never heard of before, nothing about me changes. I am still exactly who I am, with the same
weaknesses, the same paltry list of strengths, and with no advantage
at all.*

*Same thing today: a bus ticket to wherever the money in my pocket
would allow, minus a half buck for a package of instant noodles. I
never heard of this place before, and know nothing about it. Now
I am here, and nothing about me has changed since the last place
I hadn't heard of. What will happen here—and whether it will be
better, worse, or more horrifically awful than I can imagine—I
have not, as always, the faintest idea.*

(Osprey Creek, SE Washington, Dec., 1992)

Chapter 11

He turned around and said, "Mornin' bub" as if it was the most normal thing in the world for either one of us to be underneath a glacier. I stood for several moments, gaping at him with my mouth open.

"I don't mean to rain on your parade, but there's no flies in here. You're not likely to catch anything, no matter how long you leave that mouth hanging wide."

I closed it with a snap. "Thanks, I'm sure that's excellent advice. So," I said in what was inevitably a falsely casual tone, "what brings you to these parts?"

"Probably about the same thing that brings you here, though it might take some work to make that clear," Henry said. He patted the ground next to him. "Come on over, sit a spell, and tell me about your vacation so far."

I laughed aloud. "Yeah, well, it's been quite a *vacation* so far. Whatever; if you want to hear about it, I need to know how much time you have."

"I have as much time as you have breath, I expect," he said with a smile. "With a little luck, we both have lots of each to work with." He dropped the bantering tone a notch. "It's good to see you, Ray. I'm glad you're here."

I shucked off my pack and sat down next to him. "I think I'm glad to be here too, but sometimes it's hard to tell. Seriously, Henry, if you want the story it'll take a while. I'll give it to you, but could you tell me first what brings you here?"

"Why shucks, I spend as much of my spare time as I can inside the snoots of glaciers."

"That's *snouts*, Henry, and as I recall it was you who suggested we didn't need to play games."

Henry laughed, a good, full laugh. "Touché, bub. Okay, then. You've met some interesting folks since you got up here, I warrant."

"I warrant you know good and well I have. You've seen Hucklebark?"

"Not recently," Henry said. "I haven't seen much of anyone since I got back, except for Ev Longhaul."

"It figures. Did he fill you in on all my adventures? And is there anyone he *doesn't* feed?"

"Sure, he doesn't feed a hell of a lot of people, but that's because they aren't here. And no, he didn't fill me in on anything—he was in a hurry."

"All right, you're speculating instead of having heard the story already. Yeah, I've met some people."

"Then," said Henry, "You know that there are folks here who've chosen a way of life and work that's pretty different from what you've seen before."

"Yes, that is no longer news to me. Are you saying that you're one of these people, too?"

Henry shifted his weight on the rocky, uneven ground. "Not only am I one of these, I'm somewhat of a hard case even with this bunch. Most of the people who make their lives up here stay up here; you won't ever find them wandering around Pioneer Square, or a suburb of Tacoma, or wherever. But what I found up here saved my life, and I found it through somebody else who *was* wandering around Pioneer Square and had the guts to tell me I should come here and look around. Since then, I make it a point to spend some time each year in the city. I look for people like you, and when I find 'em—which makes blue moons look like every day—I try to pass the favor along. In a way, it makes me an outsider to both worlds, but I don't mind. It's good to be alive."

"So, then," I said, "You spend most of your time doing your own mysterious work around here, and the fact that I ran into you in Seattle was complete happenstance."

Henry raised one eyebrow. "You don't think so?"

"I don't know what I think." I laughed a little bitterly. "At this point I don't guess it matters."

"Not really," Henry said. "You ready to read me your version of *War and Peace*? Or is it 'How My Summer Vacation Spent Me'?"

"How'd you know? Yeah, okay, let me get some water here and I'll get started."

I began all over again—with the clear cut by the road, Hucklebark, and everything that had happened since. Henry never interrupted, not even when I ran out of steam and kept quiet for a while. But I picked it up again, and finally got through the whole thing. It took a long time. It was impossible to tell much about passing time under the glacier, but I figured when I was done it was probably well into the afternoon.

Henry continued sitting, a contemplative look on his weather-beaten face. I decided that as I had done in the restaurant in Pioneer Square, I'd wait until he started the conversation up again. Not so much to annoy him, this time, but because the combination of his presence here and the retelling of my story had given me some new things to think about.

I remembered what he had said about me: that my life had been 'stolen' shortly after my birth, and that though it may not have been my doing at first, it was up to me to fix it, retrieve it, or whatever it took. What would it mean to recover my life? I mean, what would that look like? Feel like? Who (or what) do I have to confront in order to recover it, and is that even the right way to look at it? My mind began running in circles, so I distracted it by looking around me.

With a start and the feeling of being faintly ridiculous, I remembered that I was sitting underneath the Carbon Glacier. How could you forget something like that? Instead of trying to answer that one, I tried to really see and record in my mind what it looked and sounded like. The rushing of the river, running purposefully in here before most people thought of it as "being born", was a ceaseless echoing presence. The clack and clunk of the stones it pushed along under the surface made a slow, random syncopation to accompany the water's hiss and tumble.

The light had changed since I'd come under the glacier. The full, emerald green that seemed to come from no particular source was darker now, and the shadows in the scallops that lined the ceiling were deeper. I absently dug one hand into the coarse sand and gravel we sat on, and it felt like the bank of any wild river in these parts that was busily engaged in tearing down a mountain grain by grain.

I was brought back from my reverie when Henry stirred next to me. He turned and said, "What say we take a walk?"

"A walk. Under the glacier, or back outside? No, never mind, it doesn't matter. Sure, Henry. Take me wherever."

His only comment was a grunt as he hoisted himself to his feet. I agreed with that sound when I got up myself; we had been sitting for a long time, and I was stiff. I found I was also still tired and sore from everything that had happened on Mother Mountain, though I hadn't felt it in the morning.

"Can we take it slow?" I said. "It's been a… well, the last few days have been kind of intense."

"Sure," he said. "We'll be going slow anyway, 'cause it gets a little dark farther in."

We started walking upriver along the west bank where we'd been sitting. The ground was uneven, but passable. At this point under the glacier, the river's banks still stretched about twenty feet before bumping up against the wall of ice, but I felt certain they would narrow before long.

The air grew cooler as we walked. It seemed the light grew cooler as it grew dimmer. It was difficult to judge distances, and after what I figured was only a hundred yards of deliberate walking I gave up trying to keep track. I had thought we would talk as we made our way into the glacier, but soon enough it took all my attention to walk without stumbling. I could just see Henry, about ten feet ahead of me. He was walking with calm deliberation, steadily and without hesitation. I tried to emulate that, and decided that perhaps it was the product of much practice, for I felt awkward and clumsy in the rapidly increasing dimness.

When it got to the point that I could barely see my feet, I called out to him. "Do you mind if I use a light? I can't see a thing in here."

"I mind somewhat, but more importantly it's not appropriate," was the reply. "Concentrate on using the senses you have, and don't hurry. Don't holler out, either. If you drop behind, I'll come back for you. Just keep moving, and do it well."

Since no useful answer came to mind, I didn't give one. Instead I tried to make my feet more intelligent. I quickly discovered that my feet didn't know about that kind of intelligence. Instead, they insisted on stubbing themselves on stones they couldn't expect, and forcing my whole body to lurch this way and that as they flopped into unseen holes. I was about to speak to them harshly when I realized they were as tired as the rest of me. So instead I changed tack and slowed down, reminding myself over and over that it didn't matter if Henry disappeared. If it came to that, the way out was evident, if not easy.

I settled down to paying attention to where I was, using what I had available: ears, feet and legs, and occasionally my right hand when I strayed too close to the ice wall. It only took a short time of thinking about it to learn what the water sounded like when I was about ten feet away from it, and thereafter I was able to reasonably hold to the river's course without actually seeing it. It had been thoroughly dark for some time at this point, but by following the river closely I discovered that it did some substantial meandering under the glacier. I had supposed—without really thinking about it—that the river stayed obediently in the center of the glacier, but there wasn't really any reason for that. It was, after all, the glacier itself that cut this canyon, not its runoff.

Time seemed to be losing its importance on this mountain. I stopped once or twice to drink some water, but kept moving without a food stop on what I thought of as the off chance that Henry was actually trying to get me somewhere, and it would be good to get there sooner than later. I had no idea what time it might be in the rest of the world; here it was dark, and that was that. I had fallen into a semi-regular rhythm of slow walking, feeling with my feet, punctuated by occasional stops to listen. I heard nothing but the river, and my own breath moving in and out.

It was a deep surprise to begin the slow rounding of one of the river's invisible bends and see an unmistakable glow of light emanating from around the corner. Unlike the emerald green under the glacier's snout, this light was a deep blue, and at first so faint that if I hadn't been in total darkness I wouldn't have detected it. The glow increased at the slow, steady pace of my walking. The sound of the river had begun to change somewhere behind me, but I only noticed it now; its voice seemed higher and faster. I guessed that it must be much shallower and narrower up here, though I had not found any places where streamlets, creeks or even dripping from the roof had joined it along the way.

The blue, almost purple light had increased to the point where I could see the walls of the glacial tunnel, and a deeper darkness that was the river. It was indeed much narrower than before, and I discovered that with my learned distance of ten feet from the river's edge I was hard up against the ice wall. Since I knew that the Carbon Glacier was about three miles in length, I thought I must have been coming near to the great cirque where the glacier is born, but there was no way of knowing for sure.

Another fifty feet of following the bending river, and the light had grown to where I could see Henry a short ways ahead. He was sitting cross-legged, on the same side of the river, looking much more like a cleverly carved hunk of ice than a man. He never glanced my way as I approached. When I got to him, I quietly set down my pack and sat about five feet away. His eyes were closed, and it was hard to tell if he was breathing; I had to look carefully for what seemed a long time before I saw his chest rise just perceptibly.

His eyes opened slowly, and he turned to me. "Come on a little closer, so we don't have to shout."

I moved over so I was sitting beside him, our knees about a foot apart. The light, which was so blue it was almost painful, came from a great crack in the ceiling of the glacier. It must have led to a crevasse on top, light bouncing from ice to ice who knew how many times before landing in this place. The walls and ceiling were smoother than they had been below, with little or none of the scalloped effect in them. The river here was narrow enough to jump across with only a little effort. The air was significantly colder than it had been where we entered, and so clean and sharp it tasted spicy.

Henry turned towards me and started to speak. Until now, every time he had spoken to me it had been with a sense of direct, intense engagement, even when he was being flip or casual. Now, though, it was as if his attention was thoroughly divided, and I was only a small part of what occupied him.

"Whether or not you know it, Ray, you are a Tree Speaker. Among other things, of course. It's possible—make that likely—that you are meant to be doing work you aren't even close to imagining yet. You might think of me as an Ice Speaker. This is where my work is done, and if you want to hear it, I'll tell you about how I do it." He patted the ground next to him absently, and then lifted his hand, palm up, as if cupping a glacier in it.

"The glacier spoke to me too, I believe," I said. "I asked it permission to come in here, and someone—or something—seemed to answer. I might have been making it up, I admit, but it didn't feel like it."

"Oh, I doubt you made it up," he said. "But if you knock on someone's door, and they say 'Come in', does that mean you've had a deep and fruitful conversation with them? Have you given each other your deepest life and meaning? Do you understand each other in matters of life, death, and more important issues? And are you capable of *representing* them to other parts of the world?"

"Oh." That was all the reply I could muster. Suddenly I felt infinitesimal, a fool among geniuses, crushed under the weight of my stupidity. I fought against the feeling of smallness and uselessness that wanted to overwhelm me. I resorted to self talk, as if I was calming a child: Okay, fine. So you're way out of your element, but some people are hinting that you can learn how to live and work here. Be still, ask, listen, decide nothing now.

"How," I asked, "Do you give your deepest life and meaning to a glacier? And how can you possibly receive what it offers in return?"

Henry answered with a slight smile. "I won't say it's easy. But look, Ray, you've already experienced part of this with the mountain spruce episode that went so wrong. I'm of the opinion that part of the problem was that it was a one sided conversation, and you weren't able to give anything back."

I thought for a moment "I was missing in action, that's what happened. I got lost in the act of becoming a spruce tree. Besides that, when I'm inside *me*—like I seem to be at the moment—I still don't know anything useful about who and what I actually am."

"Perhaps you can get some new ideas about that here," he said. "Are you willing to try some more work along those lines? I can guarantee that you won't be able to damage the Carbon Glacier, no matter what happens."

I had to laugh at the thought of me harming a glacier. "I think I'd be a lot more concerned about being squashed myself. If I get almost fatally lost in the heart of a spruce, what would happen to me here?"

"That's why I'm offering to sit here with you, and I imagine that's why Lyla has offered to help you too." He leaned forward. "You have contributions to make, bub. None of us has ever reached for the work we do without help; nobody gets past the beginning alone. Ever."

I thought, what work? *You have contributions to make.* What was he talking about, and was it anything more than another crazy man's fancy? I hesitated, and then remembered once more that I had nothing of value to lose.

"Okay," I said, "Let's get started. What shall I expect?"

"That's one of the most important things you must *not* do," he said. "Expect *nothing.* Be open to *anything.* It's vital you learn that when you move yourself into a landscape you never imagined, you have to be willing to see anything that's there. Otherwise, there's no point in being there."

"Easy enough to say, I guess, but whether or not I can do that is a very open question."

"Your true enemy," Henry replied, "Is inside you. It's impatience, and until you realize that *nothing useful* happens without long practice, you're the agent of your own defeat. Get over that, and get over it now."

One thing he seemed to be teaching me was to not bother answering if one wasn't needed. I nodded slightly, and waited.

"All that's required of you right now is to relax and open up. You don't have to make any declarations. The glacier doesn't need any fancy greetings or any of that. It works best for me to leave my eyes slightly open, but you'll find your own technique. The key is to not try, because right now you have no control over the part of you that knows how to do this kind of work."

"All right. But now I'm getting nervous with all this advice," I said. "I hope that's about all you need to tell me."

Henry let out an exasperated sigh. "Some people are really good teachers, but I don't seem to be one of them. A good teacher doesn't care that they are trying to lead someone to a place where they *already are*, and just won't see or acknowledge it. Don't make it harder than it is, bub. Just get on with it, okay?"

I took a deep breath, and when I let it out I did what I could to let all the possible angry responses out with it, without giving voice to them. "Okay. I'll be quiet now."

"I'll be right here," he said.

I suddenly took it into my head that I wanted to lie down for this. Without asking Henry's permission, I got up and retrieved my pack, set it behind me and lay back using the pack for a pillow. For a change, the plywood box did not instantly find my head, but stayed obediently somewhere deep within the pack. Henry made no comment about my lying down; when I glanced over at him he already looked like the clever ice sculpture he'd resembled when I first rounded the river bend and saw him sitting here. I lay back and contemplated the blue-lit ceiling, doing my best to expect nothing.

In fact I got nothing for what seemed a good while. My mind wandered constantly; it was as hard as ever to gently rein it back in without indulging in wandering over wandering. It was also hard—as usual, since I came here—to forego wondering over and over what I was doing and why. Useless thoughts and speculations circled like vultures around the foolish man that was trying to talk to a glacier.

I returned from a bout of vulture chasing, and noticed that the light seemed different again. Perhaps it was simply turning to night outside this glacier. But it wasn't getting darker. The light was changing; I inwardly recited the mantra "expect *nothing*, open to *anything*," and waited.

From deep royal blue the light had become a hazy, pearl gray. The river's musical, tenor-style rushing had receded, as if I was moving away from it. The ceiling of the ice cavern had disappeared, and in its place was an amorphous, silvery cloud. Without turning my head I tried to look out the far corners of my eyes to the walls, but all I saw was misty, shining gray.

I felt a sense of motion. It was a bit like I was moving upward, but that didn't really describe it. Perhaps everything around me was moving. Perhaps the glacier was moving into me, more than me moving into it. I felt like I was beginning to spread out, to be bigger and more diffuse.

Much as it had been when I had entered the mountain spruce, my vision began to play less and less a part in what was happening. At the same time I became aware of things I hadn't noticed before. I could feel the texture of the ice; it changed dramatically in different levels of the glacier. Down near the roof of the tunnel hollowed out by the nascent Carbon River, and in the tunnel walls, it was dense and heavy, almost like rock. Higher up towards the surface it was less substantial, more like compacted dust. I sensed pollen and soil trapped in the layers; I could move through them at will, and discovered to my astonishment that near the surface there were whole civilizations of bacteria that lived their lives in ice, feeding on the microscopic scraps of organic matter the wind laid down year after year, only to be covered by another winter's snow. I was inside an encapsulated world, as if trapped in amber. Only this amber was in constant motion.

I discovered that the glacier is simply another kind of river; not as an intellectual reckoning, but a visceral understanding. This river moves like all rivers, only at a very different rate of speed. I felt the tug of gravity pulling the whole unimaginable mass down the mountainside; the unending cycle of snow collecting in immense drifts and layers in the cirque above me, being pressed down year after year, and then beginning its majestic flow downwards, to be turned once again to water after all those patient years, when it reaches the lower valley.

I spread into the glacier. My nerves, my awareness grew into it, exploring its layers and levels, feeling the mass of ice and snow that was enough to depress the earth beneath it and carve a widening valley from living rock. I felt the river running through me, a single artery carrying me out at the low end, while at the high end I grew at a gradual, inevitable pace the like of which I would never have been able to sense, let alone feel, until now. And I began to feel the first gnawings of fear, that I would not return from this place, that my time as human was over.

It was this feeling that made me recall what Henry had told me, that I had entered into a conversation and it was my responsibility to uphold my end of it. But as it had been with the mountain spruce, this was a type of conversation so much deeper than any I'd ever known that I had no idea how to participate, other than to passively accept what was given. So far the glacier had given me a good deal of itself. I was fairly certain I had still only skimmed the surface of its life and being, despite the depth and power of what it had offered. In return I had offered nothing. I saw myself as a tiny, walled fortress of secrecy; my wall was porous one way only, taking in understanding and experience but letting nothing out. It was a pathetic little fort, quite willing to take but entirely ungenerous and *unaware of its own power* or what it might be expected to offer in return.

With an inward start I realized what I had just thought. Unaware of its own power. Did I actually have anything whatever that resembled power? What is power? The ability to push things in the world around—the willingness to exert strength over weaker things and beings? I had always doubted this meaning of the word, even though it seems to be accepted by humans everywhere. I decided that the one-way wall that surrounded my being was useless and uninteresting. The prospect of tearing it down was daunting, even though it was so puny compared to the glacier's vastness that still infused me.

It occurred to me then—was it a suggestion from the glacier, or from somewhere else?—that walls require a lot of energy to create, and more to maintain. Perhaps if I simply declined to maintain this wall it would go away, or at least become porous enough to let some of me out as well as allowing what it chose to come in. I decided to do nothing more than neglect its maintenance, and the change was immediate. I felt suffused with a sense of energy as all the work I had unknowingly put into closing myself off suddenly became available. I felt myself—the mass, if you will, of my spirit and being—become more substantial, more real. Now it wasn't simply my awareness that spread out into the body of the glacier; I could feel myself offering—what? Among other things, I'm the sum total of everything I've ever seen, felt, touched, tasted, thought and dreamed. I didn't *do* anything with all of that—I simply allowed it to be available, knowing it was still only a fraction of my being. Neglecting to pour my life energy into the wall was a profound and powerful change, and I could feel the difference.

Instead of just "seeing" the myriad parts of this glacier, I was becoming them. The sensation of bones, blood and sinew spreading out into the surrounding ice was frightening at first. But the fear of losing myself was evaporating, and soon it changed to exhilaration. A sense of rightness washed through me as I gave back, allowing the glacier to be a part of me as it had allowed me the reverse. I could feel the interstices between crystals of ice; the slowly shifting stresses and strains that work their way through the whole, shaping, twisting, cracking and joining inside me as they responded to the world's gravity and motion. The civilizations of bacteria near the surface went about their microscopic business within me, and the crust of soil and broken rock that covered the top of the glacier was a blanket that soothed and protected my body too. Far from being mortal danger or even a problem, the freezing cold was simply the way it was. I was truly *conversing* now, and doing it in a way I had never been able to do before. It felt glorious.

My awareness was drawn to something approaching me. I was mildly curious, for it was clearly not a part of the glacier. Nestled within the huge, moving equilibrium of the glacier, I was unalarmed as the approaching thing took human form, and continued coming towards me.

It was a man. His lank, black hair hung down on either side of a drawn, ascetic face. He was morbidly thin, but in movement his limbs seemed to vibrate with power. In my awareness he came before me, though I knew that no human body actually stood there. I looked into his eyes, and they were red-rimmed and filled with rage. His mouth was tightly clamped into an angry grimace, and I began to be afraid. He radiated malevolent power. He raised a hand, finger pointing straight up, and I knew he was going to drive me away from the glacier, from my conversation.

I resisted. I would not go; I was welcomed here, and he was clearly not of the glacier. Who was this one to tell me to leave? I planted myself more firmly within the ice and snow, and refused to go.

His grimace distorted into a look of pure hatred, and his eyes blazed red. The upraised hand lowered slowly as his eyes bored in on me. His gnarled, outstretched index finger floated down to a level pointing directly at where my heart lies in my normal body. It held there for several seconds, his eyes locked on me. I felt a searing stab of pain in my chest, and my heart stopped beating.

Chapter 12

I could tell it was Henry's voice, even though it was faint and far away. I couldn't see anything, and didn't know if my eyes were open, or closed, or if I still had eyes. I had to listen carefully for a moment, but then I could tell what he was saying.

"Damn it damn it *damn it* what the hell happened here, come on, Ray boy, *breathe*."

This was repeated several times, while I wondered dully what had happened, and why Henry seemed so upset. Now it sounded like he was counting. I felt a sharp, powerful thud on my chest, and suddenly air was rushing into me with a long, drawn-in gasp that tore at my throat. I could feel a softer thud inside my chest that meant my heart was beating. At the same moment my vision returned; my eyes had been open all the time, and I had to blink many times before I could identify what I was seeing.

Henry was leaning over me, watching with frightening intensity. I blinked a few more times, and succumbed to a violent coughing fit. When that was done I tried to wipe the tears from my eyes, but my arm wasn't listening; I prayed it was just a little slow, and would hear me soon.

Henry had sat back on his haunches while my body wheezed and hacked its way back to life. Now he leaned forward again and said with surprising softness, "You hear me, Ray?"

I took my time reassembling the many skills required to make a reply. My voice came out as a thin, husky croak. "I hear you, Henry. Help me sit up, would you?"

He maneuvered an arm beneath my back and with a small grunt of effort lifted. My arms were almost ready to work as arms again; they flopped on the rough ground for a moment, then remembered their jobs and pushed, palms down, so I sat up. My heart beat wildly for a moment, then slowly settled back into a reasonable rhythm.

"I'm not sure," I said, "But I think I owe you my life. What happened?"

Henry sat back on his haunches, regarding me carefully. "As far as I know, you were farther into the glacier than I would have imagined possible, and everything was going great. Then suddenly you cried out, and your whole body levitated about three inches as if you'd been hit with ten thousand volts of electricity. When I checked, you weren't breathing and your heart had stopped. I'm not exactly a CPR expert, but it looks like whatever I did handled it."

"A good thing," I replied. "A *really* good thing." Without prompting I told him all that happened, up to the point where the sinister man/spirit/whatever-he-was leveled that gnarled finger at me and did his best to deliver death. I said, "Anything you'd care to tell me about this fellow, and what his beef is with me?"

Henry was silent for so long I wondered if he was evading. Finally, he said, "This whole thing is utterly beyond my experience. And I've been working on this for a *long* time. As for this being that attacked you, I don't have a clue. But I'm beginning to realize, bub," he went on slowly, "That along with arriving here with some spectacular promise, maybe you've brought along some pretty serious problems. I feel a certain responsibility here—not only for you, but for the people and work that goes on here. But I'm damned if I know how to proceed now. You've managed to leapfrog past my abilities in one jump."

This wasn't exactly the kind of answer I'd hoped for. The longer I stayed up here, the more complicated things got. And as they got more complicated, they appeared to get riskier. Then I remembered what Lyla had said.

"I think it's time to get myself up to Windy Gap, and the sooner the better. Lyla seemed to think I'd find help up there."

Henry considered a moment, and nodded. "Sounds like a better idea than anything I can come up with. We'll have to hope that Works is around to deal with you; if anyone can sort this out, it will be him."

I laughed—feebly. "I'll take your word on that, Henry. Part of what passes for my mind at the moment agrees, and the other part wonders what amazing and lethal adventure you'll guide me into next."

Henry looked rueful. "I can only hope you don't believe I wish you harm, Ray. I've been trying—like I said before—to pass along the favor that saved my own sorry ass. If you want me to disappear, I'll do that, no questions asked and no interference, ever."

"No, no, that's not it," I said. "I'm grateful for the way you've interfered with my life. At least now there's something that may or may not make it mean something. At any rate, don't worry about it—it was only part of my mind, anyway."

Henry looked at me appraisingly. "Okay, I'll stick with you—at least to get you up to Windy Gap. But it's the middle of the night now, and I don't think you're in much condition to travel. I suggest we stay right where we are till morning, and have a go at moving you then."

"Not a chance," I said without hesitation. "I may be pretty well trashed at the moment, and I have every intention of coming back when I can to work with the glacier. But I'm out of here right now. What are we, two miles from the snout? I can handle that, if you're willing to help."

"Two and a half, as the river runs," he replied. "Well, I don't guess I blame you, though I figure if you don't actually move into the glacier—and vice versa—you're safe. You just came within a gnat's ass of dying, you know—you really feel like walking tonight?"

I thought about it for a minute, but nothing changed. "I'd be lying if I said I *felt* like it, but I feel even less like staying here. If we can take it slow, I can do it."

"You took it slow coming in, so no sweat there," Henry said. "All right, let's get a move on then."

He stood up and reached out a hand. I got up, but I had to think about every aspect of it: how much strength was in my legs (not much), how to keep holding on to Henry's hand, how to keep some semblance of balance. It was a lot of work, and when I was standing I had a moment of truly serious doubt about the wisdom of trying to walk out of the glacier before morning. Then I remembered to breathe again, and in a moment I was ready to make a start, albeit a shaky one.

Henry helped me into my pack. "Think you can carry this thing and yourself at the same time?"

"We'll see," I said.

We headed towards the entrance. At first our pace was excruciatingly slow, but it was the best I could do. After that it only took fifteen minutes or so to remember things like how to walk, which foot went where and when, things I hadn't had to think about since before I could remember.

The first mile was hard, but with Henry keeping a hand on my arm I only actually fell down once. After that it got progressively more difficult; not because of any changes in the riverbank or the ground, but because what little store of endurance I had managed to conjure was gone. When we stopped for one of many rests, I suggested that even though I knew a light wasn't appropriate, perhaps I'd be forgiven for using my towel-over-the-flashlight trick, which would produce just enough light for me to see my feet. Henry sat quietly for a minute, then said, "Sure, why not?" I imagined him asking for and receiving permission from somewhere, but I had not a scrap of will or energy with which to pursue it.

The last half mile was tortuous. By that time I was leaning heavily on Henry, panting with the exertion of taking short steps over relatively even ground. Henry was guiding me completely; the flashlight trick worked until my endurance failed altogether, and then he had had to move me this way and that as his own feet found the least resistant path. Since it was quite dark outside of the glacier, the light inside didn't change until we were fifty feet from the entrance.

Henry half-carried me through the snout. I tried to be helpful as he carefully lowered me to the ground outside, but about all I could manage was to not bring him down with me. The air in the glacier had been clean, crisp and sharp. But the air outside was filled with the soft taste of trees, and soil, and I felt an exhausted happiness taking it into my lungs again. After a moment, I looked up to see where Henry had gone. I saw a long, lanky silhouette unfold itself from the ground a short way off from where I had sat down. It moved purposefully towards me. For a horrible moment I thought my assailant had waited for us here to finish the job. A few more steps of the figure and I saw with a flood of relief that it was Everett Longhaul. He squatted flatfoot on the ground next to me, looking like a giant cranefly dressed in faded jeans and tee shirt.

I said, "I hate to be inane, but I am really, *really* glad to see you."

A shadow loomed over him, and Henry came around to settle himself cross-legged next to Ev.

"I'm pretty pleased to see you too, Ray," Ev said. "For a little while I wasn't sure it would happen again."

"You mean you already know about what went on inside there?" I had meant to incline my head slightly towards the glacier, but I was so exhausted it almost made me fall over. "How does that work? Henry, just how fast can you talk? And how would you manage to be right here at exactly the right moment, Ev?"

Longhaul raised his hands up in a 'Whoa, boy' gesture. "Henry hasn't told me much of anything, Ray. But consider it this way: if you're at home one night—we'll say you live in some kind of neighborhood—and your neighbor's garage explodes into the sky, I mean it's completely obliterated, most of the folks living around there are going to be clear that *something* is going on. Right?"

"Sure, whatever," I said. My mind was getting too fuzzy to follow a conversation, but I wasn't quite ready to give up. "But what does that have to do with me, what happened, you're being here, and all that?"

"What you haven't figured on," he said, "is that *everybody* inside a good-sized range around here knows something big happened tonight. They mostly don't know exactly what—though I bet Works does—but they know this: a member of their own community—or someone near to that—was nearly murdered tonight by some one or some *thing* none of us have ever encountered before."

I'd been leaning against my pack up until now, but I started slumping more and more towards the ground. "How is that possible? What have I done?" I muttered.

I didn't know Ev had heard me. "Oh, it's possible, and more, Ray. And it's safe to say that the people who know you don't believe you've done anything in particular, except be a little snappish and untutored on occasion. At any rate," he said, turning to Henry, "we have to get moving. Looks to me like Ray won't be doing any more of his own walking tonight. You have a plan?"

"I'd thought about Dick Creek Camp," Henry said. "It's no closer than Carbon River Camp but I warrant it's more private. I have to agree, I don't think Ray can get to either one tonight."

"Not much doubt about that," Ev said. "I tried to make some room up at Dick Creek on my way down." Through the haze of exhaustion I could still see the twinkle in his eye. "But the rumor of bears nearby didn't seem to do the trick. Far as I can tell, the only thing that'll answer for tonight is to get him up to Moraine Park. There's a ton of places up there that'll do."

"All well and good," was Henry's reply. "Who's going to fly us up there?"

Ev looked me over with a critical eye. "I'd say Ray weighs about thirty pounds more than my pack does when it's well loaded. I don't see too much of a problem."

Henry snorted. "Since when does your pack weigh that much?"

"It weighs that much," he replied calmly, "When I'm keeping you and Hucklebark supplied on the same day. Let's get on with it, Henry. Can you handle his pack as well as your own?"

"Yeah, sure. So you're gonna carry him up to Moraine Park. How'll you keep him on—staple pack straps to his chest?"

"I can cover that too." He looked reproachfully at Henry. "Oh, ye of little faith, and less than scintillating imagination."

Ev rose to his feet in a motion like steam rising from a boiling pot. He was at his own cavernous pack in an instant, and in the next had the pack slipped off its frame. He extracted a bundle of wide, buckled pack straps, carrying them over to a flat rock nearby. Slipping into the pack frame, he sat on the rock facing away from us. "Help get him sitting on the pack frame's shelf, Henry, and I'll boss you through the lashing."

Henry regarded Everett Longhaul with a mixture of suspicion and admiration. "So you're actually going to do this. What's the elevation gain up to Moraine Park, about twenty two hundred feet?"

Ev twisted around to look at him sharply. "It's twenty five hundred, and if we were trying for the summit, I'd have to think of something else. Quit wasting time, Henry, let's go!"

Henry shook his head and came over to me. I did my best to help him help me up, but by then my body was fully engaged in an all-out work stoppage, and about the best I could do was to simply not resist. Henry managed to lug me half upright and get me over to where I flopped onto the shelf of Ev's pack frame. From there Ev gave out a series of staccato instructions clear enough that Henry had me lashed onto him, with a type of bandolier harness wound around my chest, and a couple of straps around my thighs tying me to the frame. Henry stood back to examine this most unlikely arrangement and said, "Okay, Ev, how're you gonna get up now?"

By way of answer, Ev scooted his knees far up under his chest, and in one smooth, powerful motion planted his feet and straightened his legs, coming upright almost as an afterthought, like an unintended but proper consequence of just moving around. "You all right back there, Ray?" he said.

"Yeah." A single, faint croak was all I could manage, but it was enough to get us started. Henry slung my pack up backwards so that it protruded from his chest. It occurred to me that in the pre-dawn twilight we must have looked like a couple of mutant turtles, the products of a biology experiment gone horribly wrong, but I was too far gone to say so. Just as well, I think.

Ev took it pretty slowly at first, getting a feel for how he was balanced (or unbalanced, as the case may have been). He went straight to a place on the river's bank I hadn't considered when I was looking for a way across. He started into the river, and at first I thought he meant to wade across; if I could have protested, I would have. But a couple of steps in he found what he was looking for: a series of relatively flat stones just under the surface of the river. With huge, graceful strides he went unerringly from one to the next, and in seven or eight steps had reached the shallows on the other side. Before he turned around, I could see Henry halfway across, grimly eyeing the river, looking for the steps Ev had found effortlessly. Henry's stride being about half of Ev's, he made the crossing in a series of awkward leaps made all the more difficult by my pack hanging off his chest. He didn't fall in, nor did the river send any stones to knock him down, and shortly he was beside us. He and Ev waded the rest of the way to the riverbank, and moved up slope towards the trail that led to Dick Creek Camp and Moraine Park.

"Moraine covers a good bit of territory," Henry said. "Where you thinking on setting up when we get there?"

Ev answered, "I thought I'd stay with you on the way up and we can figure that out together."

"Don't let me slow you down too much," Henry said drily.

Ev chose not to take the bait. "No problem, friend, but daylight's not far away. We're running late, so whatever speed we can manage is good."

Neither one spoke after that. The trail from the Carbon River Valley up to Moraine Park rises that half mile of elevation in a little over three miles; it's a rigorous hike for most people even when they aren't carrying someone on their back. Everett Longhaul didn't seem to notice. He walked up the steep, rocky trail as if on a stroll in the park, with long, even strides that rocked me gently from side to side. The movement was rhythmic and insistent, and within a few minutes I was fast asleep with my head sunk down onto my chest.

Chapter 13

I woke with a familiar scent tingling in my nostrils. It was well known, and I knew it was a good thing, but for several moments I couldn't place it. Then, with that deep happiness that comes with recognizing an old friend, I identified it as *coffee*. I looked up to dappled sunlight filtering down through a grove of stunted fir and spruce. I was lying, fully dressed, on top of my sleeping bag. The air was warm and sweet with the tang of conifer and wildflowers mixed into the coffee smell. As I sat up slowly, Henry moved into view. He wordlessly handed me a steaming cup.

I stared at it in wonder. The night before, for a short time, I had to all intents and purposes been dead. Today I held in my hands this cup, with its heat and richness rising up to me. A wave of sentiment rolled through me, a complex emotional mix of surprise, gratitude, tenderness. I couldn't count the times I had wondered about, even considered, dying. Now I had an inkling—probably just the barest notion—of real death, and my delight at being alive was magnified a thousandfold. The wave of gratitude rose inside me until I was engulfed, and my eyes filled with tears. There was no need to sob, or wail, or even cry out loud. The tears simply flowed, running down my face and dropping to my crossed legs. They made widening dark circles on my dusty jeans.

Henry let me sit that way, holding a cooling cup of coffee and crying silently, until I was done. I set the cup down carefully and wiped my eyes with a shirtsleeve.

"You want me to come back in a while?" he asked.

"No, I'm okay," I said. "It's just that I was dead for a bit last night, and unlike most of the people that happens to, I get to be here again."

Henry went back to the camp stove, poured himself some coffee and returned. He sat down in front of me and stared at his cup thoughtfully, before looking up.

"It does change your perspective, and that's a fact," he said with a faint smile.

"So I presume you know what it feels like too."

"Oh yeah, I know a bit about that," he said. "But that's a depressing story for another time. How're you feeling?"

"Like I haven't eaten for a couple of days, but in the big scheme of things, it's way more interesting to be breathing and looking at trees. Am I correct in assuming this is some part of Moraine Park?"

"Correct indeed," Henry said. "That show-off Longhaul left me in the dust about a third of the way up from the valley. When I got to the western edge of the park he was waiting, looking smug as all get out. At least he was good enough to wait so's I wouldn't have to search the whole mountain for you. Then we chose this spot. If you're curious, it's about noon, but as far as I know, today's agenda is open."

"What about his own gear? Did he just leave that down by the glacier?"

"He ran right back down to get it, soon as we got you unloaded here. Probably took him about twenty minutes to get back down. I swear that boy's at least two thirds jackrabbit. No telling where he is by now, and I didn't ask because it doesn't matter—he'll be somewhere else in the time it takes to talk about it."

"I hope I see him soon," I said. "I owe him some serious thanks."

"He knows," Henry replied, "And will be suitably embarrassed when you say something. Don't hold back on my account. In the meantime, we'd better make sure we know what condition you're in, and how soon you'll be good for travel."

"Not that I want to sit around for the rest of my life—" I looked around me at the brilliant, sunny green of the alpine meadow where it could be seen through the screen of trees— "although I might like that if it could be here. All things considered, I appear to be in pretty good shape. I don't know what you have planned, but I could probably get somewhere this afternoon if need be."

"No need for that kind of hurry, but tomorrow we need to be at Windy Gap, if that's at all possible. Right now we're only about two and a half miles away, as the crow flies. The trouble with that, of course, is we're not crows."

I asked, "What's in that two and a half miles between us and there?"

"We're sitting at the northeast corner of Moraine Park, where it bumps up against Vernal Park." He then pointed just a shade north of west. "The Elysian Fields are a quarter mile that way, and on the other side of them are the headwaters of Dick Creek. You been up this way much?"

I shook my head, still looking in the direction he'd been pointing.

"Anyway," he continued, "It's over there and down a couple thousand feet. On the other hand, getting to Windy Gap from here means going between Crescent and Sluiskin Mountains, which is a pretty nice workout. When we get together there, we usually gather at a place a bit upslope from the Sluiskin snowfield; it's nicely sheltered from the trail, and backcountry hikers almost never get up that way."

"What do you expect to find there when we arrive?" I asked.

"If I thought I really knew, I'd say so," he said. "As it stands right now, I'd guess on a handful of folks waiting to talk and figure out what's going on, and what needs doing. Beyond that, your own guess is as good as mine. But you remember what Longhaul said last night, right? There'll be people who want to know more about why the garage blew up, and who was in it, and what it might mean for their own little garages. Don't blame 'em, either."

I joined Henry in not blaming them—whoever *they* might be. But I had to wonder what kind of reception I'd find when we showed up for this meeting, or gathering, or whatever it would be. I started wondering who would be there, and whether or not I could find a way to wiggle out of it. The first rumination stopped abruptly with the realization that I hadn't the faintest idea who would be there, couldn't have the faintest idea, and would never find out unless I showed up. In a vague and unsatisfactory way that seemed to answer the second rumination. With a deep mental shrug—in itself much less than satisfactory—I set the whole thing aside as already beyond control, never mind its being in the future.

Henry had fallen silent while I meandered through this series of thoughts, and when I looked up he seemed disinclined to start up another conversation. I slowly unfolded my legs, rose and made my way out from the grove of alpine trees that sheltered us. Since Henry didn't object, I assumed that we weren't worried about being seen, and that I could explore our refuge a little further.

It was like walking out of a lovely and magical bedroom into a great and mysterious house. I wondered if this was part of the House of Windy Gap, and decided that of course it must be. That made me think of Lyla, and I hoped I would see her again. The sun was a comforting warmth on my skin; it distracted me from my meandering thoughts, and I began to look around more attentively.

Everything in the alpine meadow was exactly as it should be: a vivid green ground cover with wildflowers dotting it. We were again high enough that there were still avalanche lilies blooming, the first flowers of the late, late summer at this altitude sharing the sun with the later arrivals—the columbine, like delicate, scarlet hanging lanterns, the deep blue of the lupine, the tiny, yet still somehow riotous yellow monkey flowers flagging the tiny watercourses that crisscrossed the meadow. They made a brilliant patchwork accented by the tall stalks of beargrass with their hairy, tufted topknots.

If I relaxed my eyes—and my mind to go with them—a little bit, I could see a grand paradox: the chaotic profusion of life lying atop the even greater chaos of the land, all of it together producing something of the highest possible orderliness and beauty. I was filled with the sense that nothing needed doing here. All of it was exactly right, and as long as I did no lasting damage, perhaps it was appropriate to be here, to drink it in and simply receive its blessing.

Gazing across the meadow, I saw a lone, stunted tree in the middle distance, and as I thought about the spruce on Mother Mountain, my mood of tranquil acceptance vanished. I had, in fact, done damage there, perhaps lasting though I couldn't know that now. What exactly had I done, and how could I repair it?

That problem was tiring, but when I tried to consider what to do about a being that appeared in glaciers and tried to kill people, my mind shied away like a spooked horse. I turned and walked slowly back to the grove where Henry was still sitting exactly as I had left him. Perhaps his mind was worrying at the same problem. I made a mental note to ask him about that later.

I sat down figuring to lay back and rest, maybe even sleep some more, but as I sat Henry looked up as if he'd made a decision about something. As I was learning was generally the case with him, when he decided something he was in a tearing hurry to act on it.

"You'll recall that I made a pot of coffee this morning," he began. When I nodded quizzically, he continued, "A consequence you might not have thought of yet is that I don't have any coffee. Meaning that I went through your pack looking for it."

"All right," I said. "I don't see a big deal there; you don't strike me as the dangerously meddlesome sort, and it's clear you take good care of your own things, so what's the problem?"

"Maybe nothing. But you already know I'm a nosy bastard, and I still can't help it. You're more than welcome to tell me where to go jump, but if you're willing to tell about the wooden box, I want to hear about it."

I never entirely forgot about it. But the events of last night had so flung me from ordinary ways and objects of thought that the idea of the plywood box was startling for a moment. My first response was anger—that he'd snooped to the point of finding it. But a short moment's reflection changed all that. Yes, the contents of the box were intensely personal, and I wouldn't allow access to them to hardly anyone, let alone *just* anyone. Henry, however, was not only something more than just anyone, he was now far more than *hardly* anyone. Henry had, beyond all doubt, saved my life last night. Granted, I had entered into communing with the glacier at his invitation; but I had entered willingly, and it was Henry's quick thinking that had thwarted a murder. On top of all this, the feelings I'd experienced on waking were still with me, and the fact of being alive seemed infinitely more important than keeping my agonized history a secret.

"All right," I said, "I'll tell you about it. Better yet, I'm going to do something I've never done before, which is to say I'm going to open it up and let you have at it."

His eyebrows rose a couple of notches as I reached over to my pack and, with a bit of fishing, unearthed the box. I unlocked it, and handed it over to him.

"I'm quite certain it won't blow up when you open it. Beyond that, I'm going to let you make of it what you will, at least for a while. Let me know if you have questions." I lay down on my sleeping bag, hands under my head, and gazed up the canopy of alpine fir and spruce with a studied indifference that fooled neither of us.

Henry lay the opened lock carefully on the ground beside him. He slowly opened the top and considered the contents. I noticed, even though I was pretending not to look, that before he even looked at it he turned the notebook back to the first page. He began to read.

October, 1972 (California, town unknown) (first year)

Papa said it's an oak tree

He said it's old and wise

Wise means smart in a big way.

Papa talked with that oak tree

All the time

And he showed me how to do it too.

He put his hand on that rough bark

And I sat with my back leaning on it

We heard all its stories: air, water, and People, How To
Live.

Papa tried to tell its stories to other people

But they got mad and said he was crazy.

They came to our house and took him.

I ran and hid behind the oak tree.

I asked it to help us. It tried to make me

Brave and strong, but it couldn't.

Everything was better when Mama was here.

Papa said she got lost, but I think he means she died.

It was a long time ago, and I can't remember.

I hid but those people found me, put me in a car.

A woman took me to a house, said I was going to live there.

I don't know anyone here.

Where is our oak tree?

Where is Papa?

Henry sat, looking down at the notebook, for a good bit longer than it takes to read that. Finally, he looked up with an unreadable expression.

"How old were you when you wrote this?"

"How do you know I wrote it?"

He said evenly, "You don't need to be coy with me, Ray. Allowing me to see it is big enough. If you don't want to tell me, that's okay."

I heaved a sigh that trembled when it came out, despite all my efforts. "I was fifteen when I wrote it down, but it happened when I was six."

"Why the nine-year gap?"

"Because," I said, "When you live in places that aren't really a home—places where you own nothing, have nothing, and there's no such thing as being safe—you don't write things down. Up to fifteen, I kept everything I knew in my head."

Henry thought about this. "Your own oral tradition, even though I bet you could write just fine, and even score the materials sometimes."

"Oh yeah, I could write." I laughed, though it wasn't funny. "At first I tore up everything I wrote; later I burned it, right after writing. I read everything in those houses that was printed, whatever I could beg, borrow or steal."

"You feel like talking about your father?"

I lay back down and looked at the green, cluttered canopy of conifer branches above us. "Maybe later. It makes me tired just to think about these things. I try not to do it very often."

"Fair enough," he said. "I'll leave you be." He closed the box, replaced the lock, and placed it next to my pack. "It's a good time of day for resting."

I silently agreed, and closed my eyes.

I woke to the sound of quiet voices. Their quality and tone told me they were friends before I was sufficiently awake to identify them. I sat up slowly, and saw Henry and Lyla sitting just outside the little grove of alpine fir, keeping their voices low.

I went out the opposite side to relieve myself, and then walked around the grove to where they were sitting. Lyla sprang to her feet, and to my astonishment hugged me fiercely. She held me at arm's length, studying my face, joy on her own turning somber as she regarded me.

"Ray, I am truly happy to see you. Are you all right?"

"All things taken into account, I'd have to say I'm quite well," I replied. "Although I seem to bring trouble wherever I go."

"Sit down and tell me more," she said.

When we were settled down I said, "Well, you of all people would know about the mountain spruce. And I suppose Henry has told you about my little adventure last night. Like I said, my middle name seems to be trouble these days."

"I think there may be more to it than just you," Lyla said thoughtfully. "Henry told me what I didn't already know from what I felt last night. I'd say there's a good chance something else is going on too."

"Why do you think so? I mean, I'd prefer not to take the job of Trouble Bringer if I can avoid it."

"You might feel like you're filling that job for a little while," she said. "But look, Ray. At around the time you were attacked last night, your villain or someone like him tried very hard to get into the tree I was working with, no doubt with a similar purpose in mind."

Henry sat up straight with a yelp. "You didn't tell me that!"

"Well, Henry," she said calmly, "It's been tough to get in a word edgewise since I arrived."

Henry flushed. "I need to learn how to keep my mouth shut."

"Sometimes you men are so hard on yourselves it's a wonder you don't all jump off a cliff at daybreak," Lyla replied. "You know as well as I do I needed to hear what you were telling, and we've already gotten around to my part, so no harm done. Anyway, Ray, there *is* more to it than your practicing to be a Trouble Bringer."

I turned to Lyla. "So tell me more about what happened with you."

"I was working with a tree only a few miles from here. It's a powerful change agent, and I've been trying to understand better how it works and if it needs or wants a partner. I was deep inside it when I felt something like a series of concussions, as if someone was battering at the tree's spirit to break their way in. Turns out someone was; I felt him starting to break through when the tree got hold of him and threw him out. I only hope he got thrown out hard enough." She shivered. "I've never encountered such an appalling malignancy before."

Henry protested, "But how could a tree defend itself from someone like that when he could walk right into a glacier? It doesn't make sense."

"I don't know with any certainty, of course," Lyla said. "You know the glaciers. I know the trees, and they have crystal-clear boundaries, easy to see and defend. Is that how it is with a glacier?"

Henry rubbed his jaw, thinking hard. "No, I don't see them that way. There's their size, of course, miles long, hundreds of feet deep, and their boundaries change with the seasons and the climate cycles. Totally different kind of person."

"Their power must be as immense as they are, Henry. Would an intruder have to batter at the gates of a glacier's spirit, or is it so huge—in all ways—that he might just slip inside?"

Henry grunted. "I don't like it, but it sounds reasonable. The real question is, what do we do about this?"

"The three of us would do well to rest and think until tomorrow," Lyla said. "I expect a lively gathering tomorrow at Windy Gap. In the meantime, though, I need to ask you, Ray—apart from resting—do you feel up to working with a tree today?"

"After the last two outings, I don't know if I can ever do this again," I said. "I want to, but between killing someone else and being killed, I don't know which way to turn with it."

"There is a tree less than a mile from here that really needs consulting, and I think you're the one to do it. I've spent some time with it, so I know it pretty well, but there are too many now that I have to deal with. What do you think?"

I studied her while I thought. Someone had most likely tried very hard to murder her last night, but the effect seemed very different on her than it had been on me. Here she was, vibrant and intent as the first time I met her, ready to continue on with her work. I felt a rush of admiration, and when it started to morph into something other than admiration I cut it off abruptly; maybe later, maybe never, but *not now*.

"I think," I started, then stopped. Was I ready to take another step, after all that had happened? What else was there to do? "I think I need to go ahead with this, now rather than later. But I have some questions. Why would this tree person need consultation—as you put it—really?"

She sighed. "There's too much to explain in less than a week, but I'll try to sketch you the barest outline. You already know that the world is filled with people, and that humans are no more than a small part of The People."

"Sure, but humans seem to have a disproportionate effect on things."

"So they do," she smiled. "Now stop interrupting, this is hard enough as it is! Anyway, you also know that different peoples communicate in ways that aren't obvious to most humans, and that to anyone with the knowledge and experience, different forms of life don't pose any obstacles to that communication. Trees, reptiles, mammals, insects, plants, glaciers—every combination is possible, and most of them happen at some point. Henry can tell you that the very stones and soil of the world are a part of this, though almost nobody in this time knows how to hear them directly."

Henry merely nodded, knowing better than me when to stay silent.

"All right, then," Lyla continued, "The point of all this isn't just that every living thing in the world gets to babble away and everyone else has to listen. What's important here is that all these different peoples have unique understandings, perspectives, and experiences. More than that, many people believe that without *everyone's* input in the Great Discussion, nothing will ever go quite as it should. Some go even further to say that without that complete participation, the world can only continue at all on borrowed time.

"The problem lies in the fact that communication is no easier for anyone else than it is for humans. Meaningful communication, that is. A tree—or a species of tree—might have some immensely useful bit of knowledge or understanding that's vital to someone else, but no way to get it across. That's where Speakers come in. Speakers are people, human and otherwise, who cross the boundaries between lives and peoples. They go back and forth, carrying things between individuals and peoples, when there is no other way for those things to move. Sometimes someone has something important to say, but no way to say it, no way to get that useful thing where it needs to go. Speakers are actually listeners, first and foremost; only after they have something that needs to be passed on do they do any speaking."

I looked from Lyla to Henry. "So you're both Speakers. Henry, you said you think of yourself as an Ice Speaker. Are you a Tree Speaker, Lyla?"

Henry took it in turn to answer. "Not really that simple, Ray. It seemed like an easy handle at the time, and sometimes it does make sense to identify the people that a Speaker has the strongest affinity with. Remember that a Speaker's job is to carry ideas and information *between* peoples."

They let me sit and think. Yes, I could understand it taking a week for a more detailed explanation. I could also understand it taking a basketful of lifetimes to actually practice it well. It opened an infinite landscape of endeavor, and the thought was intensely exciting. But having considered all that, I remembered that skeletal face in front of me, a gnarled, bony finger pointed directly at my chest, and a stab of pain.

I was about to say, "Do you really think I could be a Speaker?" but stopped before saying it. Of course I could be one; I had been doing a form of it—childish, clearly primitive—since I was six. Whether or not I could do it well enough to make a real contribution was something no one could answer yet.

So I thought of another question. "Has anything like these attacks ever happened before?"

"I've never heard of such a thing," said Lyla. "Henry, you've been at it longer, and you talk with some really long-lived people; any stories?"

Henry said slowly, "Nothing exactly like it that I can think of, certainly not in the living memory of anyone—human or other—I know. 'Course I've heard countless stories of conflict—sometimes mortal—between individuals and occasionally groups. But we're gonna need better, older experience to get that one answered."

"With luck we'll have some of that tomorrow," Lyla replied. "In the meantime, Ray, if you want to work with me, we need to get going. I'd like to start now so we can get a full night's rest."

"Yeah," I said, and immediately realized it wasn't adequate. "I mean, yes, let's go ahead with it."

"Good," Lyla smiled. "Henry, if we aren't back in about three hours, send the bloodhounds, okay?"

Henry snorted. "You pick the strangest times to joke, girl. I'm not entirely satisfied with this idea anyway, so you make damn good and sure it's three hours, no more."

Lyla's expression shifted from one breath to the next, from open and animated to completely neutral. Without replying, she turned and started off while I scrambled to my feet. When we were out of earshot, she said, "I like Henry a lot, but he can be prickly sometimes."

"Actually, I think he's got a point to be worried. Is this another 'You men' thing or something?"

She stopped and faced me. "No, Ray, it's not a 'You men' thing at all. I'm worried too. The differences are, one: I'm not going to let it keep me from my work, and two: I'm not going to get all morose about it. I'd be reluctant to work with the Carbon Glacier right now, believe me. But I know the not-human people I work with, and I know what they're like. Like a lot of human people, and I *don't* mean just men, Henry makes assumptions based on what he knows, and applies them to things he doesn't. When you're faced with complete mysteries, that may be your only choice, but when you're talking about someone else's area of experience, it means you're blowing off what they say."

"Wow. Is this Henry bringing out the prickly in Lyla, or am I completely missing the point?"

She looked at me with a mixture of surprise, consternation, and something that lay between irritation and downright anger.

Suddenly she threw back her head and laughed, all the way down to her feet.

"No, Ray, you're not missing a thing! I let him get to me. Thank you for making that clear."

"You're welcome. If I may change the subject, this body is still getting used to the fact that it isn't dead yet. Could we walk just a little slower?"

She looked startled, and studied me for a moment.

"Of course. I'm sorry if I'm pushing you; I guess I thought it would be best to have something safe and good happen as soon as possible."

I simply nodded my agreement, and she continued, "I don't expect a huge, drawn-out discussion with this tree today, but I'm hoping that this will be someone you want to work with."

We started walking again. We were moving in a westerly direction, into the Elysian Fields. The far side of this alpine valley was much drier than the side we approached, due to the slope of the land; we walked carefully through the marshy grassland until reaching firmer ground. We moved in single file, following what looked like a deer path, although I didn't think deer ever made it up this high. Perhaps it was a mountain goat path; I couldn't tell by looking, though I didn't think enough humans came this way to cut a trail into the sandy loam.

My body was actually quite accustomed to the fact that it was still alive. In fact, it seemed to take it pretty much for granted. Nevertheless, I was stiff and sore in many places. I thought about how I had felt yesterday morning—*yesterday morning?*—after the mysterious visit from the old woman. I realized that Lyla might not know about that yet, and I was interested in her reaction.

I called out to her, "Did Henry tell you about the dream, or visit, or whatever I had with the old woman after you left me night before last?"

She stopped dead and spun around. "What? No, he didn't say a thing about that. Tell me."

"You want to wait on it until we get done? I was just wondering if he'd told you."

"No, I don't want to wait. Try to tell it without rambling, but tell it now."

We stood where we had stopped, in the middle of that narrow alpine track, and I told her about awakening in the darkness to a world holding its breath; the old woman sitting there; her hands, holding the world's rivers, and how she had opened me like a pickle jar and filled me with the world. I finished by mentioning the vine maple that, as another one had after my dream of the old man, thanked me for bringing a "blessing" I knew nothing about.

Lyla stood still and silent for several moments, looking at the ground, her expression unreadable. Then, seeming to have reached a decision, she looked up.

"What color was the dress she wore?"

"What color was the—huh?"

"Come on, Ray. What color? And was her hair silver, or black, or what?"

I thought hard, but I couldn't see why it mattered, and ultimately these details refused to reveal themselves. "I don't know what color her dress was, or her hair either. What does it matter?"

Her shoulders slumped—just perceptibly—and I knew I had disappointed her badly. The knowledge hurt. "It matters very much to me, Ray. If you happen to remember, I'd appreciate your telling me."

She turned and started walking again. I thought furiously; why would it matter so much to Lyla how this mysterious old woman had appeared? The answer came so forcefully I almost smacked my forehead like some idiot cartoon character, but instead I said it aloud. "You've met her too, haven't you?"

Lyla barely turned her head over her shoulder to reply, and kept walking. "Maybe. That's why it's important, isn't it? Thanks for getting it, Ray."

I wanted to make it up to her in any way I could. I began to recount to myself every detail I could remember of those moments. I wanted to close my eyes and recreate it, but that would have to wait for a time when I wasn't walking. Just thinking deeply about it brought back an inkling of what I had felt when the whole of the earth had been inside of me, and I inside of it.

Lyla stopped again, and turned around. She seemed to know exactly what I was thinking, for she said, "I'm sorry I pushed you about it right now, Ray. It's more important to be prepared to converse, because we don't have a lot of time. If you can put that time with the old woman out of your mind for a while and just try to relax, things will go better."

I took a deep breath and told myself to take it easy, be flexible and neglect to react, in response to the flash of annoyance I felt. I was getting fed up with everybody telling me what to do, how to do it, and when to do it. Another deep breath reminded me that I was walking into a world that, only a few days ago, I hadn't known existed. And whether or not I could always remember it, I seemed to be with people who knew it well and meant nothing but good for me.

"Okay, Lyla. We'll come back to it when we can, and maybe I can do a better job of remembering."

"Great," she smiled. "We're almost there now."

The land had been sloping downwards as we moved westward through the Elysian Fields. The west end of the valley stops abruptly in a narrow bowl. Except for the notch cut by the beginning of Dick Creek, the bowl's outer ridge is steep, though not quite sheer. I had seen from the map that the other side of that ridge ran sharply down nearly a thousand feet, and I hoped we didn't need to go that way.

We didn't, in fact. A quarter mile from the end of the valley we turned northward and followed the upward curve of the land. There were more trees on this side of the valley, all of them the shortened, weathered people of the high meadows, harshly sculpted by the formidable forces that slept during the brief summer.

We followed a tiny rivulet that drained a portion of the north side of the valley. It led us into a section of slope where the trees clustered thickly, though none of them rose to a height greater than twenty feet.

I saw the tree we were making for while it was still a hundred yards off, and to our left. I didn't know how I knew it was our destination, but I had no doubt, so I was unsurprised when Lyla turned away from the little creek and started towards it.

Superficially, it didn't look any different from the other trees that surrounded us. It wasn't taller, wider, nor was it more or less twisted by the savage winds that battered it until the snows buried it completely. It was about eighteen inches around near the base, meaning approximately a hundred and fifty years old. Lyla walked up to within about ten feet of the tree and stopped. I stopped behind her.

She stood quietly for no more than a minute, and then walked around the tree to its other side. I followed, and sat down next to her when she chose a fairly level spot close to it. I had figured she would have some instructions to give me, or advice, or something, but as she settled into a sitting position all her attention was on the tree. I settled down too, focused my attention on the tree, and tried to relax.

It wasn't easy to be open to this experience after the last few days. Whether I would harm someone, or be the one harmed, was in the forefront of my mind, and I couldn't seem to get past that.

But Lyla's calm presence began to quiet my fears. She seemed to know so much, and I had already decided to trust her. I took several deep breaths, looked down towards the ground, and tried to loosen my grasp on the thoughts bounding through my mind.

Almost immediately I felt the tree's presence. I thought about the possibility of entering into conversation with it, and formed the thought into a question. I could feel it opening itself in my direction, and I responded by opening my mind towards it.

We sat about six feet away. Its lower branches touched the ground, and I could only see sections of the trunk through the branches covered all the way around with stiff, dark green needles. Most of the branches were twisted, as if someone had grasped them and turned, laterally, until they took on a slightly corkscrewed look. It wasn't hard to tell which way the wind blew most often and hardest; when I projected the direction of the skewed branches back away from the tree, the trajectory led straight up the mountain. I tried to imagine that wind tearing, roaring down from the top of the mountain, eight thousand feet up from here. The slashing of the wind-driven snow crystals, the endless beating, pushing and shoving that would go on for days, perhaps weeks—I shivered where I sat in the late August warmth, and told the tree I couldn't really imagine what it was like, but I had a faint notion.

I relaxed further, and my vision broadened. The rough patches of mottled brown bark showing through the branches grew vivid, then blurred as if they had been painted in water-colors, and a new brush of water dragged across them. As had happened both with the glacier and the mountain spruce, eye-sight rapidly became less important, and other ways of awareness slipped in to take its place.

I felt myself moving into the ground again; the hardscrabble earth, rocks large and small blocking my path down to the life giving water. I worked my way around them, so slowly. Every grain of sand I passed was an event. I was intently, intensely alive, and my thirst drove me.

I reached down farther, and tapped a vein of sweet, cold water. I drank, pulling the water into me in droplets finer than mist; it seeped through my roots and worked its way upward, filling me with yet more life. The movement of water through me felt like a river flowing through my veins, and I thought it must be the slowest, most delicious river in the world until I thought about the glacier, and realized we had something very much in common with it, only its river was even slower.

As the water moved farther and farther up, my awareness went with it. With an inward start I felt the presence of another: it was not just this tree and me. I could neither see nor hear, but someone else was here. I edged my senses a little closer to the presence, and suddenly was lifted by a pleased excitement, for it was Lyla. Within the tree she moved towards me, and we wordlessly met, greeting each other without touch or sound.

We moved upwards in the tree together, feeling the soft layer of cambium under the tough, scratchy bark. We traveled into the cool, hard depths of the heartwood, in this alpine person hardly more than a slender pole, but incredibly tough and sinewy. At the height of summer, it was crackling with life and energy.

The tree wanted something from me. I could feel the imperative, but not the thing itself. The only response I could think of was to practice again what I had learned in the glacier, quieting myself and simply neglecting to maintain the boundary wall around my being. I thought about what had happened in the glacier when I did this, and hesitated; the last thing I wanted was to test Lyla's expertise in CPR after being killed again. The tree sent a strong undercurrent of reassurance of what Lyla had said, that I was in a different place that had much stronger, tighter defenses against such intrusions. Relaxing again, I allowed the tree to take me where it wanted me to go. I traveled upwards again, and noticed that Lyla was no longer in evidence. Perhaps the tree was capable of two conversations at once; I set the question aside as I moved into the gnarled branches and felt the bristling sprays of needles in the warm air of this high, wide and shallow alpine valley.

I was facing the mountain. There was no more than the mildest breeze, warm and redolent of summer. I could feel each needle responding to air and sunlight, working at top speed to take these short-lived gifts of life and turn them—along with the water percolating upwards—into new growth. Cells divided, the tissue of trees formed, pushing upwards and outwards at a slow, measured pace. We were growing together: branch, root and needle grew along with my understanding and identification.

The breeze picked up, gradually changing from summer zephyr to autumn wind. I could sense a change in the air; it grew chill and sharp. For a short time there was rain, and I drank it in as fast as I could, watching without remorse as what I couldn't catch flowed away into the tiny rivulets meandering across the ground like capillaries. Through water I could feel them extending across the land, making arteries that followed the dictates of gravity until they reached the bottom of this valley and became the headwaters of Dick Creek, beginning their bounding journey down to the Carbon River, Puget Sound, the Pacific Ocean, and—somewhere, sometime—back to the sky.

The wind rapidly grew colder. Some moments it was filled with stinging snow crystals that worked like sandpaper on anything softer than stone. At other moments it was simply a force unto itself; it stripped any residual warmth from whatever lay in its path, like ripping a piece of paper from an unresisting hand. It began to blow steadily, ruthlessly, pounding the tree and me inside it. I grew fearful for the tree, for it felt like another boost in the wind's force would simply tear it from the ground and fling it down the mountainside.

Still high in the tree's foliage—high being a very relative term for an alpine fir—I felt the windward branches straining, bending nearly backwards as the wind tore at them. I felt the resistance as the wind slammed into the thick, bristly patches of needles that surrounded the limbs. I could sense the immediate force of the wind being throttled by them; there was no way in the world to dissipate that massive energy roaring down from the mountain, but the tree's limbs deflected some of it. I left the work of facing down the irresistible force of this wind to the branches, and retreated in towards the trunk.

The wind picked up in intensity, when I hadn't thought that possible. The branches facing it were bent as far as they could go; their tips whipped up and down, sometimes side to side, shunting aside as much of the destructive energy as they could catch. The trunk's bark on the windward side was thick, but I could still feel the mortal cold hammering on the door to the tree's heart; the sap moved inwards as far as it could go, and rested. If the sap were to freeze, the tree would die. Virtually all of its energy was directed inward, leaving only enough for the outer branches to bend and whip to and fro. I felt a wrenching snap, and realized one of the outer branches had been torn from the trunk. There was a sensation of pain that at first I didn't recognize as pain. It had no accompanying fear; it was simply a response to injury. There was nothing to do about it; it simply hurt for a moment, and was replaced by a small movement of energy towards the stump to seal it off from the killing cold. Then it was done, and nothing more than another memory.

I was living in chaos, but responding deliberately and in the way I had evolved to respond. The wind howled, screamed and ranted. I let what I could fend off go past, and marshaled my defenses to deal with what could not be avoided. In the midst of this I felt another presence approaching. For an instant I thought it would be Lyla, making her way through the storm and the intensity of surviving it to be with me again. The next instant showed how mistaken I was, for the malignancy and hatred emanated from this presence in familiar, relentless waves.

I couldn't see the skeletal form, nor the pinched, contorted face with its demonic eyes, but that didn't prevent the bolt of terror that shot through me, nor the vivid memory of a gnarled, lifted forefinger.

The buffeting of hatred and the lust for death and destruction were far worse than anything the wind could provide. I wanted to turn and flee, to run as fast as I could in the opposite direction. But I was not in a place where running made sense; I was deep within the spirit and being of a tree. The tree held me inside itself, and it was not ready to let me go.

The wind still screamed, and the tree was now resisting two immense forces. I could feel them both competing to do their work: the wind, an impersonal force that acted without judgment on the things of the world; beside and beyond the wind, the spirit of madness and destruction, hating blindly and with a terrifying singleness of purpose.

I held desperately to my sanity and my being, feeling that at any moment my courage and energy would fail utterly, and I would be swept away to nothingness, whether by wind or murder. The tree was holding its own against the wind. I could feel the evil battering at the entrance to the tree's being; it howled and raved, sending waves of malignancy before it. They washed over me like the most foully polluted tidal wave, and everywhere they touched me they produced searing pain. I screamed, a wild, hopeless shriek that heralded the descent into madness.

Chapter 14

Silence. It happened in an instant. The howl of wind, the gibbering malignancy, vanished in less than a heartbeat. The shock was almost too much to absorb. I sat, seeing nothing, in complete stillness for many moments, trying to understand where I was and what might be happening now. I heard a soft breeze making its way through the branches of the trees in the grove near us. It rustled the grasses whose seeds were almost ready to fall. From far away came the faint caw of a crow, still raucous through the distance.

I found myself sitting exactly as I had when Lyla and I had settled on the ground. How long ago was that? The sun was still shining; I tried to remember its position when we reached this spot, and realized I had been too preoccupied with our errand to take note of it. I turned towards where Lyla had sat.

She was still there. She had turned towards me, and was watching me intently.

"Ray, are you all right? Tell me you're all right."

"I believe I'm all right," I said. "But I also believe it's going to take a year or two to figure out what just happened."

"Maybe not that long, but it can wait. What I mean is, can you walk?"

I shifted around on the ground. Other than being stiff, and the fact that my legs had fallen asleep, I didn't seem to be harmed in any way. It occurred to me that if I had had this experience a week ago I would be lying on the ground right now in a trembling puddle. As it was, well, it was a terrifying experience—meaning one more in a string of terrifying experiences—and compared to being dead, it wasn't even the worst one.

"If you give me five minutes to get some blood flowing in my legs, I'm quite sure I can walk." I was still a little dazed, feeling like I was still partly within the tree. "Are we in a hurry or something?"

"I think we are," she said. "It's a good bet we've been away for more than three hours, meaning that Henry—if he keeps his word, which he usually does—will have called out everyone within ten miles to look for us."

"Oh. In that case, five minutes is probably too much." I unfolded my legs and flexed them a few times. The first attempt at standing resulted in a tumble back onto the grassy ground. The second was more successful. Lyla rose without any apparent difficulty, and we made our way around the tree and back to the creek we had followed to get here. In a few minutes we had rejoined the narrow path cut into the meadow. Lyla stopped and turned back to me.

"I doubt you're ready to talk about what happened, and I know Henry's going to make you tell it all over again. I'm sorry about that, Ray, but if you can, could you tell me what happened with you back there, while we walk back? I'll be watching to make sure I don't go too fast, and if you're willing to talk to my back, I need to hear it and maybe ask you questions that I don't want anyone else to hear just yet."

"Um, yeah, I'll try. It won't be an elegant story, Lyla."

"I don't need elegance at all. Just try to remember what happened in the order it happened, and I'll try to keep the questions manageable."

She turned and started walking at a deliberate pace, which suited the deep fatigue I was starting to feel as well as the need to think clearly. I started the story haltingly, but as I went on, it began to flow. I lost sight of the sunlit sky and the Elysian Fields while I relived my time inside that tree, and my body did its job and kept me following Lyla without falling down. At one point

I stopped short. I realized that if she hadn't made me do this I might have forgotten much of it, for the shock of being attacked again—or at least being in such close proximity to that horror—was beginning to set in.

We were no more than fifteen minutes away from our campsite when I finished. Lyla had not asked a single question, but now she stopped and faced me again.

"How close was he to you, Ray? Are you sure you didn't actually see him?"

"He felt very close," I said. "And yet, no, I really couldn't see him at all. It was as if he was just around a corner from me, but he couldn't quite make it around."

Lyla relaxed visibly. "I was hoping to hear something like that. And I hope you're right."

"Lyla. What happened back there? I can't think clearly enough right now to work it through. Help me out, please."

She paused for a moment. "I really thought this would be a simple introduction that would take a few minutes. Then we could just come back here and you could rest. If I'd known how it would go…" She shook her head and smiled. "I swear, Ray Holdman, you are a lightning rod. The tree wanted very badly to show you something, and it chose the only way it knew to show it to you."

"Show me what?"

"That remains to be seen, and I hope we can work it out together. But I think this tree was trying to teach you how to defend yourself."

"So it showed me how it defends itself against a destructive force like the wind. And then it allowed this *thing* in just enough to scare me half to death, and then shut him out in some similar way?"

"Something like that," she said.

"Needs a lot more thought, doesn't it? Right now my brain is full."

"Mine's up near the top too," Lyla replied. "But we need to get back to camp and set poor Henry's heart at ease."

We moved on. Knowing how close we were made it easier, but with every step my whole body grew heavier and slower. Would I ever be anything but exhausted again?

The little grove of firs was empty and quiet when we arrived. Lyla looked around in consternation.

"He's gone to get everybody he can to go look for us. I really, *really* wanted to avoid this."

"I don't know about you," I said, "But I'm going to lie down and sleep for the next couple of months. Wake me up when it's fall, would you?"

"Sure," she smiled. "Dream on, brother."

Brother. I wasn't exactly having sisterly feelings towards Lyla at this point. The thing about feelings like those is they won't just go over in the corner, lie down for a while and leave you alone. It takes energy to fend them off when they aren't wanted, and I had used up all the energy I had, and perhaps next year's store too. My eyes closed the moment I stretched out on top of my sleeping bag, but sleep flatly refused to come.

Fending off certain feelings about Lyla was very different from deflecting the overwhelming hatred and malice the evil intruder had flung at me twice now. Or was it? Perhaps it was simply a matter of degree, and the same technique would serve in both circumstances. Lyla's notion of what the tree had wanted to give me seemed completely right; the trees do in fact get blown down the mountain sometimes, their limbs are torn or broken off or frozen to death, and at times they are simply swept away by irresistible forces. They are not, however, defenseless. Perhaps this was what I needed to know—that no single survival technique would allow me to deal with the force that seemed bent on my destruction, but with a collection of them gathered from friends and allies, maybe there was a chance.

I heard someone enter the grove, but I was too exhausted to open my eyes or sit up. Henry's voice was pitched low.

"Glad you decided to put in an appearance. You both okay?"

"Yes, we're all right," Lyla answered. "We had a somewhat more demanding conversation than I'd anticipated."

"I told you it wasn't a good idea," Henry said severely. "You're dealing with Ray's life here, you know."

Lyla's response was sharp. Henry did indeed have the trick of getting under her skin, though I figured (very much wanted to believe, that is) that he didn't mean to. "It was a *difficult* idea, and it was vitally important. As far as I can tell, the tree had a lesson in self defense for Ray, and it also showed both of us that it was eminently capable of shutting this awful thing out."

"For how long, I wonder?" Henry mused. "I still say this was not the time, Lyla."

"Well, it's happened, and you can just get used to it," she replied. "Ray's sleeping now, so let's argue later, if we have to."

"I'm not asleep," I said, still lying down with eyes closed, "And I'd be grateful if you two neglected to bicker ever again. Henry, give me a little while to just lie here, and afterwards I'll tell you exactly what happened. We can talk it over together. Notice I said *talk*, not quarrel."

Henry and Lyla settled into an embarrassed silence. Soon I heard the quiet rustle of someone getting up and softly moving out of the grove, and decided it must be Lyla. Sleep refused to come, no matter how I tried to slow my breathing, and my mind.

My thoughts wandered back over the course of the day. I reflected on how it had started to seem that I had been up on this mountain for most of my life, and the rest of that life was a half-remembered dream. When I tried to pin it down, I decided it had been nine or ten days since I'd walked along the Carbon River Road and clambered up a hillside to visit a clearcut. Nine or ten days? I wondered if this was what life would be like if I somehow managed to join Lyla, Henry, Hucklebark, Ev Longhaul and the others for real.

My mind gave up on the unknown and scampered back to the narrow little trail we had taken through the Elysian Fields today. I remembered Lyla's bitter disappointment when I couldn't give her the details she wanted of my encounter with the old woman. Right now I seemed to have a few minutes when—with a little luck—nothing would happen, and perhaps no new thing would come crashing down from the sky to upset and bewilder us all. I stretched my limbs, drank in a deep lungful of the sweet mountain air, kept my eyes closed, and tried to remember.

The little clearing by the river where Lyla had brought me, broken and exhausted, sprang into being. I could see with the night vision granted one who has slept deeply and not seen light for hours. The starlight filtering through the trees was enough to work with; the old woman sat near me where she had been before. She looked at me and smiled, a mysterious half-smile of benediction and challenge.

Wait a minute, a part of me said. Isn't this a memory? *Why is it different?* And why is it so real?

I gazed at her, trying before anything else to learn what Lyla had seemed to want so badly. But the light would not reveal the color of her old-fashioned dress, and all I could tell of her long plaited hair was that it was shot through with silver that glinted in the faint light. There was nothing to do but let go of those things.

I looked into her eyes. They were dark pools, deeper than any I had ever looked into. They drew me in, and I allowed myself to go. Again I felt the delicious, terrifying connection to any and all things in the world. I could sense the ground deep beneath me, its crevices, faults, its places of profoundly solid rock, other places of lacy, honeycombed openings. There was water flowing everywhere; underground rivers that moved purposefully across the planet, tiny rivulets that meandered upwards and downwards obeying compulsions I couldn't fathom, and barely interconnected regions of droplets whose travels amounted to inches taken over years.

I moved up, down and outwards, all at the same time. Energy flowed through me, entering and leaving from all directions. As it moved through, it seemed to carry away with it some of the fatigue and soreness that made it so difficult to move. My senses extended farther and farther out into the world.

They were suddenly stopped, as if my awareness had run straight into a stone wall, even though up to now it had passed through stone as easily as through air. It was a jarring halt, and I let everything become still while I pondered it.

Just on the other side of the invisible thing that had stopped me, I felt resistance. It made me consider how I had been pushing out into the world, exploring and sensing. Now something was pushing back.

I wondered what might be doing that. It occurred to me that—not that it wasn't sufficiently obvious already—the world is not mine to play with or manipulate. Perhaps there are regions of it where I am not allowed to go? Or was something more generalized happening here?

My awareness pushed tentatively at the resistance. I suddenly felt a burst of malevolence that seemed to hit me squarely between the eyes. I backed away from whatever it was I'd been approaching, my feeling and spirit smarting deeply, as if I'd been bitten or clawed by something I hadn't known was dangerous.

As I backed further away from what had struck out at me, I seemed to emerge from the dark pools of the old woman's eyes. I was once again sitting facing her in the faint, dappled starlight of the tiny clearing. Her expression was difficult to interpret; it seemed to hold an immense sadness at the same moment it expressed a boundless sense of warmth and approval.

I said, "I still don't know you. Won't you tell me who you are?"

Her answer felt much as it had before: that is, no answer at all. She cocked an appraising eyebrow at me, and lightly pointed at my midsection. Even though it probably could have meant any number of things, I immediately thought of food. How long had it been since I'd eaten? It must have been at least a day and a half, perhaps two days. I guessed it had been in the early morning before entering the glacier and stumbling across Henry.

The ancient woman held her right hand out, palm upwards again. The deep wrinkles in her palm were still canyons and rivers of life; somewhere in there I was swimming, or walking, running or crawling through the world. But this time, I saw that some of the canyons and rivers looked much less inviting than others. They had an ominous, unwelcoming feel to them. She looked at me with an expression of warning, and a wish that I understand. I studied her hand, but beyond sensing that there were places I had to stay away from, I learned nothing more.

She lowered her hand and slowly disappeared. The clearing faded from view.

Chapter 15

I awoke, not having any idea that I'd been asleep. For a moment I was totally disoriented. When I had closed my eyes to recall the old woman, it had been late afternoon and the sun had still been above the ridges to the west of us. Now the light was dusky, and the air had already started to cool. I smelled coffee, and sat up.

Henry turned away from my campstove. "I don't mean to be making a habit of using your stuff, Ray, but I figured you might want a cup when you woke up. See, I need you to stay awake long enough to tell me what went on this afternoon." He brought a cup of my coffee over and handed it to me.

It wasn't too hot to drink, so I drank some. My stomach was so empty it nearly bounced back up to the top of my head. 'Thanks, Henry. I'll tell all, I promise, as soon as I've found something to eat." My pack was close by, and it yielded some now stale bread, and the eternal peanut butter. The cheese was suspect by now, so I set it aside. I demolished the bread and seized on the muesli that was left.

"Whoa, slow down, Ray," Henry warned. "I know I should have fed you earlier today when you woke up, but if you want to keep it in there, better take it easy."

"Good plan." I took a deep breath, and made a ritual of mixing some powdered milk and preparing the cereal. "Maybe if I concentrate real hard, I can more or less eat and tell the story at the same time. Where's Lyla?"

"Nearby somewhere, that's all I can tell," Henry said. She chose that moment to walk in through the trees and sit down.

She said, "Did you have a good rest, Ray?"

"Now that you mention it, I feel pretty good, except for needing to eat another ten pounds or so of food. I didn't even know I'd fallen asleep." I decided to wait until I could speak to her alone to describe meeting the ancient woman again.

I turned to Henry, and started in telling him about going into the tree, the windstorm, the intrusion of the evil being and the tree's repulsion of it. My story was a bit halting in its telling, for truth to tell I'm not very good at eating and conversing. Lyla was silent throughout. When I finished, Henry turned to her. "Anything to add, Lyla?"

"Only that when Ray moved out into the farther limbs of the tree, it held me back and wouldn't let me go with him. And that when that evil thing tried to get in, it was the same as yesterday's time with the tree I was talking to then. I could feel how near it was, but the tree just slammed the door in its face."

To me Henry said, "So you think the tree was trying to teach you something about defending yourself."

"That was Lyla's idea, and I think it's right," I replied. "I'm hoping that if I get the chance to sleep on it tonight, it'll make more sense to me tomorrow."

"Oh, it makes plenty of sense now," Henry said. "The practice ought to be pretty interesting. I'd love to hear what you come up with. Anyway, we should get some good opinions tomorrow."

I looked over at Lyla, and she returned it; there were things we needed to talk about—alone. We must have been painfully obvious, for Henry immediately said, "Well, there's lots to think about and I've spent most of the day sitting here on my duff. I'm gonna take a walk before dark, if that works out for you."

"Yeah, that's fine, Henry," I said. With no further ceremony, he hitched himself to his feet and made his way out of the grove, apparently heading back into Moraine Park.

"I don't think Henry believes we're just going to talk," Lyla said, smiling.

A stream of electricity seemed to run through me. "I think maybe I wish he was right," I said, and regretted it instantly. Lyla gave me a look of appraisal, but there was no telling what she had decided. I said, "Oh, hell. There I go, shooting off my mouth again. If you were to say it's a 'You men' thing again, I'd have to agree."

Her expression softened into a smile again. "Actually, Ray, it's a *hu*-man thing. Just to be clear—I have very strong feelings about you, but I don't know what they mean yet. Time will tell, but that time *has* to happen first."

This time I thought—hard—before saying anything. "You know, that's probably true for me too. I really envy you, Lyla. It seems like you have your feelings sorted out as you feel them. For me, it's more like stumbling around in a fog until something swats my head with a two-by-four."

"*That* might actually be a 'You men' thing," she said. "But it's not my place to judge it. And be careful about how much credit you give me for having things 'sorted out'—I'm just another human, too. We need to set this aside, Ray. It's obvious there's something else you wanted to talk about."

"Yes, there is. I wanted to tell you about the old woman." Afraid of losing this time alone with her, I launched into an account of what had happened when I had simply tried to remember my encounter, how it had instead happened again. It was still so fresh in my mind—meaning that for once nothing earth-shaking or potentially fatal had happened in the last hour or two—that all the details were right in front of me, and I left nothing at all out of the story. I finished by saying that because of the light, I simply couldn't tell about the color of her dress, or of her hair.

"But honestly, Lyla, I'm not sure it really matters all that much. Everything else about her, about where I go and what I see and learn in her presence, seems a lot more important. Have we met the same person?"

She sat silently for several long moments. "Yes, of course it's the same one. And you're right about what matters and what doesn't. Do you know what this means, Ray?"

I wanted desperately to have the right answer to this, right now. It wasn't there. Instead, I shrugged my shoulders and looked at the ground, feeling like I was failing some crucial test. "No. I don't understand it at all."

She leaned forward, and laid a hand on my arm. "Don't, Ray. Leave yourself alone for a change. I can't give it to you—it would wreck something that you absolutely have to have. Try to be patient, and let it arrive."

I looked back up at Lyla. "You know, every time you say something like that, I'm absolutely certain that I'm in love with you." I kicked myself, hard, inside. Why can't I learn to just shut up? I waited, with a lot of trepidation, for whatever would come from that.

Her response was to look directly into my eyes. "No one has ever said things like that to you, have they?" She didn't wait for an answer. "No, of course they haven't. Let's let it rest for a while, okay? I'm tired, so you must be exhausted. Henry will be back soon anyway."

We sat in silence for a little while. That was something else I hadn't experienced much of, a companionable silence that didn't require either one of us to talk. I liked it.

Henry made his way back into the grove and looked around before coming over.

"Huh. Looks like you two haven't moved since I left. Not what I expected."

Lyla looked up and said sweetly, "Perhaps we're faster, or simply more efficient than you thought, Henry."

To my astonishment, his face flushed, and with a muttered "Yeah, whatever" he went over and started fussing with the camp stove and water kettle. He looked much like a cat does when it falls off a chair or a window ledge, and immediately starts to wash itself furiously as if that was what it meant to do all along. The thought was too much for me and I burst out laughing.

Henry turned to me. "I like a good joke, Ray, what you got?"

"Not much, really," I said. "It's just that with cats it's called displacement behavior. I've done it too, but it's funny, I just couldn't help it. No harm meant, honest."

"Okay, all right," Henry replied. "I'm just a nosy old fart anyway, and they always deserve what they get. Do we have any more that needs talking about tonight, or can I turn in now?"

When I woke the night was just starting to consider giving way to day, as if it had any choice in the matter. I love the light at that time of day; you can almost see it move. I looked around and saw that Henry was already up and gone somewhere. Lyla was awake too, but sitting very still, perhaps meditating.

I got up as quietly as I could and took care of the never-ending chores that go along with living in a body. Coming back into the little grove, I saw that the camp stove was still set up. I started the ritual of making coffee. I'd once read a detailed description of the way coffee used to be prepared in old Palestine, starting with pan roasting the beans, grinding them in a mortar, all the way through the delicate and hospitable way it was served. My ritual wasn't nearly as comprehensive or elegant, but it was a comfort anyway. I was glad to have a comfortable ritual on this morning. Sometime later in the day we would move off towards Windy Gap. There would be people there; people who spent their lives doing the kinds of things Lyla, Henry and Hucklebark did, and I supposed more. I wondered if I would find help there, or judgment. The Mountain, and the work these people did seemed like a kind of rigorous paradise, and I felt like I had either attracted or brought in some lethal infection, a sickness that threatened to destroy everything here. Would I be welcomed as someone who needed help, but might have much to offer in return, or would I be driven out like a plague-ridden parasite? It wasn't much comfort to know that most people intensely dislike large unknowns; I certainly didn't like mine.

Lyla stirred while I was working on the coffee. "Good morning, Ray. How are you doing?"

"I seem to be all right, though really, I'm worried about what's going to happen today."

"I think I understand that," she said. "Maybe I can help a little bit, if you want to hear about how these gatherings have gone in the past."

'Well, yes, that'd be good," I replied. "Of course you've been to these before. What was the occasion?"

"They happen often, in a lot of different ways. Sometimes it's when someone needs to talk about something that affects more than just one or two folks. The last one was about a Change Bringer who some thought was moving too fast. It wasn't all that exciting, which was fine with most of us."

"Am I right in thinking there will be a little more excitement with this one?"

Lyla laughed. "Oh, I think so, Ray."

"Who all shows up for these things?"

"You never know until you get there," she said. "There might be an unusually large crowd today, or maybe almost no one—I really have no way of telling. It takes place in a sheltered meadow on the slopes of Sluiskin, pretty much facing Windy Gap. Since it's not exactly out in the open, we don't have to worry too much about attracting attention."

"This stove is acting up this morning," I said, "and the water's about to boil. Would you consider grabbing the coffee bag from my pack?"

"Sure." She found it without trouble and brought it over. "You may think I'm as nosy as Henry, Ray, but I can't help being curious about the wooden box in your pack—it's not the kind of thing people usually haul around. 'None of your business' is a perfectly acceptable answer, mind you."

Among this small group of people—Henry, Lyla, and probably Hucklebark and Ev Longhaul—I was starting to feel like it would be easy and comfortable to have no secrets. I wondered at that, and decided on the obvious reason—I trusted them, and they seemed to give me ample reason to do so. It was a liberating thought.

"Why don't you bring it over here," I said. "I'm almost done fussing with this stove."

When she had brought over the box and I had the coffee simmering over the balky campstove, I unlocked the box and handed it to her, opened to the first page. She studied it for a moment, as it sat there in her lap, and then without looking up she began reading. I watched her read the first page through, and then start again at the top. I was suddenly self conscious about watching, and found numerous ways to adjust the coffee and the stove flame. The trees of the little grove were suddenly very interesting, and I thought with a twinge of conscience how I had teased Henry about displacement behavior the night before.

Having found ways to not be there while I was there, I finally looked back at Lyla and saw I'd been wasting the effort. She was bent over the book, completely absorbed, still looking at the first page. She studied it with the intensity of an archeologist holding in her hands a fossil fresh from the earth. Soon she felt my attention, and looked up with an expression that was soft, but unfathomable.

"I wanted to understand this page before I went on," she said. "But there are some things here I just can't."

"That makes sense to me, and I consider your effort heroic. If you read a couple more entries it might help. Read as much or as little as you wish."

She nodded and went back to reading.

April, 1973 (California, La Cañada) (second year)

There are no oak trees at this house.

But there are others, even if I don't know their names.

There is one in the back yard that helps me be brave.

Its leaves are long, like dark green scratchy feathers.

It is tall, and talks about people from a long time ago.

They were brave, and it says I should be like them.

The grownups say I am bad. They say
Only sick boys have imaginary friends that are trees.
They say they can't pay for a doctor that can fix me.

Now I sneak out here at night, when they're sleeping
To talk to my friend the tree.
When I get caught I have to be even braver.
This tree tells me I must not hit them back.

I heard them talking in the kitchen one night.
They said I am crazy sick like my papa
And they don't want me here any more.
I went up to the room and cried.
I would love to go away. When I do, I hope I find another
tree.

May, 1975 (California, El Segundo) (fourth year)
Javier says El Segundo means "The Second".
I asked him how to say the bottom, and he said 'el fondo'.
I said this place should be called El Fondo,
Because we're at the bottom of everything.

Javier is seven—two years younger than me.
I am like his big brother. I am the only one he has.
Javier is on the bottom: I'm his big brother because
I am next to the bottom.

Everybody beat on Javier before I got here.
They beat on me for a little while, too.
There was one who beat on us the most,

Until I kicked him in the nuts as hard as I could.

He cried like a baby, and they put me in The Closet for two days.

Now nobody beats on us, but everyone is our enemy.

Javier is teaching me to talk Spanish. I'm teaching him to read English.

We talk Spanish so the keepers won't know what we're saying.

They all think only bad people speak Spanish.

Javier never knew his mom or dad.

I know my dad, but he can't come get us.

I hope he will some day, but I'm not planning on it.

When I get out of here, Javier will come with me.

He's afraid, but I'll get him to come too.

Lyla closed the book, and the box over it, with care. She set it next to my pack and then sat back down where she'd been. I handed her a cup, and we drank our coffee in silence.

As I took her cup for rinsing I said, "Questions? Comments? On a scale of one to five would you rate this person mad, sane, or simply suffering from a mysterious vitamin deficiency?"

"That last might be it," she said with a slight smile. Sobering, she said, "I'll ask later. Believe me, I'll ask. And I hope you'll give me more time with that book. Right now it might be good to pack up. If Henry doesn't show up soon, I think we should leave without him."

"It can't be much after seven right now. Will it take that long to get where we're going?"

"It's only a couple of miles," she said, "but there's a certain amount of almost straight-up-and-down, and it'll be worth it to take our time. That's not much of a reason to hurry, though. I guess I'm just anxious to get there and see if we can get some answers."

I started to fold up the little campstove, mentally filing a note to clean and adjust it at the first opportunity. "Let me put these things away, take two minutes to pack up, and we can go. I can't imagine any reason to worry about Henry." As long as he didn't take it into his head to go back into the glacier, I said to myself.

Before we had finished these few chores, though, Henry made his way into the grove. Following a few steps behind was Everett Longhaul.

Henry grunted a barely audible greeting, but Ev came over to me and held my shoulders with both hands. "Good morning, Ray. It seems like every time I see you, I'm gonna have to ask, 'Are you all right?'"

"In that case, I'll just have to say 'Yes' until I can't answer you anymore," I said. "And thank you—I owe you a great debt."

He shifted instantly into a totally different persona. In a booming baritone that would brook no response he replied, "Not at all, don't mention it, tut tut my boy, and the whole raft of other pleasant negations I can't produce at the moment."

I gazed back at him in amazement, wondering from where in his long, skinny body a voice like that could come from.

Ev turned to Lyla and slowly ratcheted himself into a low bow. His voice changed to warmth and chivalry. "And I trust this splendid morning finds the lovely Ms. Lyla in good health and temperament?"

She graced him with a warm, deep smile of greeting. "Longhaul, are you ever going to tell us what theater you escaped from?"

"Never, my dear. My secrets are dark, deep and slightly stupid, so they must remain forever impenetrable," he said with a ponderous, mock gravity, and then changed again, to brisk and businesslike. "But I came this way for two reasons. First, I always like to lighten my load as quick as possible on a gathering day. Secondly," he said, turning back to me, "I wasn't sure if you'd need to be hauled over there, or if you had your legs back."

I assured him that my legs were up to the task, and he immediately set down his enormous pack and began pulling out supplies that went towards each one of us in turn. "You know, Ray, I can't keep bringing you the same three or four things forever. You'll have to give me some ideas."

"You've hit on three or four things that keep me going, so I'm ready to practice 'food is fuel' for a while," I said. "I'm afraid there isn't room in my head for that sort of question today."

Ev looked thoughtful. "No, I don't suppose there would be. When do you all want to head over to the meeting place?"

Lyla said, "Immediately, if not sooner, would work for us."

With a grand flourish that took in ourselves, our campsite, and all of Moraine Park, Everett Longhaul said, "Then let us pack up and be gone, my friends."

We skirted the marshy eastern edge of the Elysian Fields, heading northwards towards the gap between Crescent and Sluiskin Mountains. At first the going was fairly easy. Ev kept us entertained with a non-stop stream of stories and jokes; at one point Lyla turned back to him and said with a smile, "I swear, Everett, you must spend every minute of your solitude thinking these things up."

He adopted a rudimentary imitation of W. C. Fields. "Not at all, my dear, not at all. These dulcet tones leap from my soul like an artesian spring of wit and profundity." Then, with a broad wink in my direction, "Entertainment's the thing, my boy, take my solemn word for it."

Even Ev's ebullience was muted as we climbed the short but intense, steep slope to one of the saddle ridges that separated the two mountains. From the top I could look to the northwest and downward to the Yellowstone Cliffs, a spectacular formation that towered a thousand feet above the Northern Loop Trail running along their feet. The layers of basalt and granite that had been thrust up from the surrounding mountainside were enormous books, written in a language so ancient no one alive could read more than the merest scraps of their prose. The way down from the saddle was even steeper, and we slowed down considerably, concentrating on keeping our footing in the loose talus, and trying not to start a major rockslide.

We descended nearly a thousand feet to make our way around Sluiskin's great north-facing shoulder, and then began laboriously making up the altitude, rounding the mountain and then heading up its more approachable northeastern flank. Down below six thousand feet the trees grew in ragged green patches that dotted the mountainside. Lyla pointed to one of the larger patches that lay about halfway back up the mountain and just above a snowfield that looked to cover about ten acres. "We're headed for that grove there. If there's time, there are some fir and spruce people I can introduce you to up there."

Henry, who had been almost completely silent so far, suddenly said, "Lyla, can't you give it a rest for just a little while? This is going to be complicated enough as it is."

Lyla stopped in her tracks, turned, and gave Henry a look that made me deeply grateful it wasn't directed at me. A retort sprang visibly to her lips; just as visibly, she decided against it, and without a word turned and stalked away.

We clambered upwards in silence for a while. But it only took a few minutes for Ev's artesian spring of good humor to return to the surface, and the rest of our hike was again enlivened by his sunny stories and laughter.

Skirting the snowfield that perpetually covered part of Sluiskin's north-facing slope, we began to make our way through or around the groves of alpine fir and spruce dotting the mountainside. Angling upwards it was easy enough to pick out the largest grove ahead of us. As we approached it, the grove gave no indication it was anything but deserted. It appeared to be several acres in extent, though I couldn't see within it to know if it was solid trees or a sparse collection of smaller groves.

We entered at the lower, northwest corner of the grove. The shade from the taller trees—those attaining a height of twenty feet or more—was refreshing when we walked through it. We wound around and occasionally through thickets of gnarled, stunted trees whose lives were clearly no easier than any of the myriad alpine survivors I had seen before. We approached a line of trees that seemed to make a solid barrier, grown so close together that their branches intertwined to make a virtually impenetrable wall of twisted, patchy green. Lyla took the lead, though both Ev and Henry followed her confidently enough that they all clearly knew where to go. We turned up slope, and followed the wall of trees for a quarter mile or so, until we reached a place that for all my looking appeared exactly as dense as any other. Lyla turned, and walked around one of the trees, brushing against both it and its neighbor as she passed. I thought I heard her whispering as she passed. She promptly disappeared into the foliage.

Henry followed, and vanished also. Ev turned and gave me a wink, and then he was gone too. There was nothing to do but plunge into the foliage, hoping I wouldn't make a fool of myself by not knowing some arcane trick of this place.

I took two steps into the scratchy sea of tree branches, and was stopped dead in my tracks. The limbs in front of me were too strong to push my way through, and when I discovered that small but incredibly strong limbs barred my way back, I began to panic. It took an intense effort of will to slow my breathing and stand still.

The tree limbs were pressed against me on all sides. The moment I stopped fighting and became still, I could feel them examining me. I heard soft, papery voices, not in the air, but in my blood and bones. They were speaking a tongue I couldn't interpret, but I was certain they were deciding whether or not to allow me in. I waited as calmly as I could; it occurred to me to practice opening myself up to them, making a way to tell them who and what I was. As far as I was concerned, I had nothing to hide.

I could feel it clearly when, after a few moments, the trees reached their decision. The limbs around me *relaxed*, in a way I wouldn't have thought possible for trees. Those in front of me drooped visibly, and I carefully made my way forward. Passing several of the trees in about ten steps, I emerged into a meadow.

Henry, Lyla, and Ev were waiting for me just past the screen of trees. Henry came forward with a concerned look on his face.

"You all right, Ray? What took so long? I was just about to come in after you."

"Don't the trees touch you and decide whether or not to let you in?" I asked.

"Don't the trees *what?*" was Henry's reply. "Bub, either you been out in the sun too long today or there's yet another strange thing going on."

Lyla came up to where Henry and I were standing. "Tell me what happened." There wasn't a lot to tell, so it didn't take long. She looked thoughtfully at the line of trees, then at me. Finally, she turned to Henry. "Henry, I don't think you trust me to handle anything, but I'll ask you to let me deal with this shortly. Is that acceptable?"

Henry gave Lyla a long, appraising look and said, "Yeah, Lyla, that's okay with me. No use denying that you're the one here qualified to consider it. No doubt either that if someone else needs to be consulted, it'll be someone in your group of folks."

Lyla nodded, and we turned to enter the meadow. We were facing more or less eastwards, so the slope of Sluiskin—which here faced almost due north—headed downward from right to left. The slope lessened towards the lower end; turning to look that way, I saw several knots of human people scattered about the three acres or so that the meadow occupied. We started to slant our way across and down to meet them.

The closest knot of people seemed to be a pair. When we were about fifty yards away from them, the larger of the two—a hulking, bear-like figure—turned our way. With a quick gesture to the other, much smaller person and a whoop of recognition, it barreled towards me.

PART FOUR

Sluiskin

*Bill. My father's name was Bill, and he walked with a limp from
an old Korean War wound to his right leg. I realized today I had
forgotten that I once had a father.*
*It came to me, anomalous and untimely, while I stood in the center
of a hostile circle outside the farmworkers' barracks. The circle
contained men and women: some young, strong, and tough, some
old, and wary, all of them tired and worried.*
*From a young fieldworker: "You too weird, man. You got to get out
of here, leave us alone. Take your damned weirdness and go away."*
*A circle of judgment, conclusions reached through fear and
ignorance. Bill Holdman—my father—had never acceded to this;
he had always insisted, refused to yield. And his stubbornness had
earned him entombment in a mental institution, his final eight
years an endless stretch of green-walled hell.*
*I refuse to share his fate; I will never submit to judgment, but I will
yield in order to keep what paltry freedom I have. So once again, it
is time to move on.*

(Eastern Oregon, May, 1997)

Chapter 16

Hucklebark came to a clattering stop in front of me. He wrapped his arms around my shoulders—pack and all—and gripped me in a bear hug that lifted me six inches off the ground.

"Ray! Man, it's great to see you!" He gently set me down, and I couldn't suppress a soft gasp as I let back in some of the air he'd squeezed out of me. Hucklebark examined me critically, from head to foot, as if to make sure none of me had fallen or broken off since he had seen me last. Ev and Lyla were smiling broadly, while Henry looked on with a completely neutral expression. I wondered briefly what went on between those two.

Hucklebark had not shifted his attention from me. "You all right? Heard some hair-raising stories about you, and everybody within ten miles knows somethin' really big went on the other night."

"Yeah, I guess the garage blowing up was pretty loud," I said.

Hucklebark's expression went blank. "Garage? Huh?"

"Ask Ev," I replied. "I'm really glad to see you too, Hucklebark. How's the watershed been doing?"

"Oh, you know, a little here, a little there, and wait twenty years." He laughed. "I figure by the time I'm two hundred 'n fifty, I'll have a little of it figured out."

I looked at him searchingly. Was this a joke, a hint of something, or an inadvertent slip of the tongue? After all that had happened, I wasn't willing to take anything for granted any more.

Hucklebark took in my expression and understood it immediately. A look of confusion came over him, and he stammered, "Yeah, well, just a figure of speech, you know, Ray." He brightened. "Look, I want you to come over and meet somebody."

We all began following him, trooping down the slope towards the person he had detached from to come running up to us. As we walked, he turned and said over his shoulder, "I expect you're gonna meet a lot of people today, and I figure it's good to start out with somebody special."

The woman had seen us coming her way, and started out to meet us. Hucklebark stopped, and shepherded me around him to face her. "Ray, this is Lupine."

Mad Lupine. The woman strong enough, skilled enough, and—was this right or not?—*crazy* enough to be midwife to the volcanic destruction of an entire mountain. She was much as Hucklebark's story had described her: short and trim with dark, straight shoulder length hair. There seemed no softness anywhere about her, yet there was nothing harsh either; only a sense of strength—some kind of power—that had little to do with her physical capabilities, of an origin I couldn't begin to guess. Her skin was deeply tanned and weathered, but her face was unwrinkled. Her eyes were the deep green of a glacial lake, sharp and penetrating. Standing there, perfectly relaxed, her body still fairly crackled with energy.

I realized with a start that I was staring, dumb, awestruck and unintentionally rude, as if I were a small child standing before an unfettered lioness that would soon either greet me or eat me.

No one spoke; I could feel that everyone was watching us for some reason I didn't understand. I held out my hand awkwardly, and managed to stammer, "I, uh—honored to meet you."

She gave me a reserved smile and went to shake my hand. Her touch was like the static jolt you might feel if you touched someone in the midst of an intense electrical storm—that is to say, it hurt. I flinched—just barely, though my body tried to jump a foot in the air—and held her hand for a moment while I waited for the nerves in my arm to settle. She lifted an eyebrow, apparently in surprise. Her voice was soft, round and strong, and much lower than I would have expected in someone her size.

"I'm pleased to meet you too, Ray. Hucklebark has told me a bit about you, but I gather much more has happened since you two last met."

I let go of her hand, and suddenly felt empty. What was going on? "Um, yeah, it's been a pretty busy few days." I wanted to kick myself for saying that.

But Lupine acted as if I was behaving in a perfectly natural way instead of the befuddled lackwit I felt like. She smiled again, and said, "I'm very interested to hear about what's been happening, but I don't want to make you tell it over and over again. So I'll wait until you tell us all together—but after that, I'd like to talk with you about some things, okay?"

I wanted desperately to act like a normal person. But this was *Mad Lupine*, and no matter how hard I tried I couldn't get past that. "Oh, yeah, sure. Anytime," was the best I could manage, and I wanted to crawl into a hole and disappear.

"Good. Thanks, Ray, I'll see you later," she said, and strode off up the slope towards another group. "You all, too," she spoke over her shoulder.

Lyla came up beside me and peered into my face, which probably still looked like an awestruck calf. "Made a bit of an impression on you, did she?" When I managed to focus my eyes on her, she burst out laughing. "Lupine has that effect on people she meets. Especially men," she said wryly.

I felt the blood rush to my face. I looked down at the ground, like a guilty schoolboy caught ogling a beautiful teacher. Lyla put a hand on my shoulder and squeezed it lightly. "Come on, Ray, snap out of it. You're fine, and I just told you it happens all the time." I looked up in surprise, saw her eyes filled with tolerant liking, and burst into laughter myself.

"My god, she makes me feel like I'm six years old again. How does she do that?"

"Power, and what a great poet once called 'virtuous ferocity'. Mind you," she went on, "Lupine doesn't actually throw it around, like some people would if they had tapped into the world as she has. It's just that there are times when she doesn't bother to conceal it."

"I need to sit down somewhere and think about this," I said. In an instant I felt completely overwhelmed by all that had happened, and all of the people who were casually blowing apart everything I thought I understood about the world and those who live in it. "On second thought, maybe I need to sit down somewhere and forget about everything for a while."

"I'm sorry, Ray, but I don't think you're going to get the opportunity to forget much of anything today," Lyla said. "But since we're likely to be here for a day or so, it's a good time to find a place to camp." She pointed upslope to the southeast, upward corner of the meadow. "As I recall, there are some spots up that way that are reasonably secluded, and almost level. Shall we try them?"

"Yes, sure." Then I blurted, "Lyla, I'm not ready for this."

"Ready for what?"

"That's the worst part. I mean, you've told me a little bit of what these things are about, how they go and all that, but…"

She squeezed my shoulder again, and with an inward start I realized she had left her hand there. I didn't want her to remove it. "It will be all right, Ray. Try to remember that no matter how strange or powerful people may seem, they're still *people*. There is a vital piece to that: it means that you have more in common with them than you have differences."

I placed my hand on hers, on my shoulder. It was a little awkward, but I didn't care. "You mean that?"

She smiled again. "Of course I do, Ray. Haven't you figured out yet that I don't say it if I don't mean it? Oh, and don't get too excited about what I said concerning commonality and differences. It's true for every human on the planet."

I looked at her in confusion for a moment. Then realized she was telling me not to get a swelled head over having something in common with such an extraordinary bunch of people. I couldn't help bursting into laughter again. "I like the way you can always make me laugh, Lyla," I said. I settled down and squeezed her hand. "Thank you."

"You're welcome," she said.

Chapter 17

Hucklebark, Lyla, Henry and I had set up camp in a small clearing at the southeast edge of the open, spacious grove I was starting to think of as Meeting Meadow. True to Lyla's word, there had been several pleasant, private spots to choose from. "Another good reason to come early," she had said.

Hucklebark and Henry had gone off—separately, I noticed—ostensibly to visit with some of the people who were starting to arrive for the gathering. Everett Longhaul had disappeared long before, as far as I knew without a word. I'd asked Lyla about that.

"These gatherings are the busiest time there is for Ev," she'd said. "Everyone here will need something from him. And as if that wasn't enough, sometimes people come from pretty far away – people who may not need anything from him for months at a time, though now of course they'll be hoping he has supplies for them."

"People from how far away? And what would they want that they only need every few months?"

"The farthest away I know of was when a man came here from somewhere near Mount Hood," she said. "Ev brought him several pounds of tobacco and some special kind of climbing shoes. He was so pleased he showed them all around, which is why I remember."

"Mount Hood. That's quite a ways to come for a meeting."

"Well," she smiled, "You already know from Hucklebark's story that Lupine ranges at least as far as Mt. St. Helens."

That stopped me for a few moments.

I had chosen to spend some time in private, knowing that soon enough I'd be doing a lot of talking, and probably introduced to everyone that showed up. Lyla had chosen to stay behind too, which had surprised me.

"You must know pretty much all these folks. Aren't you going to go around and say hello?"

"There'll be time for that," she had said. "I expect by the time we leave here we'll have done enough talking to last a good while."

We were both lying back against our packs, looking up at the canopy of alpine fir and spruce that shaded us. I was trying to let my mind slip into neutral for a little while. Without reflection I said, "You want to read some more of the book?"

She sat up immediately. "Yes, please."

I rummaged until I found it, and handed it over, and another notion appeared. "I don't think I'm going to say this to anyone else, but as far as I'm concerned you're welcome to read it whenever you want," and gave her the combination to the lock that purported to protect the book's privacy. "Of course, anyone who really wanted to could just smash the box. The lock is more of a statement than any real protection."

She gave me a long look that didn't say clearly what she was thinking. "Thank you, Ray." She opened the box and turned a few pages in, to the place where she had left off.

February, 1981 (California, Santa Monica) (tenth year)

I found a pad of notepaper in an alley. It was almost dry, and only had a handful of pages gone. Do you know what this means? It means that we are in the world: The Home can go to hell for all Javier and I care. They would have thrown us out in another year anyway, because we're on the verge of being too old for it. Where would we have gone when they tossed us? Where are we going now? Same mystery, but today it's our idea.

We didn't have to work too hard to get out. A second story window without bars, a loose screen, and to our

*amazement the drainpipe held. I doubt they'll look very
hard for us.*

*Javier is not very strong. Neither am I, for that matter,
but I'm the better off of us. We walked across LAX—the
airport—last night, staying out of the huge bands of
sodium light. There are lots of shadows on the edges of the
airport.*

*Now we are holed up for the day with some trolls under a
bridge. Highway 101 rattles and bumps above our heads.
The trolls are not really trolls. I want to remember to be
careful about that. They are people, just as Javier and I are
people.*

*Even though I taught Javier to read English, he never has
read very much. I have read every newspaper, magazine
and book I could beg, borrow or steal, and I have an idea
of what we have to look forward to out here. The other
people under this bridge are in the same boat. If we are at
least good enough to each other that we spend the day in
safety, we've done well.*

*For the first time, I am writing down the "stories" I made
for myself and memorized when I was too young to write
them, and later when I couldn't afford to have them around.
If they were stolen—as everything else I've ever owned was
at one time or another—life would have been a lot harder
than it already was. Now, when I'm fifteen, is the first time
it might be okay to write them down. If I forget them, I will
lose myself. That's what it means that I found a pad of paper
today.*

P.S. I got the pencil at the library. I don't figure they'll miss it.

June, 1981 (California, Goleta) (tenth year)

*Javier is gone. I don't know where, or why, or how. We've
been in this camp north of town for a couple months now.
There's work picking oranges on the coast, we've been*

getting by.

He went out last night. Didn't say a thing except 'See you later, Ray.' I thought he was just going for some fresh air, as if we don't have that already.

Maybe he found some Mexican people to go with. Lately he's been looking at me strangely. He's thirteen, and he figured out a good while back that he and I are "different". Maybe somebody's been talking to him and convinced him I'm not the right thing. I hope he's okay.

Javier grew up a lot in the last few months. When we ran away from The Home, he was hanging on my shirttail wherever we went. I think meeting his own people grew him up fast. Most of the ones that go up and down the coast picking fruit or whatever needs picking are Mexican people, just doing their best to stay alive and send something home. I'm the one that doesn't fit. Fancy that.

I'm not mad. Just really sad. I thought I'd have a brother for longer than this, once we got away. Besides, we've been brothers since I was nine. Maybe I won't bother trying to find another brother, if it's going to end like this.

Good luck, little brother. I hope people are kind to you.

September 1981 (California, Davenport) (tenth year)

Six days a week picking Brussels sprouts. And on the seventh day, I go out with the gleaners to get the rest of them.

I thought it would kill me the first couple of weeks, but I got tougher.

I haven't had to fight in a long time, and you know what? I really like that. This old guy, Nuñez, he decided to help me out a while back. I ran into him in Goleta, and then again outside of Santa Cruz. He would tell me things:

"Looky here, Ray boy, sometimes somebody mess with you, you can get away with kickin' 'em in the nuts. But it ain't

*gonna work all the time, you know. You got to have al-
tern-a-tives. You got to be able to do more than that."*

Like what, Nuñez?

*"Like you can talk your way out of a lot of scrapes if you
know how. Here it is, Ray boy: if you can figure out what
someone wants, you can figure out how to convince them
they got it already, without you."*

What if what they want is to beat the crap out of me?

*"You don' get it, boy. That ain't it—they want to feel
power, and beatin' on you is the only way they know, 'cause
they're stupid. So you learn how to make 'em feel like they
already got that power, and most times they let you be."*

So you mean kissing ass, or other places even worse.

*"Oh, you stubborn, Ray boy. No, no, NO! You learn to
talk, you learn to ne-go-tiate, learn what them politicians
know, you be safe, you get by."*

Teach me how to do that, Nuñez.

"Okay, Ray boy, I teach you when there's time."

*There never seems to be time. But Nuñez made me think,
and I'll get there eventually with or without him. I owe
Nuñez big.*

November, 1981 (California, Berkeley) (tenth year)

*Now I know, if I didn't before. I am an Undocumented
Alien in my own country. Address, driver's license, phone
number – these are for other people. All the catchphrases
you hear when people talk about "society": "under the
radar", "slipped through the cracks", and so on—it's one
thing to say them, even if you're sympathetic. Living them,
that's something else altogether.*

*A street cop tried to shake me down today. Singled me out
of four pedestrians crossing against a red light.*

*"I don't think you belong here, boy. Not very smart,
breakin' the law when you don't belong here."*

*"Yeah. You're right, officer, not very smart. I won't be in
your town for long, but I'll make sure it doesn't happen
again while I'm here."*

Thank you, Nuñez. Maybe it'll work this time.

*"Huh. I got a mind to haul you in on vagrancy. How much
money you got on you, kid?"*

*"Enough for bus fare to Sonoma, officer. I'm heading for
the bus that leaves at 3:00."*

"What's that, six bucks?"

*"That's about it. I pay my way, officer. I don't get in
anybody's face, and I don't ask for handouts."*

*"Get moving, kid. If I see you here tomorrow, I'll run your
sorry ass in."*

"Thanks officer. See you later."

*Not if I can help it. But there will be others. There will
always be others.*

Lyla carefully closed the book and its lock, and looked up at
me. "Have you ever had a home, Ray?"

"Sure. I lost it twenty eight years ago. I don't remember much
of it, of course."

"And you've never had one since then?"

I looked down at the ground, feeling embarrassed. "I don't
like to seem rude or childish—though it seems to happen often
enough. But I'd appreciate it if you read that book instead, so I
don't have to tell it again. I mean, I've had shelter: apartments
and rented houses with too many people in them, projects, tents,
picnic shelters and bridges, you name it. But I don't think I know
what a home might be, except for what I've read."

Lyla was quiet for so long that I lay back down against the pack after replacing the book. Looking up at the trees, I said, "This looks like it'd be a really nice home, this House of Windy Gap."

"It is. It's a lovely home," she said quietly.

I sat up again. "Here? You mean this meadow, this clearing?"

"No, of course not," she replied, sweeping her arm to take in the Mountain, the surrounding mountains, glaciers, river valleys. "All of here. I'm happy here. It feels like I belong here."

It suddenly occurred to me that I knew next to nothing about this woman, except that she fascinated and attracted me. "Where were you before you came here?"

"Oh, here and there, no place worth staying at or remembering."

"Come on, Lyla, what kind of answer is that? I've offered you my story, squalid tragedy though it is. Can yours be any worse?"

She looked down. "No, it's not that at all. Actually, all I remember is a city—a big city—and I didn't like it at all. I think it was somewhere in the Northeast."

"You don't remember where it was?" I was flabbergasted. "How long ago was that? How long have you been up here?"

She sat very still. "You won't believe me."

"Try me."

She sighed. "As near as I can tell, I've been living and working here for about eighty-five years."

I sat still for several long moments, trying to process that. "It isn't that I don't believe you. I just don't know how to."

She looked up at me again. "There are benefits to this kind of work, Ray, as well as risks. It's different for each one of us. In my case, a lot of the trees have given me things that I don't understand, but seem to make me age at about a tenth the rate of a normal person."

"So you're telling me that you're, what, a hundred and five, a hundred and fifteen years old?"

She shrugged her shoulders. "Something like that."

"How come you haven't told me anything about this before?"

She looked directly at me. "Because I'm afraid you'll think of me as some kind of freak, Ray. Something unnatural. I don't want that."

We stared at each other, each trying to keep our different feelings under control, each thinking furiously.

I said, "Let me get this right. You're—let's say for the sake of discussion—a hundred and ten years old. And you're worried about what *I* think?"

She was on the verge of tears. "Yes."

"And after living for over a century, with all of that experience, all those dreams, all that wisdom, all that time—you—you *like* me?"

Her tears had begun to flow, silently making their way down her face and onto her shirt. In the midst of crying, she looked up in astonishment, saw that I was serious, and burst out laughing at the ridiculousness of what I'd said. I've never laughed and cried at the same time, so I have no idea what would happen if I did. In Lyla's case, it gave her the hiccups.

"Of—of course I do, Ray! What's not—to like?"

I moved over in front of her, and took her face in my hands. Alarm klaxons were going off in my head, and I ignored them. I kissed her very gently on the mouth. "All right, I'll tell you what I think. I think you are beautiful, powerful, and fascinating. And I hope with all the hope I can scrape up that some time you'll feel something like that about me."

She took a deep breath that shuddered in the middle with a lingering hiccup. It made her laugh again, and she said, "It's a possibility. Don't lose hope just yet."

I suddenly felt like I was in danger of taking advantage of her confusion and distress, and slowly removed my hands from her face and went back to sit by my pack. "So I'm pretending that I have perfectly and correctly dealt with the fact that you are seventy five years older than I am," I said. "But we both know I haven't. Will you be patient with me while I get around to making sense of it?"

"Certainly," she replied, "But I don't think trying to make sense of it is what you need. Just accept that it doesn't make sense, Ray, and see if something comes along in time that makes it less strange or worrisome."

"Come to think of it, nothing seems to make sense any more, and most of it is *very* strange and worrisome."

"I know," she said. "That's why we came to Windy Gap."

Another thought came that demanded its turn, right now. "So how old is Lupine? How long has she worked in these mountains?"

Lyla thought for a moment before replying. "There's really no telling the age of anyone who works in this way. Most people—and I confess I'm one of them—never think about it any more. The only way to know Lupine's age is to ask her, and I can't honestly recommend that until you know her a *lot* better. She could be a hundred and twenty, or she could be eight hundred for all I know. Really, Ray—what does it matter?"

"I don't suppose it really matters at all," I said. "But how can I not be intimidated by people who've lived *centuries* longer than I have?"

"Take them at face value," she said. "If they're kind to you, and treat you with respect, what difference does it make?"

"No difference whatever," said a sonorous voice from the edge of the clearing. Lyla and I both jumped to our feet.

"Works!" Lyla exclaimed, as she ran over to him, threw her arms around his neck and kissed him on both cheeks. "I'm so glad you're here!"

He was about my height, with a comfortable build just on the athletic side of portly. The rich, dark olive-brown skin of his face, arms and hands bore the lines of great age, but his carriage and demeanor belied them. He was wearing a dark, almost black pair of light wool pants, a checkered flannel shirt, and well worn, high-topped hiking boots. He carried himself with a substantial, authoritative grace, with a dignity that managed to be warm and welcoming, yet deep and unassailable, all at the same time.

"Lyla, daughter, how wonderful to see you!" he beamed into her shining face; with a single glance he took in all the stories her expression had to tell, and gently brushed the last, already forgotten tear from her cheek. She smiled into his warm, dark eyes, and half dragged him over to me.

"Ray, this is Works. Works, this is Ray Holdman."

Works took my hand in a firm, fatherly grip and shook it. "I'm very pleased to meet you, Ray," he said gravely. "Welcome to our Windy Gap Gathering."

"Thank you. I'm honored to be here," I replied. "I hope we can get some things sorted out. And I want you to know I'm sorry for the disruption I've caused."

Works looked at me closely. I couldn't help but feel he was looking deep inside me, into places I wasn't sure I was willing to open up. But it didn't hurt, nor did it feel threatening. Clearly, here was yet another person of momentous qualities; how many of these could I stand to meet in one lifetime, let alone in a day or a week? Yet Lyla's greeting to him had been overflowing with love and the joy of seeing him, and that seemed important. I wanted to trust everyone here, but I had already stopped questioning my trust of Lyla, whether she was a young woman in her late twenties, as I had thought, or a seemingly mythical person of a hundred and twenty. I tried to follow Lyla's example, relax and allow Works to do whatever he was doing. It only took a moment, and then he let go of my hand.

"Right to business," he said. "That's fine. Shall we sit?"

Lyla spread a blanket from her pack on the soft ground of the clearing, and we sat in a triangle. Works eased himself into a cross-legged position. "What makes you feel you've created a disruption, Ray?"

"I—I don't really know how to think about all this, still," I said. "But it seems I've brought something here that's dangerous—mortally so. Lyla has already escaped it twice, only because the trees are strong enough to protect us from it. And you must already know that Henry saved my life when it killed me under the glacier." Looking down at the ground, I said, "I feel like some kind of plague carrier."

Works' eyebrows rose. "So. Something tried to kill you, and apparently tried to kill Lyla, and you believe you brought it here. Do I have you right so far?"

My voice was very small. "Yes."

No one spoke for several moments. Then Works said, "Normally, Ray, I like to take my time when somebody new enters our community. Sometimes I don't even meet them for a year or so. I allow them to take all the time they need to get to know as many of their peers as possible, to get comfortable enough with being here to make their own decisions. We clearly don't have that luxury this time. We need to know one another well, and there isn't time to do it easily or slowly. However," he went on, "We do have a little time. This will be a long day for you, and I'm sorry about that. I'll do everything I can to make it bearable for you, and to help you understand things that most people get months or years to absorb. In the meantime, there is something I want you to think about."

I had to smile at that. "One more thing to think about is probably not going to break me, sir. What is it?"

"Works, please," he said. "As I love to say, usually to the annoyance of my people, 'We don't stand on ceremony here—we sit on it'. At least on that kind of ceremony. But Ray, have you considered the possibility that you brought absolutely nothing with you when you came here, and that perhaps you have simply awakened something that has always been here?"

I sat and tried to let that sink into my mind. It was difficult; despite what I'd said about one more thing not being a problem, it was beginning to feel like my mind wouldn't accept any more.

"No," I said slowly, "I had not considered that at all. Is that possible?"

"I wouldn't have made the suggestion if it were impossible," Works replied calmly. "Just let it be a seed that does its own work for now. In the meantime, there is someone else I wish to introduce you to, and if you're willing, I need him to examine you. He's a Healer. Do you consent to this?"

"Um, well, I don't feel like I need anything right now, but sure," I said uncertainly.

Works turned over one shoulder and said, "Spark, enter now, if you please."

There was a rustle just outside our clearing, and a man walked through the branches. He was as tall as Everett Longhaul, and much more solid looking. His straight black hair was short, his expression serious without being grave. Works introduced us, and he inclined a slight bow to each of us.

"I'd like you to examine Ray now, as we discussed earlier."

I looked at Lyla. It was hard to tell if she knew him or not, for her expression was unreadable. But an almost imperceptible nod from her told me she thought I should do as they asked.

"What do you want me to do?" I asked.

Spark's voice was as calm and neutral as his manner. "Just be comfortable in whatever way works for you. Sitting, standing, or lying down—it all works for me."

"Let's begin where I am right now, then," I said. Works moved over and Spark took his place facing me.

"So do you want me to close my eyes, or breathe slow, or anything?"

"No. You can do anything or nothing," he said with a faint smile. He extended his hand, and without being sure I was supposed to, I took it in mine. Instantly I felt warm and safe, and I had no doubt of his intentions, which were all good.

He held my hand for several minutes, his expression never changing from one of abstracted thought. Lyla, Works and I all maintained silence throughout. I found myself wondering if this was all there was to Spark's examination, and how he could possibly learn anything this way. He gently disengaged his hand from mine, and turned to Works. Before he could say anything I interjected, "Is that it? That's the whole exam?"

"That's it."

To Works he said, "There's no doubt that this young man has very recently undergone rigors that would disassemble most of us like a puffball in a windstorm. There is also no doubt that he has received the kind of help and healing that only comes from the source."

Works' eyebrows rose again. "Indeed? Well, well. And his situation at the moment; does he require any more?"

"Nothing at all right now," Sparks replied. Turning back to me, he said, "You are in very good hands, Ray Holdman. I think it's safe to say there are none better. When there is more time, would you consider allowing me to study you more closely? You contain more than a few little mysteries."

"Um, yeah, sure thing," I stammered. "What do you mean by 'little mysteries'?"

"I prefer to wait until I know more before discussing those," he replied. "For now, there is one thing I need you to know: people are not generally able to sustain the kinds of abuse you have endured for very long, regardless of the help they receive. I recommend taking great care not to run any unnecessary risks."

"I'm very happy to avoid them if possible," I said, "But seeing as how I'm essentially clueless about everything, that may be pretty tough. Could you be a little more specific?"

Spark smiled, an expression that was warm, friendly and just a little sardonic.

"In particular, I recommend not getting killed again."

I can only guess that the expression on my face was part incredulous, part indignant, and part pure surprise. Whatever it looked like, Works suddenly burst into a full-bellied laugh that was so contagious Lyla and I couldn't help but join it. Spark continued to sit facing me, calm and tolerant.

"I'm sure Ray will do his best, Spark," Works finally said. "And we'll all do our best to help him continue to exist so you get your chance to learn more."

"In that case, unless you have more for me here, there are others that need tending," Spark said.

"By all means, and many thanks," Works returned. Spark rose gracefully to his feet, and with another slight bow in our direction moved serenely through the trees screening the clearing, and was gone.

I turned back to Works. "I hope you won't take this the wrong way, Works, but what was that all about?"

Works picked up a small twig lying near the blanket, and absently turned it over with his long, wrinkled fingers. "Spark is the most powerful and subtle Doctor I've ever known, Ray. I needed to know that physically you are—how shall I say it?—really who you are. I also wanted to be sure that you are physically up to telling your story again, and answering a lot of questions, some of which may be a bit uncomfortable."

"Uncomfortable? From you?"

"No, not at all. I sincerely hope that when I ask people things they feel like they can answer in perfect safety, and without judgment. But you should know that stories about you have begun circulating, and some of the people are already quite frightened. I think you've been informed that your experience under the glacier reverberated throughout the region, but you might not understand how fearful that can make people."

I thought about it for a moment, and saw his point. I already knew a great deal about the risks involved in frightening people.

"What can I do to help them understand I'm not an enemy?"

"The simple fact is that you are not an enemy," he said. "All you can do is live that way, as openly and honestly as possible. Nothing you, or I, or Lyla or anyone else can contrive will accomplish it."

I sighed heavily. "How soon will this gathering start? At this point, the best thing about it seems like its being over."

Works slowly got to his feet. "The people are already starting to assemble. I suggest that you and Lyla wait here until I send Hucklebark for you. It won't be very long; remember to be calm and patient as you can, and everything will be fine."

Lyla and I got to our feet. Works took Lyla's hand and held it for a moment, gazing into her eyes. Then he turned and, with a broad wink in my direction, left the clearing.

I went back to where my pack was and lay down propped against it. Lyla came and sat next to me.

"So now you've met Works," she said. "What do you think?"

"I have no idea what to think, except that I think I like him, and he hangs out with really strange doctors." She laughed, and it gave me a warm feeling in my chest to hear it. I wanted to make her laugh often.

"What do you suppose he meant by getting help and healing from 'the source'?" I asked.

"Don't make it difficult, Ray, because it really isn't." Looking more serious, she continued, "What do you think about where everything comes from, how it all comes about?" She swept her arm in a movement meant to encompass the whole world.

"You mean, god, or a creator, some underlying principle, or any of those other spiritual buzz words?"

"Of course that's what I mean."

I said, "I've never given it very much thought at all." She looked startled. "I guess, if I'm going to be brutally honest, I'd have to say I've spent my life totally preoccupied with getting by and staying out of the worst troubles, and when that wasn't at the front of the line, I spent the rest stuck in my own little brand of lonely misery."

She shook her head in wonder. "And yet, ever since you came here, you've been in intimate contact with it."

"I have? With what?"

Lyla sighed. "I'm still not going to hand it to you on a platter. You simply *have* to work it out for yourself, Ray."

"Are you suggesting that I've been talking to *god*, or something?"

Lyla threw back her head and laughed, a laugh that seemed to come from so deep inside I was in awe of it. I felt that warmth blossom in my chest again, and though I was almost overwhelmed with the desire to take her in my arms, I held still.

"You really are extraordinary," was all she said.

I felt confused, and a little disgruntled. I tried to cover it by saying, "So how old do you figure Works is?"

"No, you don't get to change the subject quite yet," she said. "Just consider this one thing, and we'll talk about something else. Listen, Ray—we aren't just some byproduct, some expression, of reality. Like everything else, we *are* reality. And as such, we participate in creating it. Will you think about that for a while, along with the few thousand other things you're supposed to be trying to understand?"

I took on a gruff, businesslike tone. "Yes, ma'am, I'll put it in the queue. I expect it'll reach the top in, oh, three hundred years or so."

"Okay, you silly man, I imagine that's the best I can ask for."

We lapsed once more into a comfortable silence, which to my intense regret only lasted for a couple of minutes before being broken by a rustling at the edge of the clearing. Hucklebark poked his head around a branch, as if afraid to disturb us. "Okay, kids, you ready to come out and play?"

"Not in the least," I replied. "Come back in a year or two, if you please."

Hucklebark looked startled, then blank, finally realized I was trying to make a joke, and laughed. "All right, you two, let's get on down to the gatherin'."

Chapter 18

The mid afternoon sun seemed brilliant and piercing after the cool shade of the campsite. As soon as we cleared the trees, I could see a knot of people a hundred yards down slope from us. They were facing eastwards, and there was one person standing alone in front of them. I felt a lurch in my stomach, and belatedly wished I'd eaten more recently. Too late now, I told myself. Perhaps looking forward to a good meal would get me through this.

The group looked much larger than I'd expected. Where had all these people come from? And where were they when they weren't all gathered in a meadow waiting to cross-examine a stranger? I tried to count the number of people as we approached, and gave up at around fifty. When we were within ten yards or so of the group, Lyla silently squeezed my hand and detached herself, moving over to one side of the throng. I thought I saw her standing next to Lupine, but I couldn't be sure.

Hucklebark leaned over and whispered, "Go on up front and stand with Works. Everything'll be fine, Ray, just be yourself." Good advice, I thought. But what *myself* was there to be?

Hucklebark moved away to the edge of the crowd, and I was left to walk by myself towards Works. I could feel the eyes of everyone there on me, and the wish to break away, to run down into the trees and hide, was almost more than I could resist.

Works held out a hand as I approached, and when I reached him he took my hand in his, and turned me around to face the group with his other arm around my shoulder. He felt warm, strong, and filled with purpose, and I could feel my courage returning, at least to where I could stand with some semblance of dignity.

"Folks, this is Ray Holdman," he began. I was surprised to hear a low murmur run through the group, and I was sure I heard things like "Hey, Ray", and "How's it going?" I thought I heard other things too, that were far less reassuring.

"We've already talked about why we're here, what we know about what's been happening. Ray has a lot to tell us, and it's going to take a little while. I assure you it will be worth your patience and attention." He turned to me with a light squeeze of my shoulder. "Okay, Ray, it's all yours."

That's all? Just start talking? My mouth felt like a desert, and my tongue refused to listen to any commands that it start working. I stood there, feeling like an idiot. I finally managed to look at Works and stammer, "Wh-where do you want me to begin?"

"Start with when you got here—up to the mountain, I mean—and we'll move backwards as the need arises," Works said calmly. He looked at me closely, and then signaled into the crowd. "Everett, could we have some water up here?"

Ev Longhaul emerged from the crowd and hustled towards us, carrying a couple of water bottles. He set one down on the ground in front of me and made to hand me the other. In an undertone he said, "Looks like it might be a two-quart story, Ray." He punched me on the shoulder, so lightly that it might have been mistaken as an awkward part of handing me the bottle. I accepted it gratefully, and without ceremony unscrewed the top and swallowed a third of it before breathing.

"Looks like it might be as long a story as I thought," Works said to the assembled company. "Let's get comfortable, folks." People began to sit down on the rocky ground. There was a short interlude of rustling and arranging, and by the time that was done my mind had settled to the point where I felt I could try to start.

"My name is Ray Holdman," I said, and immediately felt stupid. Hadn't Works just told them that? "I'm going to start this story in Seattle. In Pioneer Square, to be precise."

I began slowly, with long pauses, trying to marshal my thoughts and suppress the stage fright that periodically threatened to halt the story completely. But the story began to take hold of me, as if it had happened to someone much more capable and interesting than me, and it started to flow of its own accord. The first time people laughed was when I told about my first meeting with Hucklebark, when I thought I was being addressed by a grizzly bear. The tension eased after that, and I began to lose myself in the telling.

I left nothing out, except for my feelings about Lyla, and many of the conversations we'd had. It took hours; I remember at one point Ev unobtrusively coming forward to replace the now empty water bottles. I briefly wondered how I could hold that much water, and realized with a start that I was drenched with sweat. I talked on as the sun fell behind Sluiskin Mountain, and the twilight crept over us.

It was nearly dark when I finished with, "And we arrived here this morning." I had not been interrupted once, not even by Works. My voice, now husky from unaccustomed use, and the breeze that rippled the trees in the groves around us, had been the only sound for hours. Now that the breeze had died down for the evening, the silence was thick and heavy, and it seemed that time had stopped. No one stirred; people sat or stood, looking down at the ground or up at the sky, still deep in thought perhaps. I wondered how long we would stay here like this, but I was not willing to be the one that broke the moment.

Works took on that job, cheerfully and without ceremony. "Now *that's* what I call a *story*. All right, folks, I was going to ask for questions before we get down to discussing this, but I think we could use some time to think on it. We'll break for tonight; back together an hour after dawn, if you please."

People began to get up, stretch themselves, and wander off to their campsites. There was a certain amount of horse trading going on with campsites; apparently Meeting Meadow, as I thought of it, wasn't normally host to a crowd of this size. Hucklebark, Lyla, and Henry came up to where I had been standing with Works. Hucklebark got to me first.

"Nice job, Ray!" he clapped me on the back. "You had 'em hangin' on every word."

"I didn't know it was a performance," I said with a grin.

Lyla had come up to us. "It wasn't," she said. "But you told it well, and honestly, and that counts for a great deal."

Henry arrived, and with his characteristic bluntness said, "Nice job, Ray. Too bad it was so long my ass fell off while I was listening. Takes a lot of food to grow a new one, so let's get going and get something to eat."

Hucklebark looked pained, but Lyla and I laughed, and we turned to go. I looked around, and Works was still standing where he had been the whole time, looking as if he could stand there for fifty winters with no effort or discomfort. Without knowing if it was even appropriate, I said, "Works, would you care to join us?"

He stirred, and turned with a smile. "Thank you Ray, you all go on ahead. I'll probably see you sometime this evening. Good night until then."

Lyla walked beside me as we made our way back up slope. She said quietly, "Lupine wants to talk to you tonight. Alone."

I slowed down, almost to a stop. Hucklebark and Henry walked on ahead of us, unaware we were falling behind. A sense of dread entered me. Why should I be so terrified of Lupine? I fervently wished I knew, so perhaps I could do something about it. I leaned towards Lyla and whispered, "I'm afraid of her, Lyla. What should I do?"

"The same thing we keep telling you to do, Ray," she whispered back. "You are what and who you are—just be that. Since you don't have any control over anything else, why worry about it?"

"Yeah, I know you're right. I just wish it was as easy to do as to say."

She laid a hand on my arm, and I felt a brief, pleasurable tingle. "Lupine is on your side, Ray. Try to remember that."

I wondered how Lyla could be so sure Lupine was on anybody's side, but chose not to say it out loud. We walked the rest of the way to the campsite in silence. Hucklebark and Henry were already there. Henry had appropriated my camp stove, but instead of lighting it he was studying it with a scowling intensity.

He looked up when we approached. "Doesn't seem to be working. Got any suggestions?"

"What's it doing?"

"Not a thing—that's the problem."

I held out my hand. "Let's have a look. It's had a long, hard life, not unlike some fine new friends I've acquired."

Henry handed it over with a grudging smile. There was a tiny bag of miniature tools that came with the stove, and I got them out and began disassembling the business end of it. The needle valve that fed the burner was gunked up as usual, and in its typical way refused to be cleaned out. I was focused intently on it when a battered pair of sneakers came into the periphery of my vision and Lupine's voice said, "Hey, Ray. Stove acting up on you?"

I looked up, as afraid of turning again into a stammering six year old as of anything else. "Oh, yeah, well you know, I'm not the maintenance fanatic I could be, I guess."

Lupine chuckled and squatted on her haunches, even with me. "I have something that works well on those. Give me a shot at it?"

Was this the woman who had scorched me with the ferocity of her energy? How many Lupines were there? "Sure," I said, handing over the tiny valve.

She took it deftly between two fingers, digging into an inner pocket of the plain brown vest she was wearing. She finally extracted a small canvas pouch and pulled it open, removing a piece of wire with its ends jammed into bits of cork. "Amazing number of things this little beast is good for," she said as she pulled off one of the cork ends and ran the wire expertly through the needle valve. She handed it to me, and put the wire away while I reassembled the valve and tested it.

"Good as new," I said. "Thanks, Lupine."

"Don't mention it. Ray, I expect you're tired, and you have a right to be. It's not every day one is required to stand up in front of a bunch of strangers and deliver an epic. Even," she said smiling, "if you don't have to make it up, it's a lot of work to talk for that long, especially after all that's happened to you recently."

It took me a minute to work through this, but I did it.

"So you believe my story?"

"Of course I do. For one thing, Works would never waste our time and energy if it weren't true. But there are other reasons, and those are the ones I need to talk to you about. Urgently. Would you consider going for a walk?"

I looked longingly at the camp stove, which Henry had re-appropriated and was busily using to make coffee. It seemed vastly unlikely that I could summon the nerve to make Mad Lupine wait for coffee. My stomach had other ideas, though, and it didn't care if I made everyone in the world wait.

"I can't even think for much longer, unless I get some food in me," I replied. "Let me scrounge something to bring along, and then sure, I'm ready."

Lupine smiled. "Good. I'll be right outside your campsite."

She sprang to her feet and stalked out of the clearing, tossing a "See you guys in a bit" to Lyla, Hucklebark and Henry as she left. I turned to Lyla and raised an eyebrow. She smiled reassuringly, but I could tell she was nervous.

"What is it?" I said.

Lyla came over to where I was still sitting. "It's nothing, I'm sure." She hesitated. "I'm not frightened of Lupine, but she works at levels of intensity that should scare just about anybody. Don't get me wrong, Ray, but be careful. Think over whatever she's going to suggest, and don't rush to any conclusions, okay?"

"I don't think I could come to a conclusion tonight if it stepped on my toes," I said. Lyla made a face at me. "Yes, I'll think slow and careful, I promise. Honestly, I don't understand how I could have anything to do with any kind of work at Lupine's level anyway."

"There are a lot of things you don't understand—yet," she said.

Chapter 19

THE NIGHT WAS CLEAR, AND THE MOON WAS nearly full. Out from under the trees there was enough light to move freely without the need for any other illumination. Lupine had waited a few paces beyond the trees that screened our clearing, and when I emerged she turned wordlessly and headed up the slope, away from the meadow.

We walked uphill at a pace that made me realize the sandwiches in my pocket were going to have to wait a bit longer. I groaned inwardly, but kept up with Lupine as she strode up the mountainside. When we had gone up about a half-mile in distance, and five hundred feet in elevation she turned in a northerly direction, taking us around the shoulder of Sluiskin. We traveled diagonally, mostly around and a little bit up. I saw what appeared to be a glow around the bend of the mountain from us. Its luminosity grew as we went on, and as we crested a small ridge, the Mountain burst into view, filling my eyes with so much light I had to stop.

The moon was shining down on Mount Rainier from a sky so clear it seemed to vibrate. The Mountain's bulk, vast beyond any real understanding, shone with a silvery white so bright I thought it might blind me if I stared too long. Lupine had discovered I was no longer following, and had returned to find me.

"Are you all right, Ray?"

"I—yes, I'm okay. All the times I've come up here, and somehow I've never seen it this way before." I felt like I was in a place too grand, too powerful, for mere humans occupy. It was hard work to resist the urge to steal another moment of soaring beauty and then run howling down the mountainside, away from it.

"Just a few minutes more, and then we can stop, okay?"

All I could manage to say was "Lead on."

We walked around Sluiskin's shoulder for a little longer, and then Lupine abruptly turned and headed straight up its side. The going was rough, but not impossible, tired though I was. Lupine had to wait for me several times, and when at length I struggled up to where she was waiting she said, "This is good. Let's stop here."

I turned around and faced the Mountain again, my chest still heaving from the climb. It seemed enormously closer now. It filled the sky before me, and I felt utterly overpowered. I sat down heavily. "I hope I'm not expected to do any thinking up here, Lupine."

She sat down lightly beside me. "The most natural thing for you to do right now is be grateful, and to eat. Take some time to settle down, get yourself fed, rest a bit, and we'll see what happens then."

Gratitude. Yes indeed, I thought as I pulled the now rumpled sandwiches from my pocket. Sure, there are lots of people who come up here at some point and are privileged to see the Mountain like this. But compared to those in the world who never get to see anything like this, anywhere at all—it's like being one in a million, or maybe even ten million. I thought about all of the times in my life when there had been no sandwich to pull out of a pocket, and realized that what could easily be taken for granted as simply a really nice time in an unusual place was much more than that. It was, in fact, an incredible gem on a stunning necklace of similar experiences, the handful of which had somehow miraculously arranged themselves during a life of lonely misery around the neck of a single human who thought of himself as Ray Holdman. How was this possible? What cosmic lottery did I win, and why? For now that my breathing had slowed and the muscles in my legs were relaxing, it was clear that if nothing ever happened to me for the rest of my life, this moment would do. It would be enough. I remembered other times, particularly times up in this region that had held similar moments of brilliant clarity and what should have been life-altering beauty. Oh yes, more to be grateful for than I could recount, despite anything and everything else. The air was clear and still, and the Mountain gazed back at me with implacable calm.

I ate my sandwiches and drank from the water bottle I'd brought, drinking in too the sight of moon-stippled glaciers cascading down from the summit. I pointed to a nearly sheer wall of rock about five miles away in front of us. It rose three thousand feet high; its upper edge was shrouded in snow and ice, and the lower edge was shielded from our sight by Old Desolate, a "minor" peak between ourselves and the Mountain. "That's Willis Wall, isn't it?"

Lupine's voice was studiously neutral. "Yes, I believe that's what it's called these days."

Open mouth, insert foot, I thought. One more try, and if I screw it up again, I won't say a thing till we get back to camp.

"Lupine, I'm sorry if I was ignorant or offensive. There have to be other names for it that are meaningful, or truthful. Would you tell me the name you think of it as?"

She turned to me with a smile. "Nicely done, Ray. I'm not really that delicate but yes, I'll admit that place names can be a sore spot for me. The name for that place over there," she pointed to the wall, "that has been around the longest and makes the most sense to me, is 'The Home'."

"The…" My voice trailed off. Those words meant one thing to me: a crumbling, multi-story house in Southern California that been the storage dump for a couple of small boys everyone seemed to think were useless and crazy. A place of squalid, sometimes violent politics among powerless children, and their equally powerless keepers. And here was Lupine indicating a place of almost supernatural grandeur with the same name. "What does that mean—*The Home?*"

She looked at me in surprise. "Well, let me see if I can say it properly. It refers to the chosen dwelling place of some of the most important and powerful people who live in this region. They've been here since the Mountain was born. Why does the name shock you, Ray?"

I told her briefly what it meant to me, and then said, "There isn't room in my head for both of these places to have the same name. It's too much, Lupine—how can it be?"

She sat quietly, thinking. "Perhaps what you're really asking is how the two places can be in the same world, never mind their names. Does that make sense?"

"Yeah, I'll accept that. But the question stands: How can these things—one beautiful beyond imagination, the other a sordid pile of misery—both be here?"

"It's a mystery, isn't it?" Before I could come up with a retort, she went on, "If you're going to get through this next part of your life, Ray, you're going to have to get comfortable with mystery. The more you see, and the more you learn, the less you'll understand. Take my word for it, and learn to be patient, because your patience will keep you alive."

"How much mystery is there in the world for you?" I challenged.

Lupine laughed. "For god's sake, do you think I know everything? Let's just say that for every mystery that my experiences unravel, two more pop up to replace it."

I shook my head. "It seems hopeless, Lupine."

"Why ever would it be hopeless unless you've misplaced your hope? You're making a supremely common mistake, Ray. There is a distinct difference between the drive to understand, and the notion that humans have to understand *everything*. Make that distinction, and you'll make your way through things you never imagined. Fail to make it, and you'll drown the next time something truly new confronts you. As," she added a little ominously, "Has already happened."

We sat in silence for some time, gazing at the Mountain, soaking in the moonlight that washed over it and flowed towards us like a living thing. I thought about names—of places, people, and things, how important they could be, and at other times how trivial. What's in a name? Beats me. Why do some names insinuate themselves into the being of something, while others never seem to do more than lay on the surface?

"Lupine, what do you call The Mountain?"

She stirred, returning from some deep place she'd been visiting. "Of the recent names, I prefer Tahoma, like a great many people. There are older names, and some *very* old names. But a lot of those refer to this place when it was part of a huge sea bed, so though they were right at one time, the newer names succeed them."

"Who in the world was giving places names when this was a sea bed? That must be, what—two hundred million years ago?"

She looked at me in surprise. "The people who lived here, of course. And no, it was only about twenty million years."

"I don't get it. As far as I know, humans as we understand them go back about two hundred thousand years. Are you saying there were humans here that gave places names twenty million years ago?"

"I'm saying you need to expand your understanding of 'human'; that should come with work and experience. I'm also saying—again—that your welfare depends on dealing with mystery without panic, which is something I can hear in your voice, just below the surface."

She was right, and it stung. "So what if I feel like panicking? Wouldn't you feel the same way? How long have you had to learn these things?"

Holdman, you *idiot*. Why can't I keep my temper in its rightful place? *Because I'm scared, of course.*

Lupine replied calmly, "That's a good question, Ray, and it leads us where we need to go now. Before I answer, is there any chance you want to rephrase that into something more constructive?"

I felt chastened, scolded by someone so vastly superior and more powerful there was no hope of ever being on an equal footing. I felt like… I was six years old again. With astonished anger, I felt tears hot against the backs of my eyelids. *There isn't time for this, and I don't want it*, I told myself furiously. Someone said—was it Lyla's voice?—*then don't. You are who you are; just be it.* I took a deep, shuddering breath, and the tears receded. I would probably need them some other time. I tried instead to think about what was before me, here and now.

"Yes," I said, "Maybe I can try that again sometime. But I'd rather change the subject. Lupine, why are you spending this time and effort with me? I mean, here you are, a person who works with unimaginably powerful forces to bring about change on the planet. And here am I, some goof who's been more or less on the run most of his life, who happens to talk to trees. Where is the connection?"

"That's a change, all right," she replied, "And maybe it will get us even closer to the heart of the matter. Don't you see it, Ray? This being that attacked you; where do you suppose it comes from?"

"I have no idea. I wish I did."

"Then I will tell you, by way of experience I have and you don't, that a thing that malicious and powerful comes from deep within the earth. And we—or someone much like us—are usually at least partly responsible for its existence."

"All right, I'll go with that as a working hypothesis and leave the rest to mystery for the time being," I said. It made Lupine smile, which felt much better than making her angry or impatient. "So this means that since you have a lot of experience with things and forces that happen deep in the earth, you might know something about all this."

"Very good, Ray."

"But what do I have to do with it? I'd think you'd just get whatever I can remember of all this from me, and then go about dealing with it?"

"I might be able to *help* you with this, Ray, but it's not mine to deal with. It's yours, and yours alone."

"How can I deal with something like this? I already said I'm just some fool that talked to a few trees!"

"Try to understand this, Ray. *Try.* You are probably as powerful as I am, if not more so. I'm willing to work with you on this, but it's absolutely necessary that you make your changes *now*, not in ten or a hundred years."

"I'm trying, but I can't accept it Lupine, what do I have to do with forces like that? This just isn't possible!"

Lupine was clearly trying to keep her temper, which was making it harder for me to concentrate on what she said.

"Ray, have you ever heard the term *idiot savant*?"

"Huh? Yeah, sure. It refers to someone who's a genius at something, but an idiot in every other aspect of normal human endeavor."

She looked straight at me. "Well?"

What she was proposing began to sink in. It was worse than I thought. At the same time, it was hilariously, sublimely, ridiculous. I couldn't decide whether to laugh or run away.

"Oh, no—no, no," I said. "I'm thoroughly used to being thought of as the *idiot* part, but for the rest, I really don't think so."

"Then it's time you changed your mind."

I tried to take a deep breath. My lungs felt small and tight, and though we sat in a sea of the purest air, I could not get enough of it.

"All right. I know I'm trying your patience to its limit, and I'm sorry. Do you have anything else available that will help change my mind?"

Lupine heaved a gusty sigh. "Okay. At least we're making some progress here. Let's consider the alpine spruce that invited you into itself on Mother Mountain. Give me your brief impression of *why* that happened."

"Human went nearby, human honored tree, tree invited human inside."

Lupine laughed. "If I didn't know Henry, I'd say you might be the most exasperating person I've met in a very long time." She got serious again. "Do you honestly think it was that simple?"

"I don't know."

"Well, I do. Ray, that tree sensed your presence from ten miles away, or more. From that moment on, you were going up Mother Mountain whether you wanted to or not. It *chose* you. And not because you were 'human passing nearby'. It was because of two things: one, it had something you need, and two, *you have something that everything and everyone here needs.*"

"I…"

She interrupted. "Take it, let it in, and move on, Ray. We can't even talk about what's truly happening here until we can teach you enough of who and what you are to make it sensible."

"Okay. I'll try."

"Not much more I can ask for, I guess," she said. "Another point, then. Who do you think the old man and old woman are that you've encountered in 'dreams'?"

"Again, I don't know."

Lupine hesitated. "I've been told that I'm not to talk with you about this, that you have to get it yourself. I don't agree with that. We don't have time for organic self-discovery, or whatever you want to call it. I'll take the consequences if I'm wrong, but I'm going to lay it on you now."

She had me quaking in my boots at this point. I chose not to answer.

"Since you've spent some time with Lyla, I imagine she's told you that we are part and parcel with reality, and that as such we help shape it. That knowledge is more important to her than to some, because of some of the people she works with. Most humans who worry themselves about the concept of reality want it to be—in fact insist on it being—immutable, totally concrete, not subject to negotiation. Unfortunately for them, nothing's further from the truth. Each one of us who harbors some concept of god, creator, creators, guiding principle, or whatever, has our own way of perceiving that. Yours happens to be one that many people have worked out for themselves in their innermost beings. But they worked it out by seeking it. The mind boggling thing about you is that as far as any of us can tell, you have *no* concept of these things, and yet they come to you anyway!"

I sat very still, listening to my heartbeat for a while, before I tried to deal with this. "Lyla did try to tell me something like this. You're saying that I'm talking to, or being visited by, God."

"Whatever, whoever you want to call it," Lupine said. "When people tap into the original source, it takes whatever form works for them. You'd be amazed at what some people experience. But once more, Ray—the point is not that you've tapped into it. The point is that *it's tapping into you*."

Think, Holdman. Do something intelligent. *This can't be happening to me!* But why not? Isn't the world full of stories of people who've had this sort of thing happen to them? I looked up at the Mountain, sitting in its immensity under the moon, and I asked it, *What do you think about this? Got any tips for an idiot savant that's getting pinged by God?* No response. I wasn't too disappointed, for I hadn't expected one. Perhaps I'm deaf to mountains, and if I could hear them I'd get some really good advice.

Another question came to mind. It was a surprise to have thought of it, and I wasn't sure I wanted an answer. I asked it anyway.

"Not that I'm complaining, Lupine. Why did you bring me up here?"

Her gaze swept out over the Mountain, the smaller, surrounding attendant mountains with their meadows, trees and rock, then up to the sky and back to earth again.

"Whatever your own work is, this is where it's to be done, Ray. We need you to see that, to know it and live it in the strongest, deepest way you can find."

She turned her gaze directly on me. "And nothing less than all of this is what is at stake."

I looked where she had looked, and felt like a worm that lives its life in a few square yards of dirt, never going or seeing beyond that. What could all this have to do with me? And yet I was certain Lupine was not, would never even consider, lying to me about this or anything else. How was I to believe in this? How could I ever tolerate this much mystery? Now that I had come to this place in the world, my choices seemed to be dwindling rather than growing. As far as I could tell there was nothing to do but try to understand, and either drown in it all or learn to swim in the effort.

"All right," I said quietly, "We'll say that who and what I really am is very different from what I thought. Obviously, I need to understand what to do next. Any suggestions?"

"First, do whatever you can to remember everything we've talked about here," Lupine replied. "Next, consider the fact that you belong here, no less than the rocks, the glaciers, and the trees do. Take that knowledge in, accept it, and keep moving. After that, work on eliminating every scrap of unnecessary fear that keeps you in the *idiot* state and out of the *savant.*"

"If I ask you one more stupid question, and promise not to ask any more—at least in the next five minutes—can you be patient?"

Lupine laughed again. "Go for it, Ray."

"How do I get rid of 'every scrap of unnecessary fear'?"

She sobered. "Doesn't qualify as a stupid question, but that's fine. It's a crucial question, one that people of all types have wrestled with since the beginning of everything. Fortunately for us, a few of them have learned a bit. So: the single most important thing is to *remember.*"

"Remember what?"

"Stop and think about that word, Ray. *Re-mem-ber.* The Latin roots are *re,* the prefix that means 'to do again', and *memor,* which means 'mindful'. Unnecessary fear is that which drives all useful things from your mind, and leaves you with the *idiot.* The *savant,* on the other hand, is able to ignore unnecessary fear and maintain the understanding needed to survive and get done what needs doing."

I have done that before. The stories I told myself, over and over, so that I would never lose myself. Those tiny little stories had kept me in this body, in this mind—diminished, beleaguered, perhaps, but still there—when others much more powerful were doing their best to tear me apart.

"Yes. Yes," I said, "I see it. Thank you, Lupine, you've reminded me of something—something whose meaning I'd almost forgotten."

She looked at me in surprise. "You're welcome, Ray." She raised her arms, stuck out her legs and stretched hugely. "I'm about talked out. It's time to head back down."

"But you haven't even started telling me about what's going on," I protested. "I still don't have a clue how to move forward!"

"Easy. I'm going to leave the next step to Works. He'll tell you more, and maybe kick me around the meadow for telling you what I did. At any rate," as she stood up, "We need to get back down so nobody thinks we fell off."

Chapter 20

I walked slowly down the mountainside behind Lupine, exhausted but still thinking furiously. I retold our conversation to myself over and over, trying to go through it rapidly but clearly, so nothing would be forgotten. I stumbled over the rough ground frequently, paid just enough attention to keep from falling, and went back to my telling. I mentally checked the book in my pack: yes, there were still a handful of blank pages in the back. The things Lupine had told me tonight would need to be recorded one way or another, even though I was already trying to burn her words into my memory.

We had rounded Sluiskin's shoulder, and Tahoma had been obscured by the smaller mountain. I realized with a start that I had called it *Tahoma*, and wondered if it was slavish imitation or the adoption of a worthy change. I decided that it was the latter, and it would not matter if anyone thought otherwise.

When we were a hundred feet above the ring of trees that surrounded Meeting Meadow, I chanced to look up and saw a figure standing a little ways down from us. Lupine walked on with her ferocious grace intact, but I thought I detected a slight tensing in her movements. I must have been making it up, I decided.

A few more steps down the slope, and I could see that Works was waiting there for us. We came up to him and stopped. He smiled pleasantly at Lupine and said, "Good discussion, daughter?"

"Yes, Works, we made a lot of progress," was her reply. Her tone was even, but I felt sure there was an undercurrent of nervousness. If Works noticed it, he didn't let on in any way. Lupine said, "I'll head down to the camp and tell Lyla and the others Ray will be back presently."

"Thank you, Lupine." Works turned to me. "I wish we were done for the evening, Ray, but it isn't so yet. I have to ask your indulgence for a little longer, but I'm not quite as athletic as Lupine." He glanced towards a large, flat rock about twenty feet away. "That will do nicely, if you're agreeable."

"Yes, sure." We made our way across the slope, which was slippery with loose gravel, and seated ourselves on the rock, looking down on the ring of trees that screened the meadow.

Works looked tired. So, I imagined, did I. The moon had risen higher, and shone down on us with a benign intensity that made every pebble and stone cast a shadow on the rough earth. Works took in the view for a moment, and sighed.

"I have an extreme dislike for the need to push young people beyond decent limits of learning and hardship," he said. "Whenever there is any other way to get something vital done, I do it. Consider this an apology if you will, Ray. If you accept what I need to tell you, you'll understand that you have one coming to you."

I sat quietly, realizing that some kind of reply was required, but not knowing what to say. Finally I gave up on saying anything useful. "That's fine, Works."

"I imagine Lupine told you a bit more than I might have intended her to," he said with a smile.

Without thought, I rose to her defense. "She did what she felt was necessary, and I –"

He held up a hand and stopped me gently. "I don't pretend to perfect wisdom, or even comprehension, Ray. As well as loving Lupine dearly for who and what she is, I value her judgment more than I can say. You need have no worries on her account. It would be a great help to me if you would tell me the conversation you had with her."

I recounted for him what we had talked about, including the struggles Lupine had had to make me understand, finishing with, "I'm trying as hard as I can to make sense of all this, Works, I really am. I still don't know if I'm up to it."

Works thought for a time. "It may be some time before you realize what she's given you. If nothing else, I urge you to act on her advice—remember it *exactly*."

"But Lupine seems to think I'm some sort of seriously powerful person," I protested. "Works, it's just not true!"

"Have you considered the possibility that what you need to learn is no more important than what you need to *unlearn?*"

"No," I said slowly, "I hadn't gotten there. What do you mean?"

"The world is not some mechanical, reactionary system where everything in it salivates at the sound of a dinner bell. On the other hand, since the very first event that heralded the beginning of us, all that followed has been a response to what went before. Ray, I gather that all of this lifetime you have been taught, ruthlessly and endlessly, that you are nothing: useless, unimportant, someone who merely consumes oxygen that could have been better used elsewhere."

"That's a very harsh way to put it," I said, and the bitterness I felt was there in the words. "And absolutely accurate."

Works turned to me and held my gaze with an irresistible strength that firmly overrode his age, and his tiredness. His eyes were so deep they felt like the old woman's eyes had felt as I had looked into them, and seen the entire world.

"Here is something else to *remember*. You have been taught a great lie, perhaps the greatest and most destructive lie. There is *no living thing* that meets that description."

My instinct was to look away, to look anywhere else but at Works, but I could not. "I want to believe that. I really do."

"You must, Ray. A great deal depends on that. I need you to understand," he went on, "Logic is an excellent tool, but it has very definite limits. There is a vast region of thought and feeling that lies between rigid logic and blind faith, and that is the place you need to work towards. Use some logic to help yourself believe that you have been lied to; when that will carry you no further, pick up the feelings that help you to live, and keep moving. Along with all the other things you're being expected to remember tonight, add what you have felt when you survived against all odds, when you and someone else connected in a way that defies logic, and the two of you felt or did something neither one of you could do alone."

"All right, I'll work with that." I gave him a small, exhausted smile. "I'm sorry, Works, but if I don't start writing some of tonight's stuff down, I'm afraid I'll forget it."

Works smiled back. "A little bit more, Ray, and then I can let you go until the morning. Lupine told you, I recall, that the being that attacked you came from deep within the earth, and that we—or someone like us—probably had a hand in its shaping. Am I correct?"

I nodded.

"I want you to think back on what I said a moment ago, about everything in the world that has happened being a response to what happened before. Now think about the emergence of life; its beginnings, its flowering, and finally its outpouring. The world abounds in life, it's everywhere. What kind of response might you expect to something so spectacular?"

I thought hard, but my mind was nearly at an end of thinking for the time being. It felt like there wasn't room in my head for another idea. But Works was speaking earnestly, and I wanted to please him. It felt like an incredibly stupid idea, but I came out with it in desperation.

"Um, well, some kind of anti-life?"

To my amazement, he said, "That's exactly right. I prefer to think of it as an *opposition* to life. Not merely death, mind you; death is an integral part of life. I'm referring to something much more profound, and much less understood. To me, at least, the abundance of life and the opposition to it seem to spring from the same all-encompassing ways of the world. Now consider once more that Lyla and Lupine have told you since we ourselves are a part of reality, we have a hand in shaping it. Do you see any connections here?"

My head felt like it was stuffed with rocks, and nothing less than dynamite would penetrate it. It was starting to ache, but I sensed that I was close to what Works wanted me to understand. His sentences wound through my mind like ponderous, laboring snakes; seemingly of their own accord, two of them coiled together in slow motion, and presented me with an idea.

"You're trying to tell me that this 'being' is a—an expression of some *opposition* to life that's arisen in response to all the living things in the world, and that we—or someone like us—" I stopped cold. Works waited patiently for me to finish.

"—or *I*—have somehow given it this form, this ability to harm us."

Works released a long sigh, as if he had been holding his breath while he waited for me. "I'm proud of you, Ray. No one so tired, who's had a day like you have, should be expected to do that well, let alone any better. Before you decide to take responsibility for this being's presence among us, I want you to *remember* everything you've heard tonight. I will not ask any more of you until tomorrow."

I laughed, a little shakily. "That's a good thing, because I'm really, really close to losing a lot of it."

Works got up slowly, dusting off the seat of his pants. I stood up, lightheaded and wobbly. Works took my elbow and steadied me; in that instant I was filled with a different kind of lightness, and a warmth that felt like the comfort and cheer of a thousand campfire-lit nights. I looked at him in surprise, but he appeared to be concentrating on his footing. After a few steps he let go of my arm. The memory of that feeling stayed, though the lightness left me.

When we got to the trees that ringed our campsite, he took his leave. "I sincerely hope you get some rest, Ray. There is more we need to talk about tomorrow."

"I guess I'll see you an hour after dawn," I replied. "Though I'll probably be depending on someone else to wake me up!"

Works smiled broadly. "That would be Henry, I believe." He turned and walked through the moonlight towards the other side of Meeting Meadow.

I wound my way slowly through the trees that screened our campsite. There was a pool of moonlight near the center of the little clearing, while the edges were swathed in darkness. On the far side, where my gear was stowed, I saw a tiny pool of light. Walking slowly, and trying not to stumble across the moonlit opening, I saw Lyla sitting up with a little candle lantern next to her. It gave enough light to read by (if you kept your book within a foot of it), but she wasn't reading. She was simply sitting, eyes closed, her face serene. I felt envious of her stillness; my legs were starting to tremble from fatigue, and my whole body felt like it wanted to sleep for a week. My mind was so full of what I'd been told that it was randomly jumping from one thing to the next in a lurching, purposeless gallop.

The slight rustle that came when I lowered myself to the ground caused her eyes to open. "I'm sorry," I whispered, "Didn't mean to disturb you."

"I was waiting for you to get back," she replied in the same low tones. "Is everything all right?"

"At this point, I have no idea. Lupine and Works both opened up the top of my head and poured in three or four truckloads of new ideas. How I'm even going to remember it all, let alone sort it out into some kind of sense, is beyond me."

Lyla looked closely at me through the dim light of the lamp. "You don't look as bad as you did after coming out of the mountain spruce, but it's uncomfortably similar." She thought for a moment, and then seemed to arrive at some sort of decision. "I don't know what they gave you tonight, but there's no doubt you have to hang on to it. I'll be right back. Whatever you do, Ray, don't fall asleep in the next five minutes."

Before I could ask where she was going, she rose and strode away into the darkness.

Falling asleep in the next five minutes sounded like a wonderful idea. But at this moment my mind chose to pull up, in

Lyla's voice, the words *I don't say it if I don't mean it*. I forced my eyes to stay open and my body to continue sitting upright. That took all the energy I had left, so there wasn't much to think about while I waited for her to return.

She came back in what was probably less than five minutes, though I was becoming so dazed with exhaustion it was hard to tell. Lyla took my hand and hoisted me to my feet. I wanted to protest, but it didn't seem worth it; her sense of purpose was clear and strong.

"Come with me now. It's not far and it won't take long, I promise."

I leaned heavily on her arm as she led me to the edge of the clearing. The darkness seemed impenetrable under the trees as we entered a thicket. I stumbled frequently, and Lyla had all she could do to keep me upright. Fortunately, whatever we were seeking was not far; after only ten yards or so of struggling through the thickly growing alpine trees, we stopped.

Lyla reached up around eye level and grasped a limb of one of the trees. It was too dark to see exactly what she was doing. She held it silently for a moment, then dropped her hand and took mine.

"The trees held you back from coming here this morning because they know a lot more about you than we do. They had to decide if you are what you seem, and they have decided. They want to help you in any way they can.

"Hold this branch, right where it joins the trunk. The tree will tell you what to do next."

She moved my hand to the branch. I could barely see it, but I grasped the branch that she had guided me to, and held it. My hand fit easily over the rounded ridge where the branch joined the trunk.

Immediately I felt calm wash over me. The exhaustion that threatened to overwhelm me receded, and I could think again. Inside my mind I heard a thin, papery voice say, *I will hold them for you. Open, and share.*

I was instantly afraid. Was this tree going to take from me all that Lupine and Works had worked so hard to give me tonight?

Not take them, no. They will be kept safe here, as with you. Relax, and trust.

So, another decision to make. All I could think of for a moment was that I was utterly sick of making decisions; if I never had to *decide* on something again, that would be fine.

I felt a small movement, and realized that Lyla was still holding on to me, helping me to stay standing. She had brought me to this tree; she knew so many things I did not. Did I trust Lyla? Yes, that was good enough. I tried to relax, as I had been instructed to, and let the tree do whatever it was going to do.

I began to feel my resistance to letting anything happen with this tree slowly drain out of me. There was a sudden burst of energy inside me, and then there was no barrier between the tree and everything that lived inside me. The movement was so strong I thought I was being lifted off the ground, but after a moment I could tell that it was a torrent of thought, feeling and experience that flowed from me into the tree.

It only lasted for a few seconds. When it subsided I wondered for a panic stricken moment if it had indeed taken away all that had moved between Lupine, Works and the others, and me. I started to ransack my mind as I would a cluttered closet that I was sure hid something I needed desperately. But there was the time with Lupine, sitting on Sluiskin's west-facing slope; I could hear her talking. There was Works, sitting next to me on the flat stone, his deep, quiet voice sending more mystery for me to get comfortable with. This tree had told the truth; nothing was lost to me, at least for the time being.

Return when you can, if you need. You will be here.

I stood in wonder. Never in my wildest imaginings had I considered that a tree could offer this kind of gift. Did I really understand what had just happened? Of course not; I was beginning to accept that everything happening to me was a mystery, and that I would understand some of it in its own time, and some of it never.

Thank you, I said to it. *When I need to come back, will you be able to help me find you?*

Get yourself near, and you'll find.

All right, I replied. *You have my gratitude.*

Go see Him.

What? Who is 'Him'?

You know Him. He has come to you, and you need his help now.

I didn't answer, thinking about it instead. Was this tree referring to the old man I had dreamed?

I felt a sudden, inward lurch and I let go of the branch, my hand seeming to move of its own volition. Lyla was still holding my other arm, helping me to stand. I turned to her, barely able to see her features in the darkness.

"Do you understand what just happened?"

"The tree offered to listen to some of what's inside you," she replied. "It heard it, and is keeping it safe. If you lose some of it—meaning mainly if you forget—you can come here, and it will give it back to you."

"I had no idea this was possible." I stood, thinking hard and trying not to tremble, both from exhaustion and from wonder. "You were holding onto me. Did you feel what I felt, did my experiences go into you too?"

"No," she said, "It went straight from you to the tree. I was paying attention to something else, anyway."

"Can I ask what occupied you so?"

"Keeping you upright," she said, smiling. "It's a big job right now."

"Let's get back to camp, so you can be done with that job."

I made sure not to lean so heavily on Lyla's arm as we went slowly through the trees towards the tiny pool of light still shining at one edge of the clearing. With her help I eased myself down onto my sleeping bag. It was a warm night—and uncomfortably close to dawn anyway, considering we would have to meet soon after that—so I lay on top of it. Lyla went over to her spot and with a soft "Good night, Ray" blew out the little candle in its lantern.

The darkness that enveloped us was accentuated by the pool of silver light that filled the center of the clearing. The moon was sinking behind Tahoma; in a little while it would leave the stars to shine on their own. Sleep seemed like the only thing in the world worth having right now, yet it wouldn't come. I lay looking up into the varied patterns of black that were the trees overhead, and tried to empty my mind.

It was full to bursting, and though it was too spent to be capable of any useful work, it caromed here and there without letup. After a few minutes it settled on the words *Go see Him* and refused to move on.

Who else could that mean but that old, old man who had sat next to me in a dream? Perhaps it would work as it had when I had tried to remember my encounter with the old woman. I closed my eyes and tried to envision the tiny clearing, the surrounding vine maple, and the old man himself.

For a few moments I couldn't get anything to hold still, and the images I was concentrating on danced and wavered as if I was trying to find the faint signal of a distant broadcast. I almost gave it up as too much for an exhausted mind to accomplish, but I hung on to it for just a little longer. The memory settled into stillness, and I entered into it.

This time I wasn't as startled to notice that there were differences. I sat facing him; his silver hair cascaded down his chest, and his head was lowered, as if contemplating something tiny on the ground before him, or perhaps meditating on something else altogether. I saw that he was barefoot. His feet were thin and heavily calloused, so much so that I thought he could walk to the top of Sluiskin that way without discomfort.

I was drawn to him; the trees, the clearing all faded away and there was nothing to see but him. I could feel the power that emanated from him, and as I began to pay attention to it, the intensity of it leaped upwards and out, in every direction. I could feel it ripple through me as if I wasn't there. It felt like what was required to make the earth rotate, like it was the stuff of the world. I began to feel afraid. I suddenly thought about what Lyla had said about Lupine: *sometimes she just doesn't bother to conceal it.*

He raised his head and looked at me. His eyes too were much like the old woman's: deep beyond reckoning, unfathomable. I didn't fall into them as I had into the old woman's. He smiled, and an image presented itself in my mind. It was a high, huge rock wall, with The Mountain rising precipitously beyond it. The top of The Mountain was lost in the clouds. There were no trees wherever this was; there was only rock, and snow, and ice.

The image faded away to be replaced by another: a gnarled, wind-battered mountain spruce that I realized with a start was the tree I had entered so disastrously on Mother Mountain. Then this too faded, and I was left facing the old man. He extended his hand, making it clear I was to take it in mine.

I hesitated. The power, the energy that surrounded him was so strong I wondered fearfully what would happen if I took that hand. I was afraid I would be consumed in some way, whether burned up, or evaporated, or simply disassembled and dispersed to the winds, I didn't know. He looked at me steadily, hand held very still. His eyes asked me if I had the courage to do what was necessary. I decided I didn't, and in the same moment reached out and grasped his hand.

Something exploded inside me. I couldn't tell if it was in my mind, my heart, my body itself, or all of them. It hurt with an intimate, urgent and lethal agony, as if something deep within that had been welded in place was being forcibly torn open. It happened so quickly I was shocked into silence while I seemed to be coming apart.

The energy that seemed to come from the old man, that had felt like it was passing through as if I wasn't there, began to move differently. It followed pathways in me that hadn't been there a moment before, as if a great river had suddenly been rerouted and was purposefully digging new channels. It seemed to be entering from any number of places—the top of my head, the bottom of my spine, my extremities, and it was leaving from all of those places at the same time.

The pain, which had felt like something I couldn't possibly survive, was beginning to subside, and soon I could think again. The old man had let go of my hand, and it had dropped lightly into my lap with the other. The river of power running through me continued on; I was tethered to the universe by it, and I thought of all the stories I had read or heard where the phrase 'Heaven and Earth' appeared. Now, it would seem, I knew what that really meant, for all that passed between them was running through me.

Soon the feeling of the river flowing within me began to subside, slowly but surely. The feeling of being so intimately connected to all that is began to fade. Not all at once; it was as if the energy moving through slowed from a river to a stream, to a creek, to a trickle. It never stopped altogether, but there came a moment when its movement was so faint that I became aware of my surroundings again, felt the ground I was sitting on, the air on my skin, and saw the old man still sitting before me.

So many different and conflicting feelings ran through me I couldn't sort them out. I was empty, I was filled to bursting. I was terrified, I was calm. I was angry and confused, I was composed and at peace. I wanted desperately for the ancient man to talk to me, to explain it all. I was sure that if he didn't just *tell me* what I needed to understand, none of it would ever make any sense. Instead, a deepening of the twilit darkness began to fill the little clearing; the vine maples, the old man and the ground itself began to slowly fade away.

I looked directly into his dark, infinite eyes and pleaded, "Talk to me. Help me understand, please!"

Just before it all faded into a warm and complete darkness, he leaned forward with a broad smile, lightly rapped my knee with his knuckles, and spoke.

"Get to work, child."

Chapter 21

I woke to the sound of Henry's voice, but he wasn't talking to me.

"Lyla. Time to wake up, girl. It's time."

Lyla. Hearing her name triggered a landslide of thought and feeling, even to a mind that was not truly awake, that was complicated and simple at the same time.

There was so much I didn't know. How had she spent eighty five years on the Mountain? How could I even accept the notion that she had done that? And if I set that intolerable mystery aside, what had led her here? None of it seemed to matter as much as how I cared for her, and my fear, borne of a lifetime of losses, that if I dreamed and wanted it would only hurt that much more to be denied when the inevitable happened, and it all came to nothing.

Nobody had made me feel like this in a very long time. For years I had actually thought that I was inured to never having that kind of love or friendship; now that I had met Lyla, all that time of self-deception had vanished as if it had never happened. There was a whole host of thoughts urgently drumming on the doorway to my consciousness, and I resolutely left the door shut tight, for they would have to wait. I had been reckless beyond any sort of reason, telling and showing her the things I had, letting her know how I felt. I knew that she was a person of immense integrity, and honesty, clarity, and kindness. But I was afraid of what might happen if I kept laying my heart on the line, and the fear was overwhelming. Who was I to think that someone like Lyla would come into my life and then choose to stay?

I wanted to stop thinking, and I couldn't. My mind had run itself into a well-worn pattern of fear, loneliness and worry, and I knew from long experience that it wouldn't be able to find its own way out. It began circling over the same weary fears and recriminations. The thoughts that so badly needed my attention still waited outside, powerless to make their way in. It was Henry who opened the door to them, and freed me too.

"Hey, Ray. You need to wake up now. Come on, bub, rise and shine."

My eyes flew open. He was kneeling beside me, one hand gently grasping my shoulder.

"Thank you, Henry. And I really mean, thank you."

Henry looked down with a mixture of surprise and consternation. "Yeah, sure thing. You okay?"

I sat up. "Better now. Did you happen to get that cantankerous camp stove going this morning?"

"As a matter of fact, I did," he said. "Gather your rumpled, sleep-deprived self together and come on over for a cup."

I got up and started to move toward the trees to relieve myself. The simple act of moving brought back everything from the night before, with a suddenness that made me sit down again abruptly. The time and talk with Lupine, with Works, Lyla taking me to a tree that offered to store my innermost thoughts and experiences, and finally, the time with the ancient man that I had thought at the moment must tear me apart. How would I ever make sense of all this in less than fifty years? How in all the world did I get here? The days were running together, but I still knew that less than two weeks ago I had been trudging through a drab, unsatisfied life of useless alienation and conflict, in places that now seemed to be from some other world. And then a man—the man who had made this morning's coffee on my own stove, no less—had bummed a meal in a Pioneer Square café. That was the last thing I could remember that made sense, feeding someone who was hungry. Lupine had told me to get comfortable with mystery. But I was drowning in it…

My vision had tunneled down to a tiny spot on the ground before me, but I became aware that someone had crouched beside me. Lyla's voice was soft.

"Ray, are you going to be all right? Talk to me."

I turned and looked at her, and all I could feel was fear and confusion. For a long moment I had no idea what to say, and when I spoke it was to say something I hadn't known I would say.

"Lyla, I don't know who I am any more." I looked down at the ground.

She gently lifted my chin until I was looking at her again. "Tell me true, Ray—did you ever actually know who you are?"

Not at all what I expected. How can you not love someone who surprises you endlessly? She made me think.

"I thought I did. I really thought I knew."

"And it's hard and frightening to have that torn away from you, even when what's offered is better beyond your dreams," she said. "I know how that feels."

"You do?"

She smiled, perhaps I thought, a little wistfully. "Maybe there will be time to tell you. I hope there will."

"I hope so too." I heard a theatrical clatter of pots and utensils over by Henry. "Lyla, I have to tell you what happened."

Hucklebark's rumbling voice came across the clearing. "Hey you kids, get a move on—you're holding up *The Works*," followed by a belly laugh at his own joke.

"Hang on, Hucklebark, we'll be over in a minute," Lyla yelled back. "Can you tell me quickly?"

The things that happened with the old man were something I thought needed to be told deliberately and carefully, but I did my best to recount it without wasting time. Even still, I sensed the mounting impatience from Henry and Hucklebark. I chose not to care, though. Lyla needed to hear this now, even if I wasn't sure why it was so important.

She listened intently without interrupting. When I was done she thought for a quick moment. "Ray, I can't take all that in so fast, but with a little time I'll get it. In the meantime, can I make a suggestion?" I nodded. "Don't tell anyone else, except perhaps Works if you feel you need to. Or," she added, "knowing Works, if he asks you first."

"How would Works know about something like this?"

"You have enough mystery for now," she said with another smile. "Now, if I was reading you correctly, you had somewhere important to go, but you sat back down instead. Hopefully we can talk about it more after this meeting."

"Hm? Oh!" I scrambled to my feet and this time made my way into the thicket surrounding the clearing. There was something different in the way I felt, but I couldn't place it. I thought about the river of energy that had ripped through me last night, ripping down everything that stood in its way. Was something gone from me, or had something new arrived? Or perhaps both?

I had just returned to the clearing and was gratefully downing a cup of coffee from Henry when Lupine came through the trees. Her demeanor was serious, and it struck a chill in me.

"It's time, folks. Everyone else who's going to be here is here."

"I thought this was a continuation of yesterday's gathering," I said. "What's changed?"

"Works decided to send most of the people off, and asked that a few stay behind to represent differing viewpoints," she replied.

"What kind of viewpoints?"

Lupine looked pained. "There are a lot of folks who seem to feel you should leave here, hopefully by choice, by other means if necessary. Works is much more charitable about it, but as far as I'm concerned they're behaving like idiots."

I mulled this over for a moment. "Too much unnecessary fear?"

Lupine looked at me in surprise. Her expression lightened suddenly, and she laughed. "Outstanding, Ray! There's hope yet," she said. "Ready or not folks, let's get going."

Henry and Hucklebark, who had been taking all this in silently, led the way. Lyla, Lupine and I followed them through the thicket and down slope to where a nearly-closed circle of people were sitting. It looked like there was just enough room in the circle's opening for the five of us to sit.

I didn't notice exactly how they did it, but Lupine and Lyla maneuvered me so that each sat on one side of me, Lupine to the right, and Lyla to my left. I surveyed the faces of the people already in the circle, and recognized only Works and Everett Longhaul. The expressions of many of the others were grim, and glancing to my left and right, I began to feel like a vulnerable and clueless male flanked by lionesses, ready at an instant's notice to leap to his protection.

Works was sitting a few people to my right, and after a moment of silence he spoke.

"All right, I think we're all here now." He turned to Lupine. "Did you have the opportunity to tell them what we learned last night?"

Lupine shook her head silently. Works sighed and continued, addressing our little band. "Late last night we heard that three other Tree Speakers have been attacked in the last couple of days." I heard a sharp intake of breath from Lyla. "None of them were killed, but one was injured seriously, which is why Spark isn't here to help us with his wisdom this morning. In light of this, we must have a clear way to move forward, and we must have it immediately." Works turned to address the entire assembly.

"We will halt all work, all projects, until further notice. This extends to everyone, not just the Tree Speakers. I depend on all of you to get the word out to every one of our people. I cannot tolerate any more needless harm. We already know that if it was not for Henry's quick and proper action, we would by now have a death on our hands," as he nodded towards me.

"That is my message for today. Now I want to hear from each of you. Ash, would you begin?"

A short, youngish, sandy haired man looked up, his face bearing a deep defiance along with its clear dissatisfaction. "I speak for a great many of the Speakers when I say we feel this Ray Holdman," and he looked directly at me, "should leave here immediately and never return. He has brought this thing here, and he needs to take it away with him. If he refuses to leave, we should assist him in doing so."

Works nodded almost imperceptibly. "Very well. Jarra?"

An older woman spoke next. She appeared to be another kind of Speaker, though she didn't identify herself. Jarra had much the same to say as had Ash.

It went that way around the circle. Different types of Speakers, and a few Change Bringers all said pretty much the same thing, in ways varying from strong disapproval to vehement promises to use force to drive me away. A number of familiar sensations were making their way into me, and they were most unwelcome. I didn't belong here, I brought nothing but trouble, I didn't fit here, I should just go away *now*. I hated these feelings. They had accompanied me all my life, dogged my footsteps everywhere, and I was sick to death of them. But perhaps the most important reason that I was alive, and my father was dead, was that whenever people had pronounced such judgments on me, I had left them behind. Leaving had always made more sense to me than fighting that kind of ignorance and prejudice.

Now, in my mind I began preparing to leave this place too. The thought of never seeing Lyla again was like a knife already tearing into me. The thoughts of never getting to know Works, or learning more about Lupine, of losing my friendships with Hucklebark, Ev Longhaul, and even Henry, were just as painful in a different way. But it had always been so, and there was no reason to think it would be otherwise today. Did these Speakers and Bringers, with all their fine work and superior knowledge, think I'd never before been the center of a circle of hate and fear?

I stole a glance down the line of people to my left. Henry sat like a boulder, impassive and silent. Hucklebark was quivering with an indignation that wrote itself plain on his furrowed brow. Lyla seemed coiled tightly in place, ready to spring in whatever direction was required, her eyes mobile and studying the people across the circle from us. I looked surreptitiously the other way at Lupine. She was sitting in total stillness, her face composed. And yet, seeing her from the corner of my eye, it looked like the air around her was roiled in some subtle way, as if at any moment bolts of lightning would erupt from her.

Then it was Henry's turn to speak. As he swept a look around the circle his eye rested squarely, with undisguised contempt, on each one who had spoken so far. He said slowly, as if talking to willfully stupid children, "I have nothing whatever to say at this time," and closed up again. Hucklebark, on the other hand, could hardly keep his emotions in check enough to speak.

"Y-You people don't know what you're talkin' about," in a voice choked with feeling. "I'm here to tell you that Ray isn't goin' anywhere, not unless he wants to. Nobody's askin' for your help, so I guess we better just agree to stay out of each other's way for a while."

He lapsed into a heavy silence. Across the circle from us, Ash slowly stood up. Four or five others stood up with him, as if they had planned to act together.

"Hucklebark," Ash began, "I have never crossed you before, not even when I totally disagreed with your way of doing things, which I've never liked anyway. But you're in over your head here. We intend to make sure this Holdman person is gone from here this morning. What you do is up to you, but I warn you not to stand in our way."

Hucklebark's response was a growl, and it did not bode well for anyone foolish enough to challenge him, no matter how many. He was on his feet in one swift movement that should not have been possible for one of his size and bulk. He began edging forward, angling to stand in front of me. Ash and his friends began moving forward, very slowly.

I drew in a deep breath to shout them still, to tell them to stop this stupidity, that I was leaving and no one would have to do anything about it. Just as I began to make the words, an elbow slammed into my left side, and the air I had been holding—all the air inside me, in fact—was expelled in a rapid, silent whoosh. I bent down almost to the ground, gasping. When I could straighten up I turned with watering eyes to see Lyla, looking at me with a ferocity that silenced anything I might have said, before I considered saying it.

"Whatever you were going to say, leave it!" She spoke with the kind of quiet, powerful anger that brooks no response. I stared at her in disbelief, at a complete loss.

Ash and his companions were still moving inexorably towards our side of the circle. Hucklebark had moved to stand directly in front of me. I was still sitting, and he towered above; even from the back he radiated fury, and I had to think anyone who would try to force him aside must indeed be an idiot. Lupine had risen to her feet, as had Lyla, and they were both close on either side of Hucklebark, slightly behind him and in front of me. I seemed to be the only one in the circle still sitting, the one cause of all this strife, but Lyla had shocked me so deeply I sat stupidly, idle and uncomprehending. It was all spinning out of control, and it seemed at any instant things would break loose into useless, mindless violence.

"*Stop.*"

The voice, calm but with an immense undercurrent of dignity and anger, was like a slow motion whip. All the people froze instantly, and all eyes turned toward the owner of that voice—Works.

He went on, in the same measured, precise, quiet tone.

"No one has made me this angry in a very, *very* long time. And I had relished that long stretch. Now you betray the very work you purport to do. You have thrown your intelligence and your experience aside, like valueless trash, while you wallow in baseless, destructive fear and ignorance."

His gaze swept the entire circle, excusing no one. "I promise you—and you know I keep my promises—that anyone who attempts violence here will never again work within this land. I give you the count of five to resume your places in the circle."

Like people wakened from a dream that had gripped them without mercy, they turned and gracelessly made their way back.

Hucklebark had flushed to the roots of his hair with shame and embarrassment, and it was clear that angering Works hurt him far worse than any human's blows could have, while Lyla and Lupine moved back to seat themselves beside me with faces carved of stone. The rest sat down again in the circle with expressions that warred with themselves, revealing shame, fury, and fear.

Works waited until everyone was seated again.

"I have not devoted my life to this work only to see it thrown away the first time we are confronted with a mortal threat we do not immediately understand. I have taught you—all of you, excepting Ray, who I have known for one day—better than that. I require a moment of silence, while you reconsider what you have been taught. And following that, I require this conversation to continue, in the only way through which we will get done what needs to be done."

Most of the people were already looking at the ground directly in front of them. I stole a glance at Lupine, and found her gazing at Works, concern and worry large on her face. A short glance across the circle showed me Ash, who still stared defiantly at Works. Works returned his look with one I suspected must have felt like the first time he looked at me: a look that had penetrated my soul and uncovered all that was there, whether I wished it or not. Ash tried to hold his defiance, but in a moment he seemed to melt, and looked downwards in defeat.

There was no sound but the breeze playing in the trees a hundred yards away. I worked on settling my breathing, trying to become calm, and to understand what I should do next.

Lyla had seemed to know what I was about to say, and had taken drastic measures to prevent my saying it. She had already told me she meant everything she said, and I was prepared to believe her actions matched that clarity. I trusted her more than I could ever remember trusting anyone, and that was what told me to hold my silence.

It was, as it was meant to be, Works who broke the silence.

"This interruption should be—*shall be*—forgotten. Until a short time ago, we were having a discussion about matters whose import amounts to life and death for us. We have not yet heard from everyone. Lyla, I wish to hear you next."

All eyes rose up from the ground and turned to Lyla. She did not seem any more ready to resume this discussion than anyone else but Works, but she took a deep breath, allowed herself one more moment to think, and spoke.

"I need to know more about these three new attacks before I can reach a decision that counts," she said. She turned to Works, who nodded shortly as if to say as soon as this was over, she'd hear it. "But I don't believe that Ray brought this thing here with him. If he had that much to do with it at all, I'd guess it's possible that he woke something up that's been here all this time." She paused to take another breath, and think. No one stirred. "In either case, I've seen enough of who and what Ray is to know that he is an important part of dealing with this. Whether or not this person or that person agrees with him or supports him doesn't matter much, but to drive him away right now would be asking for disaster."

One of the men across the circle—one of those who had not been with Ash—said, not unkindly, "I appreciate your viewpoint, Lyla, but is it possible you're a bit, well, prejudiced in this matter?"

I felt my face flush at the implication. But Lyla fixed him with an icy glare. "I would have *thought*," she began with painstaking clarity, "That with all the time you've been here, you would have outgrown that penchant for making *assumptions*."

I thought for a moment he might wither and die on the spot. But after a moment taken aback, he recovered. "Point well taken, Lyla. I withdraw the question, and ask your pardon."

"Given, with no harm done," she replied a little stiffly. "That's all I have to say."

The air was still thick enough to slice, and the energy running through it was still sharp and hostile. I thought, with the way things had gone, that I was expected to speak now. But before I had collected my wits and drawn a breath I heard Works say quietly, "Lupine now, please."

I had hoped that nothing would happen to ratchet the tension any higher. The hope was in vain; as I looked around the circle, I saw most of the people stiffen perceptibly, their eyes narrowing a little. I glanced at Lupine. She hadn't burst into flame, or changed color, or anything else. Then I realized that I was a little slow; without any movement or outward change, Lupine was drawing our attention in to her as if our minds were on strings, and she simply yanking them towards her. There seemed to be no resisting the force of her personality, and as I looked around the circle of people I could sense the new and different fear that many of them felt.

Oh—of course. *Mad Lupine.* There were likely a lot of good reasons to be afraid, most of which I wouldn't even know of. What would she say, and how would she say it? What was she capable of doing? Considering what little I did know, anything was possible, particularly as perhaps I alone had seen her reaction to Works' distress and anger. As I gazed at the circle in front of me, I saw expressions ranging from wary reserve to outright terror. I began to feel afraid myself as Lupine allowed the silence to stretch near the breaking point. But I thought again of what she had said to me the night before, and I wondered how much of this fear was unnecessary. The answer was: probably most of it, as usual. I made an effort to look squarely at the fear I was feeling, and when I did so, all but a scrap of it simply disappeared. Lyla had told me Lupine was *on my side,* and I would stay with that. A feeling of relative calm washed over me, and I figured I was ready for whatever she would say.

Her voice was low and even, and pitched to just reach the people on the far side of the circle. But it would not have been clearer had she been shouting.

"I have been working, down inside the heart of this world, for a very long time. I have been to places that are never mentioned, not even in the oldest stories I've been told. I've seen things, and *escaped* from things, that I'm not going to tell you about now, and will probably never tell you about. And I have been waiting for this time to come to us, knowing that someday it would.

"I can tell you that this thing that threatens us is as old as anything we know, and in the right circumstances, as powerful as life itself. I think, as Lyla does, that Ray's arrival here may well have awakened it. And I want you to consider this before you make any more *decisions*." Her gaze swept slowly around the circle; no one avoided it, but there was clearly courage involved in meeting it. "I have worked with the forces of the world, in all these places, for year after year. Nothing I've ever done has awakened this. And yet—if we're right—Ray has awakened it merely by *showing up*. What does that really tell you about him?"

She stopped to let that sink in. I wished with all my heart she hadn't said that, and being somewhere else began to sound good again. But Lupine wasn't finished.

"This man, this Ray Holdman here, means to do well for the world and all the life on and in it; I'm not mistaken in this. He is just beginning to get the faintest idea of who he is and what's been given to him. *I* want his help to deal with this, and I'm going to ask you all to consider once more: wouldn't you rather have a man like this on your side?"

Lupine sat back, ever so slightly. It was as if she had been holding each one of us by the shirt-front, her face inches from ours, and now she had relaxed her grip and released us. The tension began to drain out of the air surrounding us, and it looked like most everyone felt like they had just run three or four very hard miles. I stole a glance at Works, and saw that he alone was sitting still, calm and alert, as he had since the talking began, his anger notwithstanding. I wondered if I imagined a tiny trace of amusement struggling with his unfathomable expression, but to look at him left no doubt about the seriousness of the situation.

Works gave the circle a few moments to breathe, and then spread his hands slowly in front of him.

"You are the ones who represent everyone else in this decision," he began. "And here is what the decision is *not*. We are not deciding to drop everything in our lives and form some kind of army that will do battle with the thing that threatens us. Nor are we deciding we will place all our hopes and confidence in one person, asking him to tell us what to do."

Thank all the gods who ever lived for small favors, I thought.

"We *are*, however, deciding that not only is this man," he gestured towards me, "going to stay here and help us deal with this danger, we are going to assist him as we can, if he—or any one of us all, for that matter—should happen to ask for it. Nothing more, nothing less. Now, is more time needed to reach this or reject it?"

The man who had questioned Lyla spoke up. "I don't need any more time. And it's quite clear that I have made more than one wrong assumption," as he looked with a slight smile towards her. "Perhaps I understand things a little better now. Ray Holdman, I fervently hope that you won't need any help at all from me. But if you should, ask for it and whatever I and my friends and colleagues can do, will be done. My name is Douglas, and we are Speakers to many of the plant peoples."

I looked back at Douglas, feeling like a third-rate actor mistakenly cast into a sweeping epic populated by masters, and wondered what I was supposed to say. In the end, I said, "Thank you. Thank you very much."

He nodded, and I was relieved to conclude it had been enough. Works turned to the circle again.

"I need to know if there is sufficient dissent to prevent our working together. If you are still in direct opposition to this decision, or if you are undecided, you must say so now."

There was a long silence, with much looking at the ground and sighing from certain quarters. But there was no response.

"Very good," Works said. "Return now and tell everyone you represent that all work must stop until further notice, and that a group of people, including Ray, may need help of an undetermined nature sometime soon. Believe me," he said with a wry look, "We'll try to make it short. The last thing I want is to have the whole lot of you running around with nothing to do."

That brought the short, nervous chuckle that was the best he could hope for, and the circle broke up. People rose, in various attitudes of worry, dissatisfaction or sullenness, and stretched themselves as if they'd been sitting for days. I understood exactly how they felt.

There was no idle chatter or bantering as there had been yesterday. The people headed purposefully back to their camps to pack and be on their way, and within a few moments there were only Lyla, Lupine, Henry, Hucklebark, Everett Longhaul and Works remaining.

Ev came over to where I was still sitting and hunkered down in a squat, his great feet flat on the ground. "If there's anything in particular you need, Ray, let me know now. I'll be back tonight."

Even squatting as low as he could get, he still towered over me. I looked up and replied, "Thanks a lot, Ev. Nothing comes to mind right now, so I guess it's more of the usual—as usual." My stomach chose that moment to growl ominously.

Ev's eyebrows rose. "Would I be correct in assuming you didn't have time to eat much of anything this morning?"

"Um, yeah, that's a good assumption."

He reached into one of the voluminous pockets in his vest, and produced, conjurer-like, a pair of sandwiches. A short fishing expedition in another pocket produced a small water bottle. I stared at the sandwiches as if I didn't know what they were, then took them and the water with thankfulness. I unwrapped the first of the sandwiches and began to wolf it down.

Between mouthfuls, I said, "Everett Longhaul, will you ever stop amazing me?"

"I really hope not," he said, and his smile was sardonic, frank and open, all at once. "I cherish that blank look of astonishment you always give me."

END

OF

BOOK ONE

Acknowledgements

Though many of the places (particularly on Mount Rainier) that are described in *The Fireweed Entrance* and *A Mountain Spruce* are physically, intimately familiar and dear to me, others are places I have only visited in wishful imagination and by way of excellent topographic maps. For their descriptions and many of their remarkable details I have Floyd Schmoe to thank. Mr. Schmoe first arrived at The Mountain in the winter of 1919, as caretaker of the lodge at Paradise, and stayed as a Park employee off and on for many years, eventually becoming the first Park Naturalist. His eloquent and observant book *A Year in Paradise* has been a treasure trove of information and inspiration.

I also owe a deep debt of thanks to several people still with us: Joe Schonbok and Rex Morris, for careful readings and crucial feedback; Larry DuBois and Gates Johnson, the other two thirds of the world's nearly-smallest Writer's Group; Jim Burke and Mary Shackelford, for an irreplaceable friendship and some important hikes. And finally, my deepest love and gratitude to Nancy Olszewski, without whose support, wisdom, and occasional good, swift kicks this work would not have been possible.

Richard Jones
Puget Sound, Washington, July, 2019

Richard Jones has spent decades hiking in the wilderness areas that are the setting for Speakers of the Earth, and many years imagining and creating the work he has set there. He lives on an island in Western Washington with his wife, where they share the land with an elderly pygmy goat and an alpaca.